Praise for the novels of

Love Creeps

"A fast-moving surrealistic sex farce about fear, seduction, and stalking in Manhattan—a place where everybody is spying on everybody else—that's part suspense comedy and part philosophical treatise on the neurosis of love. This is, by far, Amanda Filipacchi's funniest and most accomplished novel."
　　　　　　　　　　　　—Bret Easton Ellis, author of *American Psycho*

"Filipacchi has *such* an original voice and this book is her most hilarious and thought-provoking yet—entertainingly complex!"
　　　　　　　　　　　　—Tama Janowitz, author of *Slaves of New York*

"Whimsical and subversive, *Love Creeps* takes the hot, tragic issues of our day (stalking, child abuse) and cools them down to wry comedy. The result is both shocking and philosophical."
　　　　　　　　　　　　—Edmund White, author of *The Flaneur*

"Inventive . . . hilarious . . . [Amanda Filipacchi's] style is reminiscent in certain ways of Muriel Spark. It's brisk, witty, knowing, mischievous. . . . *Love Creeps* is a rare treat. It's intelligent, and perceptive about the slippery nature of desire. And it's extraordinarily funny."　　　—*The Boston Globe*

"With a flair for delightfully silly dialogue, Filipacchi's third novel portrays romance as the tricky, prickly game that it is: Her characters fall in love for all the wrong reasons. Flirting is a complex process, requiring wit, patience, and elaborate displays of disgust."　　　　—*The Village Voice*

"A whimsical look at the connections we make and the desires that drive us."　　　　　　　　　　　　　　　　　　　—*Publishers Weekly*

"Always entertaining."　　　　　　　　　　　　　　　　　—*Elle*

"A hilarious glimpse at dating in NYC."　　　　　　—*Star* magazine

"It's a love story of stalkers in New York. It's great. It's the funniest book I've ever read."　　　　　—Brian Dannelly, director/cowriter of *Saved!*

Nude Men

"Hilarious, full of plot surprises, and completely original." —Louis Malle

"Playful, perverse, and wonderfully funny. . . . An irresistible introduction to a sublimely precocious writer." —Kathryn Harrison, author of *The Kiss*

"Filipacchi is fearsomely witty. . . . [*Nude Men* is] a truly clever first novel, one that makes *you* feel clever as you read it." —*The Village Voice*

"A quirky, unpredictable comedy of contemporary urban morals. . . . Entertaining and provocative." —*Chicago Tribune*

"An enchanting fable, a sobering tale . . . [an] exhilarating pleasure." —*Newsday*

"Even at its most twisted . . . *Nude Men* somehow has the charm of a fairy tale." —*New York*

"A sly look at contemporary sexual politics and mores." —*Vanity Fair*

"Witty and unpredictable to the end." —*Vogue*

"An optical illusion novel: savor the shimmering wit and sharp writing from a distance; or get close and risk seeing something that may shock you." —*Details*

"Exuberantly inventive . . . Droll, mesmerizing, and memorable." —*Publishers Weekly* (starred review)

"Filipacchi's [writing] is truly funny, [and] she has the self-mocking, well-chosen arrows of John Fante; I look forward to more writing with that directness." —*Paper*

"This is one of the most bizarre, challenging novels I've ever read. It's also one of the best. . . . *Nude Men* is, by turns, shocking, funny, moving, perverse, and very, very clever." —*New Woman*

"How come Britain can't produce young writers as fresh and inventive as Amanda Filipacchi?" —*The Face*

Vapor

"Amanda Filipacchi has pulled off the rare feat of writing a novel that is at once great fun and extremely thought provoking. She takes the Pygmalion myth and through a surreal twist, helps us to see the reality of human relationships with new, valuable clarity."

—Alain de Botton, author of *How Proust Can Change Your Life*

"Rewardingly escapist."

—*Time*

"Wildly imaginative and intelligent, *Vapor* is as good as any long-awaited second novel can get."

—*Time Out New York*

"Mercilessly witty and outrageous . . . [Filipacchi's *Vapor*] showcases a prodigious postfeminist talent. Her energetic originality never falters and her unforgiving eye for the fluidity of human weakness never blinks."

—*Publishers Weekly*

"Original and beguiling."

—*Kirkus Reviews*

"A saucy stomp through a slightly surreal New York City."

—*Paper*

Also by Amanda Filipacchi

Nude Men

Vapor

Love Creeps

Amanda Filipacchi

ST. MARTIN'S GRIFFIN

NEW YORK

www.stmartins.com

Library of Congress Cataloging-in-Publication Data

Filipacchi, Amanda.
    Love creeps : a novel / Amanda Filipacchi.
        p. cm.
    ISBN-13: 978-0-312-34033-9
    ISBN-10: 0-312-34033-8
    1. Women art dealers—Fiction. 2. Manhattan (New York, N.Y.)—Fiction.
3. Triangles (Interpersonal relations)—Fiction. 4. Stalking victims—Fiction.
5. Male friendship—Fiction. 6. Stalking—Fiction. 7. Stalkers—Fiction. I. Title.

PS3556.I428L685 2005
813'.54—dc22

                                                                    2004066386

First St. Martin's Griffin Edition: June 2006

10 9 8 7 6 5 4 3 2 1

For Richard

Acknowledgments

For her brilliant insights and constant encouragement, I am especially grateful to my mother, Sondra Peterson.

For their valuable support and advice, I thank my agent, Melanie Jackson; my editor, Diane Reverand; Priscilla Cohen; Martine Bellen; Mark Woods; Mark Gimpel; Walter Biggs; Richard Stahnke; Jim Horowitz; Barbara Scrupski; and, as always, my father, Daniel, and my brother, Craig.

I would also like to extend a special thank-you to Randy Dwenger, Jennifer Cohen, Shelley Griffin, Lee Klein, Catherine Cusset, J. B. Miller, Ben Neihart, Heather Chase, Ken Foster, David Smith, and, most of all, the ever-inspiring Richard Hine.

Love Creeps

One

Lynn stalked. She had taken up stalking for health reasons, but it was not paying off as handsomely as she had hoped. Lynn was not in poor physical health, but she was in rather poor mental health.

At the age of thirty-two, she had suddenly found herself wanting nothing. Lynn had never before wanted nothing, and she missed wanting. No one around her wanted nothing. She became envious of everyone who wanted. She wasn't impressed so much by what, specifically, each wanted, but rather by how much. That is why she became especially envious of her stalker, who wanted her very badly.

He clearly did not suffer from the same mental health problem Lynn had. If anything, he had the opposite problem. But since Lynn, like most people, foolishly believed that any problem opposite her own is a lucky problem, she envied him. And because she envied him, she copied him.

Alan Morton, Lynn's stalker, had first noticed Lynn at the gym. He enjoyed sitting at the weight machine opposite hers, staring at her. He was allowed. There was not a club rule that said, "Do not sit at the weight machine opposite the one at which women open and close their legs.

Do not sit there and look at them." He intended to exercise his rights, as well as his body, which weakened every time she opened her legs.

He was a plump man, but one day he planted himself before her and began turning in place. "Excuse me," he said, "could you please tell me if I have any muscles I could tone further for your pleasure?"

To show her he had not meant anything offensive by this—he was sensitive enough to notice the subtle expression of aversion on her face—he added, "I'd be happy to return the favor. For instance, I don't mind telling you that I feel you're wasting your time toning those arm muscles. You should be toning your stomach muscles instead, which don't get much of a workout from everyday activities like shopping and carrying groceries."

She was staring at him blankly, as if in a trance. This was an improvement, he thought. Vacancy was better than aversion. He would take advantage of her receptive state. "I know all this, because I had a personal trainer for three sessions. I don't know if you've ever had one."

She made no reply.

"I don't mind passing on some of his pointers. For free," he added, raising his eyebrows.

"No thanks, I'm fine," she said.

"Well, I certainly won't argue with that!"

She must have been done with her workout, he assumed, because she went to the women's locker room. Alan went to the men's locker room and changed. He followed her out of the gym, at a distance. He saw her enter a gallery a few blocks away.

Two weeks later, standing in her art gallery, her assistant, Patricia, by her side, Lynn pointed to her stalker on the sidewalk. He was peering in at her, his forehead pressed against her gallery window, his hands cupped around his eyes.

"Patricia," Lynn said, "am I going crazy, or is there not an alarming difference between his face and mine?"

"There is quite a big difference. But it's in your favor, and you should be grateful for it."

"No, I'm serious, Patricia. His face glows, it's alive. My face is dead."

"I would not say your face is dead." After a pause, Patricia added, "Speaking of dead, he's been stalking you for two weeks now. Why aren't we more scared?"

"He doesn't make it easy. He's so goofy looking."

Alan was not a man of great stature. He was only about an inch taller than Lynn, who was five-six. He was not a slim man, nor muscular. But he had blue eyes and blond hair, the thought of which cheered him up when he was feeling insecure about his appearance. He did not have a full head of blond hair, but the few strands he did have were absolutely, incontrovertibly, blond. He tended to dress in black or dark colors because he'd heard they were slimming and secretly believed they were cool.

"But at least his face is alive," Lynn said. "I really think my face looks dead."

"Men don't like women with dead-looking faces. Yet you have lots of guys after you. Therefore, your face cannot be looking dead," Patricia said, studying Lynn. Lynn often wore panty hose and cream-colored things and taupe things. She was the kind of woman referred to as "elegant" or "classic" by people who weren't on the cutting edge of fashion. She sometimes even wore her dark blond hair in a ballerina bun. To be that conservative looking was quite daring,

Patricia thought. Lynn was sleek and hairless, except in appropriate places. What Patricia didn't know was that one of Lynn's great pleasures in life was getting rid of her undesirable hair. She wasn't a particularly hairy creature to begin with, and she wouldn't have minded having a larger quantity of undesirable hair, just for the pleasure of getting rid of it.

"There's no one I'm attracted to," Lynn said.

"I know."

"Art that used to stimulate me no longer does. Where do I have to go to find beautiful art and a beautiful man?"

"A therapist?"

"I've seen many, and none of them was ever beautiful, and neither was the art on their walls."

Lynn Gallagher, one of the five most influential contemporary-art gallery owners in New York, had had a relatively normal dating life. Her longest romantic relationship had been a year, her shortest a night. Her longest period of celibacy had been six months; her shortest time between two men had been two hours. That only happened once.

For Lynn, relationships and singlehood both had their pros and cons, but she, unlike many women, only slightly preferred the former to the latter.

Lynn watched Patricia spit a thoroughly chewed piece of persimmon into a paper napkin and drop it in the wastebasket. She wasn't a bad-looking girl, with her long dark hair. She held a striking resemblance to Frida Kahlo. Her eyebrows were thick, giving her otherwise beautiful face a slightly cavewoman look. Had she known, she would have plucked them more. Lynn was sure of it. Lynn, who was never without her own tweezers except when they were confiscated by airport security, often had an urge to pluck Patricia's eyebrows because she found them distracting. When Patricia spoke to her, Lynn usually averted her eyes in order to be able to concentrate on what Patricia was saying.

"Shall we look at slides?" Patricia asked.

"If we must," Lynn replied.

Searching for new talent used to be the best part of Lynn's job. Now, it was an ordeal.

She heaved herself up and went to the light box. Patricia opened envelopes, pulled out slide sheets and transparencies. She held them in front of Lynn, one after the other, as Lynn shook her head and said, "No." While the minutes passed and the images kept passing in front of her without provoking the slightest twitch of enthusiasm, Lynn became progressively sadder. These sessions were a lot shorter than they used to be.

The gallery door opened, and in came Judy, a slightly less successful gallerist who had been Lynn's friend and competitor for six months. Lynn switched off the light box and spun around. She preferred not to be caught looking at art in vain.

"Hi. I'm on my way to a meeting, but I just wanted to say hello. How are you?" Judy asked, kissing Lynn's cheeks.

"The same."

Judy looked at the empty walls. "Yes, I see." She sat on the edge of Lynn's desk, her short, red, pleated skirt hanging from her knee in an arc. She always dressed entirely in red after having decided four years ago that creating a memorable and consistent look greatly increased one's chances of succeeding in life. "You know, there is a simple solution to your problem."

"What is it?"

"Addiction."

Lynn frowned.

"I highly recommend it," Judy said. "One of my greatest pleasures is promising myself I will not drink, or smoke, or take coke, or do heroin, or eat cookies, then doing it. It's a pleasure that can be repeated daily. The desire renews itself incessantly, and you can always rely on it unless you screw it up by going to rehab or something. But even then, the damage is not irreversible. The key, though, is making the resolution, making yourself *think* that you will be deprived, and indeed depriving yourself for a couple of hours to allow the desire to build up, then, suddenly, caving in. I bet heaven is caving in."

"You're dangerous," Lynn said. "Your weapon is logic."

"Thanks, but it's really just common sense. And I'm not dangerous. I mean, you know I'm not a huge junkie. Just a little hooked on coke, a little on alcohol, a little on heroin; just enough to have that interesting tension in my life between wanting and satisfying."

Judy's attention was distracted by Alan. "Who's that man? He's been standing there peeking in this whole time."

"I don't know, some creep, just ignore him," Lynn said.

Judy obeyed. "So anyway, as I was saying, my addictions are all under control. And yours can be, too, as long as you remember to maintain that all-important balance between deprivation and allowance, needing and fulfilling."

"I'll remember that, but I'm just not sure addiction is what I need at the moment."

"Fine. It's always something you can fall back on if you find nothing better. Let me ask you this: Have you really, really searched? Is there nothing at all that you desire?"

"I desire to desire, but I don't think that counts as a desire."

"I think it counts," Judy replied, to be nice, even though she didn't really think it did count.

Lynn shrugged. "So, you don't have any other ideas, along the same lines, only more . . . humdrum?"

"How about antidepressants?"

"I don't want to resort to those. They don't seem right for my problem. I mean, I used to feel desire. There's no reason I can't re-capture it."

"Do you know why you lost it? Have you thought about it?"

"Of course I've thought about it! Haven't we thought about it?" Lynn said, turning to Patricia.

"Yes," Patricia said, "we've discussed and analyzed and dissected it for hours. We couldn't come up with a cause."

"Desire for what, exactly, did you lose?" Judy asked Lynn.

"All sorts of things. Various men. Travel. Discovering new artists, launching their careers, seeing my efforts pay off. Shopping. Acquir-ing things, beautiful clothes. I used to look forward to the ballet sea-son, to certain parties, to hearing updates on my friends' lives. I used to feel really passionate about all these things. And I got a lot of plea-sure out of wanting them. I miss yearning strongly for something. I used to be like him," she said, motioning toward her peeping stalker, then adding, "Inwardly."

Judy nodded. "You're suffering from anhedonia."

"I'm not so sure about that. I still derive as much pleasure as ever from all sorts of things, like the smell of a rose, the company of a good friend, the feel of a beautiful day." *Plucking,* Lynn added, in her thoughts. "And I still have strong emotions, I experience happi-ness and sadness. I've just lost the great hunger. I crave the hunger. I don't even feel ambitious like I used to feel. And a sort of nausea washes over me at unexpected moments."

"Sounds like a pain. I'll try to come up with more ideas, but right now I've got to run. I'll call you." Judy left.

"Listen, I've got an idea," Patricia said. "Perhaps it would help if you tried to be interested in something outside yourself, in another human being, for instance. People often do volunteer work for this purpose."

"Hmm. I'm not sure that would make any difference. Do you suppose he does any volunteer work? And yet look at him, he's happy," Lynn said, pointing at her peeping stalker.

"Well, he is interested in another human being."

"Oh. Maybe I should become a stalker, too, since I'm sure you'd think it would make me less self-centered. At least there's some pep to it."

Patricia stared at her with an expression Lynn read as exasperation. Lynn had learned from experience that the only way to cope with being stared at by her assistant was to ignore her and charge right ahead. So she muttered, "The problem is that to be a stalker, you have to want someone . . ."

Patricia had learned from experience that the best way to deal with Lynn's annoyingly sensationalistic comments was to top them.

"Not necessarily," she said, feigning absentmindedness and absorption in her work, in order to add authenticity and innocence to the sensationalistic comment she was about to make. "The chicken or the egg. Maybe to want someone, you have to stalk him first."

Hearing no response, Patricia looked up to find her boss staring at her, unblinking. Lynn murmured, "What you just said is completely absurd and lame, yet it has great depth, and you don't even realize it. It reminds me of that old theory about smiling, which says that people can feel happier by smiling first, instead of waiting until they feel happy before they smile."

Lynn did not lose time. She frequently lost other things, like her keys, her hat, her desire, her wallet, but never time.

She chose a man in a Chelsea bakery, across the street from her gallery, thirty-seven minutes after she had decided to find someone to stalk. She had bought herself a meringue to get energy in her quest for a victim, and then—*boom!*—it happened. He walked in, and she thought, *He'll do.* She had seen him before in the neighborhood. He never smiled. He seemed to be in his mid-thirties and was good-looking in a bland way, dark-haired, tall, and tan. She disapproved of tanning but was willing to disregard it for now. Her only concern was the sweater tied around his shoulders. A gay man was not the prime choice for heterosexual stalking. She held out hope that maybe he was just European.

With relief, she noted a slight French accent when he asked for a *pain au chocolat* and a *croissant* and a *palmier.* Despite his large order, his body was muscular. The pastries were possibly for friends. Or perhaps he was an obsessive gym-goer. When he turned around to leave, she was ruffled to notice that around his neck he wore a locket. She remained standing, uncertain for an instant, but decided to chalk up the locket to his French citizenship as well, then followed him out of the bakery.

She was glad she'd seen him before in the area. It was convenient if he lived nearby. She had no intention of stalking someone who lived far away. Long-distance stalking had to be annoying.

Right then, possessed by the enthusiasm often accompanying the onset of a new hobby, she was willing to follow him far, which was why she was unpleasantly let down when he entered a building less than a block away. She almost muttered "Ow" from the sheer discomfort of being left standing on the sidewalk with her stalking enthusiasm still swollen.

At a loss as to what an average stalker would do next, Lynn took out her cell phone and instructed her assistant to replace her at the building until her prey reappeared. She returned to her art gallery to wait for her assistant to call and tell her the prey was ready for further stalking.

At five-thirty Lynn got the call and resumed the tailing herself.

The man walked a few blocks and entered an apartment building with a doorman.

This new postponement was maddening. She really wanted to get going on her stalking project.

Approaching the tall, gray-haired doorman, Lynn asked, "Does that man live here?"

"Yes."

"What's his name?"

"I'm sorry, I'm not at liberty to divulge that kind of information."

"Oh. He just looks like someone I know," she tried. "I wonder if he's that person."

"I'm sorry, I'm not at liberty to divulge his name."

"Is there anything you are at liberty to divulge?"

"Yes. That if you would like, I could ring up Mr. Dupont and—" He seemed abruptly shaken by his slip.

"And ask him if he'd mind disclosing his first name?" she teased.

"Something like that." He placed his hand on the house phone, threatening to pick it up.

"No, no. Please don't bother Mr. Dupont for such a trivial matter."

Not actually caring about his name, but aware that typical stalkers are at least slightly pushy, she added, "Do you mind if I try to guess his first name?"

"I don't have time to play guessing games. I'm busy," the doorman said.

"You are?"

"Yes, I am. I'm working. You are interrupting my work."

"I'm interrupting your standing there?"

"That's right. I get paid to stand here and do nothing. You are interrupting what I'm paid to do."

"Please tell me his name."

"No. What seems to be the problem?"

She hesitated. "I've lost something, and I think he may be able to help me get it back."

"What have you lost?"

"That's nosy of you."

"Just doing my job, miss. What have you lost? Perhaps I can help."

"I'm sure you can't."

"Can't hurt to try me."

She finally said, "I lost my desire."

"I don't have time for this."

"I understand. Time is precious, but desire is even more precious."

"Hardly," he said. "Desire is a curse. You're lucky to be free of yours."

"I am? I guess you're not free of yours?" Lynn asked.

"No, I'm not. And I would do anything to be. How, may I ask, did you manage to get rid of yours? If you tell me, I'll tell you Mr. Dupont's first name."

"I didn't get rid of mine, I told you, I lost it. Accidentally. I don't know how. I'd do anything to get it back. I think he can help me regain it."

"All the more reason not to help you. You should realize your good fortune, your fortunate loss, but you don't. And I know why. Your loss is a lie. You claim to have lost desire, and yet you desire to know Mr. Dupont's first name. Do you not?"

"Actually, no. I'm asking for medicinal purposes."

"Shall I inform Mr. Dupont of your alarming presence?"

"No, don't worry, my presence is neither alarming nor worthy of informing him about."

"Good. Then I really must get back to work, so if you'll excuse me," he said, averting his eyes slightly and unfocusing them.

"I understand," Lynn said. "You're paid to do a certain amount of nothing every day, and you might get in trouble if your superiors see you haven't done as much nothing as you were hired to do."

He remained standing perfectly still. So struck was Lynn by his resemblance to a Duane Hanson sculpture, that she instinctively brought her face closer to his, to marvel at his detailing, at the realistic imperfections of his skin, at the small hairs sticking out of his nostrils. He didn't flinch under her scrutiny, so absorbed in his work was he.

She walked away.

Stalking Mr. Dupont every day required tremendous willpower for many reasons, not the least of which was that Lynn always wore moderately high heels not made for long walks at a tall man's pace.

Unfortunately, the more Lynn forced herself to want Mr. Dupont, the less she did.

I need help, she thought. So she ordered her assistant to help her stick to her stalking, to be her coach in this matter, and harass her to follow the man.

It didn't take Lynn's stalker, Alan, long to realize that sometimes, while he followed her, Lynn was following another man. Alan hoped it was his imagination, but he soon had to accept that it wasn't. He was confused. This was not the way this type of thing usually unfolded. Granted, he'd never stalked anyone before, but from what he'd seen in movies and in books, a victim of stalking does not engage in stalking another man while she's being stalked. Alan told himself not to worry about it too much, that it might pass.

Instead, he turned his attention to finding a way to become part of her life. After a while he came up with this: he could try to sneak it past her, could try to let his love creep slowly into her life.

She was the kind of woman not bothered by a stalker. In fact, she was so absorbed in other things that she might not notice if he entered her life. Before she realized, they'd be friends. One day she might even absentmindedly accept an invitation to dinner. And another time he might manage to have sex with her while she was doing something else. Before she knew it, maybe he'd move in. And one day, if an attractive man said to her, "I'd love to take you out to dinner. Do you have a boyfriend?" she'd think about it for a second and be forced to reply, slightly stunned, "I guess I do," wondering when, exactly, it had happened.

It was a perfect plan. He would seep into her life.

Alan started sending Lynn gifts. First he sent her cookies, then movie tickets, then a bonsai tree, then pink and yellow lingerie. He also sent her notes. With the cookies was one that said, "I hope you'll enjoy them. I know you don't need to watch your waistline." With the lingerie, the note said, "You are visually sleek. Your colors blend so well with each other. You look airbrushed. These colors should complement you nicely." The note that came with the bonsai tree said, "Please take care of this small life-form, and know that it not only excretes oxygen, which is good for you; it also excretes my love for you, which is even better."

Alan could not help noticing that Lynn continued stalking the other man. Alan was extremely perturbed by this. He had never heard of such a thing. Was it just a weird coincidence, that the woman he happened to stalk was a stalker herself? Had she only begun stalking recently? He'd only noticed her doing it for a few days, but maybe she'd been doing it all along. To make matters worse, the man she was stalking was taller than Alan, better-looking than Alan, and had more hair.

It didn't take long for Alan's degree of frustration to reach intolerable levels. He decided he had to meet the man Lynn was stalking. He wanted to see him, face-to-face, wanted to know what he was like, hoped to understand what was going on.

Alan joined the gym the man belonged to and immediately found an ideal way to meet him.

In the locker room, he saw the man adding his name and number to the signup sheet for racquetball partners.

Two

One day, Patricia had just left work and was giving a few coins to a red-haired homeless man at the corner. She'd seen him roaming around the neighborhood for two years, and she liked giving him money regularly because he wasn't pushy or intimidating. Other than to say "Thank you," he had never spoken to her. Until today.

"Excuse me," he said, "I know you work with that woman at that fancy gallery at the corner. I was just wondering if you might be able to tell me why she follows a man every day while she herself is followed by another man?"

When Patricia had gotten over her surprise that he had addressed her, she asked, "Is it very noticeable?"

"A bit. To me. Why do they do it?"

"Who knows."

"You know."

"Not exactly."

"But enough. You know enough. I would be truly thrilled to know. I'm a different kind of homeless person."

"Isn't that what they all say?" she answered, hoping she didn't sound mean.

"No. They say, 'Give me money.' I say, 'Give me answers.' I beg you to give me an answer. It'll keep me warm tonight."

"But I don't really know."

"And I don't really believe you. Have a nice evening."

Ray watched her walk away, disappointed that she hadn't enlightened him. He really wanted to know why the elegant gallery owner was going around every day following a tan, unsmiling man while she herself was being followed by a man who managed to appear clownish despite wearing black; quite a feat, in Ray's opinion. The three of them often gave him money, one after the other, as they passed him by. He'd seen them before in the neighborhood, but had never paid close attention to them until recently, when they'd begun following each other. He diagnosed them as nuts. Displays of this kind were not easy for him, considering the fact that he used to be a psychologist whose practice had been ruined by his unfortunate ECD, or Excessive Curiosity Disorder. Curiosity about the slightest peculiarities in human behavior. The opposite of those therapists who fell asleep while their patients spoke, Ray was too interested in the soap opera of their stories. The suspense was both thrilling and intolerable for him. He called most of his patients at home many times a day, to ask for updates on their situations. Once, he had a patient whose boyfriend had stormed out after a fight, and she was waiting for him to call. Ray phoned her every hour asking if her boyfriend had made up with her yet. His obsessive behavior destroyed his practice, not to mention the sanity of his patients.

Two weeks after Judy had advised Lynn to take up addiction, Lynn and Patricia were shocked to hear from a mutual acquaintance that Judy had been hit by a truck. She was fine, with nothing but bruises. She had been kept at the hospital overnight for observation after the accident and was now home recovering.

"It must be all the drugs," Lynn said.

Lynn knew she had to take her stalking more seriously. She began writing notes to Mr. Dupont. They were not as good as the notes her own stalker sent her. He wrote things like, "Your concentration blows me away. It is blinding. I love the way you stare at my gifts. I have many other gifts you haven't seen. One in particular. It yearns for you." It was disgusting. Why couldn't she come up with something like that in her own stalking? Instead, she wrote things like, "You intrigue me. I hope you don't mind my following you. I hope you are flattered by the attention I give you." Another one she wrote was, "You look really intelligent and good. I mean 'good' as in 'attractive,' of course, for how should I know if you are good or not? For that matter, how should I know if you are intelligent, but you might be. And that's good enough for me."

She was bad at writing notes, and on top of that, she had stalker's block. She felt she had exhausted all the obvious statements. She was amazed that her own stalker was able to come up with fresh ideas all the time.

So, out of frustration, she began copying her stalker's notes and sending them to Mr. Dupont. She sent the ones that said things like, "I watch you all the time. Even when I'm somewhere else, I watch you in my mind," and, "To my little pooky bear. I pook you." What did that mean? She didn't know. All she knew was that she couldn't have thought of it herself.

Eventually, she got tired of even the transcribing process, and decided to save time by simply covering up her stalker's signature with Wite-Out and signing "Your fan" over it, before sending the notes on to Mr. Dupont.

Riding the elevator up to the courts, Alan looked at his new racquetball partner and broke the silence with, "Nice locket."

"Thanks."

"What's inside?"

"It's personal."

They played for the first time. Lynn's stalking victim won. Not a bad player, Alan thought, for a Frenchman.

After their game, Alan suggested to Roland Dupont that they go to the juice bar for a smoothie. Roland hesitated, then accepted the invitation. They ordered their drinks, Banana Lipgloss and Blueberry Beach Sand, and sat at a table.

Alan complimented Roland on his game. The Frenchman returned the compliment.

They engaged in some small talk. It turned out Roland had only recently moved to the neighborhood.

"How do you like it?" Alan said.

Roland fingered his locket and looked at Alan without answering right away. "I don't think I like it very much, actually."

"Really? Why not?"

"It's the people," he said. "The people are creepy here. Much more than where I lived uptown."

Alan's heart was beating fast at how easy it was. The progress was rapid. "Creepy how?"

"There's a woman, for example, who's been following me."

"Oh. Do you know her?"

"No."

"Why do you think she's following you?"

"I have no idea. I guess she's just a stalker, or something. And she's been sending me notes. Stupid, weird notes." He produced an exhausted chuckle.

Roland Dupont spoke well for a Frenchman. This annoyed Alan. "What do the notes say?"

"In one note she calls me a teddy bear, or pooky bear, or something like that. I can't really remember."

Alan was silent. Was Lynn using his wording? Or was "pooky bear" very typical, universal wording among stalkers? Alan was perplexed. "What else does she say in her notes?" he asked.

"Oh, let me think . . ." Roland stared down at the table while tapping it with his fingers. "She wrote something like, 'Seeing you makes me happy every morning.' And she follows me. And she'll sit across from me during lunch when I'm with a client."

"A client? What do you do?"

"I'm a lawyer. And you?"

"Accountant."

Roland nodded. After a moment of silence, he said, "You know, in France, stalking doesn't even exist. There isn't a word for it in French. I was trying to tell my family on the phone that this woman is a stalker, and I realized a French translation of the word does not exist."

"That's probably because in France stalking is such a normal part of everyday life that they don't need a special word for it. They probably call it living." Alan chuckled.

Roland seemed taken aback. "It's really horrible to be stalked. It's one of the worst crimes."

Now Alan was taken aback. "Really? I don't mean to belittle your experience, but it strikes me as one of the mildest crimes."

"How can you think that?"

Alan stirred his smoothie, stared at Roland's locket meaningfully. "I mean, I'm sure at some point in your life you must have been very interested in someone, unrequitedly, and engaged in similar behavior vis-à-vis this person."

"You mean stalking someone?"

"If you want to call it that, sure."

"No. Have you?"

"Naturally. Who hasn't?"

"Well, you're very open-minded," Roland said, "very forgiving, I guess. Of yourself. But then again, I doubt you've seriously stalked anyone."

"Your doubt is unfounded."

Had Roland been the type who ever laughed, he would have laughed. He rarely found anything amusing, and even when he did, such as now, he never felt comfortable laughing. Even a smile looked odd on him, as if the particular facial muscles that created his smile were nonexistent, and he had to resort to using a combination of surrounding muscles, such as the muscles of his neck, forehead, eyes, nose, and ears to produce one. It came out differently each time.

"You've actually been a stalker?" Roland asked.

"I wouldn't call it that, no, but you probably would."

Alan didn't want this man to call him a stalker. It was racist, or something. Hate language. The nice word was "admirer." Calling him a stalker was like calling someone who refuses to risk his life "a coward," instead of "smart." Or like calling a promiscuous woman "a slut" instead of "liberated" or "sensual."

"When were you a stalker?" Roland asked.

"If you don't mind, please call it 'admirer.'"

"Okay, when were you that?"

"Not long ago."

"But now you've quit?"

"Of course not. I'm not flighty. I still admire the person."

Roland suddenly looked alarmed. "It's not me, is it?"

Alan burst out laughing. "No! It's a woman. I'm not gay. Are you?"

"No!"

They stared at each other in silence.

"I pity her," Roland said. "You don't know how unpleasant it is to be stalked."

"I pity the poor woman who's stalking you. You don't know how unpleasant it is to have one's efforts be despised. Do you find her at all attractive?"

"She's not fat, if that's what you're asking."

"No . . . that wasn't what I was asking."

"She looks good," said Roland, "but I could never be interested in a woman who pursues me. And I think you should stop stalking your woman."

"Easier said than done. Anyway, I don't see how it's your business."

"I'm sorry. I guess I've just become sensitive about this issue." Roland got up, placed his unfinished smoothie in the trash. He then cordially took leave of Alan, until next time. No, the neighborhood was not treating him well.

As Roland walked out of the snack area, he discreetly took a paper clip out of his shorts' pocket and dropped it on the floor. Yes, he had some of his own eccentric habits, but he was decorously ashamed of them and would never dream of going around parading them. He was proper and continent and did not appreciate the absence of these qualities in others.

Indeed, Roland Dupont had never had a high tolerance for weirdos.

Alan was unusual in plenty of ways Roland did not even suspect. For example, almost every day, Alan walked down the seventeen flights of stairs in the stairwell of his building, stopping at each floor to make sure all the stairwell doors were shut. It usually took him about four minutes.

Patricia didn't enjoy playing the bully, but she couldn't stand Lynn's reproachful glances if she let up on pressuring Lynn to stalk.

"Have you been taking care of yourself lately? Have you been stalking?" Patricia said.

Lynn was pleased with Patricia's pushiness. The extra lessons were paying off. "Yes, I have done more stalking."

"What stalking have you done?"

"I followed him."

"You better have done more than that," Patricia said.

Lynn lowered her eyes. She understood that Patricia was tough not because she was a mean person, but because she cared, and because she knew how important it was that Lynn take her stalking seriously in order to regain her desire.

"I did do a little more," Lynn said.

"What was it?"

"Notes and such."

"Notes? What did they say?"

"The same things any stalker's notes would say."

"What do you mean by that?" Patricia asked, squinting suspiciously under her bushy eyebrows and not letting go, just as Lynn had taught her.

"What do you think I mean?" Lynn squinted back, mockingly.

Patricia did not enjoy being parodied, especially when she was only following orders she didn't want to be following in the first place and that were not part of her job description. In a gesture that was unexpected to the both of them, she grabbed a nearby flexible metal rod that was used to hang paintings, and whipped it against the top of her desk. It made a shattering sound. Lynn's eyes opened wide, thrilled.

"What did your notes say?" Patricia asked.

"Oh, uh, one of them said, 'To my little pooky bear. I pook you.'"

Patricia frowned. "That's what your stalker wrote you."

"Yes, I thought it was a good one. So I used it."

"You copied your stalker?"

"Yes," Lynn murmured melodramatically, turning her face away suddenly, her hair fanning out in the process.

"It's a crime to plagiarize. It's illegal," Patricia said.

At that moment a man entered the gallery. The two women fell silent, watching Mark Bricks, who was one of Lynn's rival gallery owners. He was in his late twenties. His gallery was three blocks away.

They all smiled at each other, said hello pleasantly.

He looked at the walls. "Ah. Still not feeling well?" he said to Lynn.

"No." Lynn felt embarrassed about her naked walls, but she would have felt even more embarrassed had they been clad in works she didn't like. It was known throughout the art world that Lynn was going through a crisis. Her walls had been blank for two months.

"That's a shame," Mark said. "Judy's not well either. You heard about her accident?"

"Yes, it's terrible. My problem seems trivial by comparison," Lynn said.

"Not at all. What's more, Judy's doing better, and you're not. Isn't there anything that can get you out of this funk? I want my competition back! I hope to see your walls with a little meat on them before long," he said, sweetly. "What about your family. Can't they help?"

"My family?" Lynn asked, puzzled.

"Well, I don't know, loved ones? Can't they give you advice? What do your parents do in life?"

People from the art world often asked Lynn what her parents did. "My mother's a cop, and my father's a collector," she always said, as she did now, to Mark.

"Oh yeah? What kind of art?" he asked.

What constituted art was subjective. "He's fond of objets trouvés."

Lynn's father was a garbage collector. Her mother was a police officer and had first met her father one night when they were both on duty. They had made eye contact, and it was love at first sight. Her mother had just stepped out of a patrol car that had gotten called about a ground-floor apartment's shattered window. At the same moment, a charming man jumped out of a garbage truck, grabbed a trash bag from the sidewalk, and flung it into the back of the truck. He had spotted this pretty cop who was watching him. He felt shy, and he felt dirty, which he was. They just stared at each other, wondering who would speak first. Lynn's father did. "Hi. Any idea who mighta broke the window?"

"Beats us," she said. "Me and my partner were wondering if any of that trash was used to break it."

Since the only trash around was sealed in plastic bags, the charming garbage collector knelt next to a bag of trash. "Let's see if there are any shards of glass stuck in the plastic, which could indicate this bag was swung at the window in order to break it."

They both knew the bag of trash could not have broken the window. It was full of soft things. But it didn't matter; they needed it to keep talking.

When Lynn was young, her parents were coarse and jovial. They liked to go bowling. They liked motorcycles. And trailers. And they had a dartboard. They were full of mockery toward a dandified relative of theirs who was interested in art and dressed in an elegant manner that they found stuck-up. They scoffed at refinement.

Lynn loved her parents' scorn of pretentiousness, but she also loved the pretentiousness they scorned. She derided the haughty with them, but secretly started accumulating elegant clothes. And she discreetly wore them. When her parents began making little comments like, "Those shoes you're wearing, aren't they a bit la-di-da?" she'd exclaim, "NO-O-O!" with disgust. And she'd turn away, her feet prickling with shame.

But it happened again. Not more than a week later, her mother noticed that Lynn was dressing rather well. She said, "Isn't that a little ladylike, that style?"

Lynn said it was not ladylike in the least, but that was a lie, and she knew it. She was a closet ladylike-clothes wearer. She loved flipping through fashion magazines and followed their more conservative styles.

After college, Lynn got a master's in art history at Columbia. She then spent a year working as a researcher for Christie's in Contemporary Art sales, and spent two years working her way from a sales position at Luhring Augustine gallery to its director. There, she established such good contacts with important collectors that several of them agreed to back her when she moved to open her own gallery.

The first time Lynn's parents visited her gallery, they looked at the paintings hanging on the walls and said, "Like father, like daughter." It took Lynn a moment to realize they were implying she was a garbage collector, too. She wondered from whom she had gotten her good taste. Certainly not them. Maybe taste skipped a generation, like insanity.

Just as Mark Bricks was about to leave the gallery, Judy walked in wearing a red pantsuit.

"I was worried about you," Lynn said, hugging her gently.

"We were just talking about you," Mark said.

"Sorry I haven't been in touch," Judy said, "but life has accelerated. I'll get to the point. Go and get yourself hit by a truck. All three of you. But you, especially, Lynn. I highly recommend it. It clears the head like nothing else. It will help you regain your desire for things, lots of things. Forget all the other tricks, the addictions and all that. This is much more effective. Foolproof. If your lack of desire ever drives you to the verge of suicide, first try walking in front of moving traffic."

Mark said, "You're not, by any chance, trying to eliminate your competition, are you?"

"No! I'm absolutely serious."

"Hmm. You do seem well," he said.

"Yes, you do," Patricia said.

"I am well. It was a very violent blow, but evenly distributed over the length of my entire body, and therefore it was more traumatizing to my soul than to any one part of me. Now I have an incredible zest for life. There are all sorts of things I want to do, vacations I want to go on, people I want to meet. That's why I thought of you, Lynn. I feel the opposite of you. Getting hit by that truck was the best thing that ever happened to me. But I'm aware that the benefits might wear off. The euphoria, the divine perspective might fade, so one day I may have to do it again to refresh my zeal."

She paused, and they all watched her. "Well, I just stopped by to tell you that. Lynn, your walls are still empty, so think about it."

She kissed all three of them and left.

Mark left shortly after that, and as soon as he was gone, Patricia said, "As I was saying, it's a crime to plagiarize. Do you know that certain authors have committed suicide because people found out they were plagiarizers? They killed themselves out of shame. Have you done anything else, other than follow him and send him notes?"

"I sent some lingerie."

"What? He's a man! Stalking will never treat you well if you treat it with mockery."

"I didn't do it with mockery. I enclosed a note that said I could wear this lingerie for him. It was the lingerie my stalker sent me."

"Lord! That is worse than derivative. You'll get nowhere fast this way."

"I'm sorry. I won't do it again."

"Tell me you'll come up with your own ideas."

"I'll come up with my own ideas."

Lynn did try to come up with her own ideas, but in the meantime she simply continued following Roland down the street. And she, in turn, was often followed by Alan.

Ray, the homeless ex-therapist, continued observing them. People sometimes interested him, like this chain of stalking, but he had been disillusioned by so-called intriguing people. And they had cost him one year of his freedom. While trying to pierce a mystery of human motivation, he had overstepped the bounds of lawfulness and had ended up serving a one-year prison sentence for coercion in the second degree—a class-A misdemeanor—and getting his therapy license permanently revoked.

The incident had begun innocently enough when one of his patients had informed him that a female acquaintance had told him not to bother pursuing her romantically, because she was not interested in dating him.

"Do you have any idea why she didn't want to date you?" Ray had asked.

"No. And I don't care."

"You don't care? But it would be useful to know, for future reference, like the next time you meet a woman you want to date."

"But I didn't want to date her."

"Then why did you ask her out?"

"I didn't."

"Then why did she tell you not to pursue her romantically?"

"Beats me."

Ray leaned forward in his seat and spoke very clearly. "What did you say to that woman that made her think you might want to date her?"

"Nothing."

"What do you mean, nothing? She just said that, out of the blue? She rejected you preemptively?"

"Yes. It hadn't even entered my mind to date her."

"It would be good for you to know why she said that. I think you should call her up when you get home and ask her."

"I don't know about that."

"Well, I do. It's important that you do this. We can't make much progress if you don't."

That night, Ray called up his patient and asked him if he had called the woman yet. The patient said no. So Ray called him back an hour later and asked him if he had called her yet. The patient said no. This went on a few more times, a few more days, until finally Ray managed to get the woman's phone number from the patient and called her up himself and asked her why she had told the patient not to bother pursuing her romantically. There was a long silence. The woman said, "Who are you?"

"That's not important," Ray said.

"You're a friend of his? Why didn't he call me himself?"

"He didn't want to, but I think it's important that he know why you said that."

"You think it's important?" she said. "Who are you, his therapist?"

"Yes."

She laughed. "No, really, who are you?"

"I *am* his therapist."

She snorted, still not believing him. "Listen, I don't have time for this."

"Wait, can't you just, please, answer the question?"

"No. How's that? No." And she hung up.

No? No? Why, no? He punched his pillow.

"She's a bitch," Ray informed his patient.

"Yeah, she might be."

"No, I'm telling you, she is. How can you not see it? I mean, that she would presumptuously tell you not to try to date her, for no reason! Why doesn't that make you more mad? That's not healthy."

"Well, it did annoy me a little bit."

"That's my point. Why not more? That doesn't make sense. It's as though you're hiding something, as though you perhaps know why she said that, know what you did to make her say that, and you just won't tell me."

"Yes, you've already told me you think that, but it's not true."

"Then why aren't you more mad that she was so presumptuous? You don't seem at all tormented by the mystery of it."

"No, I guess I'm not."

"Well, you've got to work on that."

This patient, who at first hadn't cared why the woman told him not to pursue her romantically, was gradually transformed, thanks to Ray, into a neurotic wreck who ended up resorting to alcohol and drugs to endure the stresses of life caused by his therapist.

As for the mystery of why the woman had told his patient not to bother pursuing her romantically, Ray pierced it. He found the woman, tied her to a chair at knifepoint, and forced her to answer the question. Her answer was: "He had asked me to dinner." And for that banal answer, Ray served his one-year prison sentence. He had been disappointed before by patients, but this one took the cake. No matter how enticing patients seemed at first, they let him down. The human was a less interesting animal than he had thought. With little personality, no real character—the human was all just meat. Meat, meat, meat. And Ray had been fooled so many times. Now, when he saw nuts, he steered clear. He had become suspicious of strange behavior—he suspected it wasn't as strange as it seemed.

Ray was sorry about the damage he'd caused so many of his patients. By being a homeless person, he had chosen to condemn himself to the hell of human banality. It was like standing in a stream of disappointment, day after day. He had become desensitized to strangeness and would not let this weird stalking chain—comprised of the three nuts—reawaken his curiosity disorder. He was comfortable with his new identity as a blasé bum and determined not to be seduced again.

Ray was relieved, in a way, that Patricia hadn't answered his questions about Lynn. Asking questions was playing with fire. Patricia's answers might have aggravated his curiosity disorder. He never again asked her any questions, nor did he accept money from her when she walked by.

Lynn was trying to get ready for a lunch appointment with a collector. She couldn't find her tweezers. She never left home or her gallery without plucking a couple of hairs first. This preparation was mental more than physical.

She usually kept tweezers in her desk drawer, but they weren't there; she had looked three times already. She searched on her desk, under her desk, around the light box, in the wastepaper basket, in the bathroom, all the while mumbling to Patricia that she couldn't find her red tweezers. Patricia's silence suddenly made an impression on her. Lynn looked at her assistant, who was staring back at her placidly. The tweezers were on Patricia's nose, clamping it shut, pointing forward and up, like a strange beak.

"I've been looking for those for the past ten minutes. You know I'm running late for lunch!"

She marched toward her assistant, arm outstretched to grab her tweezers, but Patricia yanked them off her nose and hid them behind her back, shaking her head and saying, "No plucky before stalky. You haven't stalked yet today. Stalk first, pluck later."

They should put an expiration date on those pita rolls. There was no question about that. Those supermarket people were in the wrong. And they lied to Alan. They told him the pita rolls were replaced every day, but they were not, Alan was sure of it. To prove it, he had secretly marked them when no one was looking, made a tiny X with a pen on the label on the back of the package. And five days later, they were still there.

To soothe his nerves he added two six-packs of beer to his shopping cart and headed toward the checkout. The female cashier carded him. He thought she was just trying to flatter him, to make up for the lie about the pita rolls. He searched for his driver's license but couldn't find it.

She wouldn't let him buy the beer without ID.

"But I'm thirty-four and look even older," he said.

"I'm sorry, it's our policy."

"Okay, I'm flattered, I appreciate your attempt at making me feel better after the fiasco with the pita rolls, but please ring up this beer. I need it to help me get over the pita rolls. I need it more than flattery."

She still refused.

"If you don't ring up this beer I will be more pissed off than ever about the pita rolls, and you will have defeated your purpose."

She didn't seem particularly knowledgeable about the pita-roll reference. Perhaps not everyone was in on it.

"Okay, whatever. This supermarket sucks," he said, paying for the rest of his merchandise.

Just as he had promised, he walked home feeling more angry than ever. The disappearance of his driver's license didn't help, but he knew he was also irritated at himself over an entirely different issue.

It was bad enough that the woman he loved and stalked loved and stalked another man, but that on top of it she was using his precious words to seduce her prey was tough on Alan. No matter how hard he tried to shrug it off, it came back, the torment. He came up with an idea he hoped would get her attention, perhaps even bring her to a halt in her pursuit of Roland.

At home, he screwed his Polaroid camera onto a tripod, took off his clothes, pressed the timer button, and stood in front of the camera. The flash went off and the picture slid out. He waited for his nakedness to appear. It did. His entire body and face were very clear. He slipped the photo into an envelope, got dressed, and dropped it off at Lynn's gallery.

Later, Lynn opened the envelope, was assaulted by the sight of her naked stalker, and, refusing to remember that she had promised Patricia she would come up with her own ideas, she slipped the Polaroid into another envelope and addressed it to Mr. Dupont. She attached a little note to the picture.

Roland Dupont, later, opened the envelope and was assaulted by the sight of his racquetball partner naked. He grimaced and read the note.

Later, Alan waited for Roland at the racquetball courts. When Roland finally showed up, he thrust something into Alan's hands and said, "Explain."

Alan stared at the naked photo of himself. The volleying racquetballs in nearby courts sounded like explosives, blasting into his brain.

Alan had not expected Lynn to send Roland that photo. After he'd mailed it to Lynn, he'd deeply regretted doing so when he realized Lynn might copy his idea and send Roland a nude photo of herself. He'd felt like a complete idiot and was beating himself up about it. He, Alan, was the one who deserved a naked photo of Lynn, not Roland. He'd tried to comfort himself with the thought that maybe Roland would at least let him see the nude photo of Lynn. Maybe Roland would even let Alan buy it from him, or at least make a Xerox of it.

Alan had to think fast. He couldn't let Roland know that their meeting as racquetball partners had been deliberate; otherwise, Alan was sure Roland would get paranoid, would want nothing more to do with Alan, would think Alan and Lynn were psychos who were probably in cahoots and purposely tormenting him. Alan was not ready for that to happen. He wanted to continue his acquaintanceship with Roland; he wanted to know him better and understand what Lynn saw in him.

In order for this to happen, he had to act at least as shocked as Roland by this turn of events.

"How do *you* explain it?" Alan shouted.

"I got it from my stalker. I think it's pretty self-explanatory. Read the fucking note."

Alan read, "Dear Mr. Dupont, Here is proof that I am a desirable person and that you should give me some thought. This is a photo of my stalker, which he sent me this morning. You see, I have one, too."

"Are you my stalker's stalker?" Roland asked.

"I am no one's stalker. Apparently, the woman I admire may be the same woman who's been admiring you." Alan carefully changed his expression, trying to appear as though he were making a sudden realization. "Oh my God. She's copying me! She's sending you the same notes I sent her. I *thought* those notes you told me about sounded familiar, like when she called you 'My pooky bear.' I mean, that is not the universal language of stalkers, I don't think." Alan felt the need to discuss with Roland the strangeness of Lynn copying his stalking style.

Roland said, "The notes she sent me are in my briefcase in the locker room. Let's check."

They went. Alan's chest was puffed out, his stride brisk with indignation. Roland took a penny out of his shorts' pocket and covertly dropped it on the floor.

When Roland opened his briefcase, Alan gasped and clenched the fabric covering his heart. It was no longer acting. "These are the *actual notes* I sent Lynn," he said, picking up a note and scratching off the Wite-Out. "What else did she send you?"

"Flowers, candy, a bonsai tree, lingerie."

"She copies my stalking mindlessly, without even thinking or making sense. She's a machine, a factory of stalking. Why would she send you lingerie? For you to wear?"

"No, her note said she could wear the lingerie for me."

"Hmph. What did it look like?"

"Yellow with a pink lace border."

"I bought it at Victoria's Secret. It was expensive."

"I can give it back to you if you want."

"That would seem fair. It's not the money I'm concerned about. The item was special to me. And it's weird that you would own it."

"I agree. In a roundabout way, Alan, all of this makes you my stalker."

Alan turned red. "I asked you not to call it that."

"Very well then—my admirer."

"How ironic, then, that I don't admire you."

The two men stared at each other. Alan finally added, "No offense."

"Fine, none taken. Listen, if you've been following this woman a lot, why didn't you notice she was following me?"

Alan had to be careful and persuasive. "I stay a certain distance behind her and she probably stays a certain distance behind you, so the distance between you and me is pretty significant."

Roland nodded.

"Plus, I lack powers of observation," Alan said, "especially in those crowded streets and when I'm focused on Lynn. Also, I have poor skills in recognizing people, particularly from the back. I do remember noticing she had an air of self-centered single-mindedness—which I found very appealing—but I didn't attribute that to the fact that she was following someone."

Alan noticed Roland was staring at him with an air of suspicion, which was exactly what Alan had feared. *Think! Think!* he told himself. And then he got an idea. *Turn the tables.*

"This is all strange," Alan said. "Is it really just a coincidence, or are you in on this with Lynn? Are you a friend of hers who's helping her get back at me for stalking her?"

"No, I'm not a friend of hers! And I could say the same to you!"

"Well, I'm not a friend of hers, believe me. I wish I were." *Good. Now, use distraction.* "But there are two questions that are driving me crazy. The first one is, Why is she copying my stalking method?"

"Well, that seems pretty obvious," Roland said. "This woman wants me, but she's too lazy to come up with her own stalking methodology. Too cheap to buy me her own lingerie, and probably her own flowers, too, and her own candy."

Alan was surprised by this theory, but it made some sense.

"We can't let her get away with this," Roland said. "What she's doing calls for retaliation."

Alan was even more surprised by this comment, but his fixation on another issue prevented him from getting sidetracked. "And the second question that's driving me crazy is, Why does Lynn prefer you to me?"

Roland stared at the Humpty-Dumpty man addressing him. He shrugged modestly.

They played their game of racquetball. The Frenchman won. Before leaving the gym, he took a shirt button out of his pocket and dropped it on the floor. He always had a fresh supply of buttons, pennies, paper clips, and movie stubs in his pockets to avoid the discomfort of finding himself with nothing to lose.

One of Lynn's artists was showing her a just-finished abstract painting composed of brilliant colors and geometric shapes. Lynn was gazing at it without liking it, making polite but unenthusiastic sounds.

The artist suddenly said, "The title of this painting is, *You Should Stalk More*."

Shocked, Lynn asked, "Why did you call it that?"

"Patricia suggested it. Said you'd like it."

Ray the homeless man found himself overcome by the urge to whisper therapeutic comments to Roland, Lynn, and Alan as they passed, but he tried to resist exercising his influence and deploying his power of suggestion. Sometimes he failed.

The first time this urge overpowered him, he whispered to Alan,

"Get a life. Manhattan is a city rich in possibilities. Inject some variety into your stalking. Pick someone else for a day."

Lynn was tired of Patricia's pranks. One time, Lynn took a bite of a sandwich she had bought earlier, but the layer between the ham and the cheese was not appetizing. She slid it out. It was a piece of paper on which Patricia had scrawled, "Why aren't you stalking?"

"How can I make you stop doing these things to me?"

Patricia handed her a typewritten document.

Lynn read.

STALKING ASSIGNMENTS

In order to avoid any further annoyances, at least one or a combination of the following has to be done daily:

- *Follow Mr. Dupont for an hour.*
- *Loiter outside his building for an hour and a half.*
- *Say something to him. Make eye contact. Let your presence be felt.*
- *Write him notes, call him, spy on him, go up to people he's hanging out with, talk to his doorman some more.*

Three

By the next time the two men met, Alan had come up with a theory as to why Lynn preferred Roland to himself, and he was excited to share it.

"It has to do with color," Alan said, pausing dramatically, clearly waiting for Roland to say "Oh?" So Roland humored him and said, "Oh?"

Alan nodded with delight. "It's the colors you wear."

"What colors?"

"Any colors. You wear those things called colors. I don't. I mostly wear black. I was watching a nature show last night on birds. And bingo. Our little Lynn, she's like a little bird, haven't you noticed? So it's normal that she would respond favorably to men adorned in bright colors."

It was strange to Roland that Alan was so blind to Roland's more obvious attributes, but Roland didn't see how he could inform him of them without being offensive or sounding monstrously conceited.

Lynn came back to her gallery after having spent hours stalking. Exhausted and achy, she lay down on the floor.

Patricia stood over her without pity.

"Stalking makes me feel humiliated," groaned Lynn.

"Good," Patricia said. "As you said yourself, you've been on top of the world for too long. A little humiliation once in a while is healthy, it's part of the human experience. It's like gravity. If you don't have it, you're like those astronauts who've been in space for ages. Your muscles get weak. You start having problems, unless you're on a special exercise program. Your exercise program is stalking."

Charlie Santi entered the gallery. Lynn promptly picked herself off the floor.

He wanted to show her some of his new paintings. Lynn had been representing Charlie for five years and had always been his staunchest supporter until the sudden disappearance of her desire. She took him to the dreaded light box, remembering when she used to call Charlie up almost every day, begging to know what he was up to.

Charlie began laying out transparencies of paintings. They were in his usual style. Charlie's canvases were always fairly large, covered in textured white paint. In a corner, or at least off center, was always a tiny shape, which looked vaguely like a person, but that was never certain. In Lynn's all-time favorite painting of Charlie's, the little shape looked as though it might be lying on its side, sleeping, possibly with its hands under its cheek. It was a very peaceful painting, which, along with all the other paintings in the world, she no longer liked.

Lynn stood rigidly over the light box, making polite but reserved sounds.

Her stalker, whom she hadn't yet noticed, was standing outside the gallery window, staring at Lynn through the glass fondly. He was wearing red pants, a green shirt, a blue tie, a yellow jacket, orange shoes, and a purple hat with a white feather sticking out of the top. He looked like an elf. Or a parrot.

When Charlie was done showing Lynn the transparencies, he said, "So, what do you think?"

She glanced at him almost pleadingly. "Oh, Charlie. I think you should trust your instinct. I'm not the right person to ask right now."

"I want an answer. An honest answer. Yes or no. Do you like them?"

"Charlie, I'm not . . ."

"Yes or no, Lynn! Yes or no, goddammit!"

The cuckoo clock Patricia had recently bought for Lynn did its hourly thing. Its doors flew open, the yellow bird came out, but instead of saying "Cuckoo!" it said, in Patricia's voice, "Stalk! Stalk! It's four o'clock! Do you know where Mr. Dupont is?"

Unwilling to be distracted, Charlie said, "Just answer me, Lynn, do you like them?"

"No," she said gently. "But it doesn't mean anything."

"Shh! I brought two canvases with me." He quickly unwrapped them. "This work is phenomenal," he said. "I'm no longer asking you, I'm telling you. Because I don't have the slightest doubt."

"That's great," she said.

"Really? You like them?"

"Well . . . I meant it's great that you feel so strongly about them."

"But do you like them?"

Lynn scrutinized the paintings, searching for the faintest speck that might thrill her. In one painting, Charlie had, for the first time ever, painted not one, but two tiny shapes. One appeared to be strangling or hugging the other. In the second painting, the single tiny shape was in a fetal position, or possibly just thinking in a position like *The Thinker,* by Rodin.

The little shapes became blurry through Lynn's tears.

"Can I ask you a question?" Charlie finally said.

Lynn nodded.

"Do you think I suck, or do you think you suck?"

"I think it's probably me," she said.

"What do you mean it's *probably* you? I won an American Prix de Rome, a Guggenheim, an NEA, and an NYFA. I'm at the forefront of academic interest. Doesn't that speak for my work?"

Patricia laughed softly. Lynn frowned with alarm at the lack of tact.

"Did you take a look at your stalker today, Lynn?" Patricia said, pointing to the window.

Lynn looked at her stalker. "Why is he dressed that way?"

"Who knows," Patricia said. "Maybe he watched that nature show last night on birds and decided to dress colorfully to attract your attention."

Charlie packed up his art and left without saying anything.

Roland dropped quarters into the hand of the homeless man, who looked into his eyes, and whispered, "You're being followed."

When Lynn gave him change ten seconds later, the homeless man said to her, "You're on a downward spiral of self-destruction. Don't put all your eggs in one basket."

And after Lynn, he said to Alan, "Take a class, a vacation, a multivitamin. Take your mind off romance, take control of your life and your future." Alan stared back at Ray, who was screaming, "Go and see a movie, take a self-improvement class. You're better than them!"

At a small café near the gym, before their scheduled game of racquetball, Alan told Roland that his color theory hadn't worked.

Roland was pleased, and said, "That's terrible."

Alan was silent, looking down at the table morosely.

To be nice, Roland tried to change the topic. "So, what did you do last night? Did you go out?"

"I walked down the stairs of my building, making sure the stairwell doors were closed on every floor."

"Why?"

"In case there's a fire. It's really important for the stairwell doors to be closed. It prevents the fire from spreading too quickly. I check the doors every day."

"Doesn't it take time away from your stalking?"

"It only takes about four minutes."

"Did you do anything else last night?"

"No. I tried to understand why my color theory didn't work." Alan looked disillusioned. "I really thought it was the key. I mean, it made so much sense. Look at us. Color was the only difference between us. Now that we're both colorful, we could be twins. Well, no, I'm exaggerating, but you know what I mean. We're both fine-looking guys, relatively charismatic, intelligent, pretty well educated, somewhat athletic."

Roland could no longer be polite.

"Where did you go to college, Alan?" he asked.

"Putnam."

"I went to Harvard."

"Same difference," Alan said, nodding. "Both good colleges. Don't tell me you're going to quibble over which is better?"

"Who always beats whom in our games of racquetball?"

"I think we're pretty well matched. So far, you may have beaten me more often. I don't really keep track of these things."

"Which one of us is a lawyer, and which one an accountant, not even a CPA?"

"You know the answer to that."

"Who is six-three, 190 pounds, muscular, with a full head of hair? And who is five-seven, 190 pounds, not muscular, and bald?"

In a small voice, Alan said, "Well, who has blond hair and blue eyes?"

"Excuse me?"

"Well, who has blond hair and blue eyes?"

Roland stared at Alan for a few long seconds, then said, "You are a short, fat, balding man with blue eyes and a few patches of yellow fuzz. You're like Danny DeVito with blond hair and blue eyes."

"But you don't have them at all."

"That's right."

"Wait, let me get this straight," Alan said, smiling. "Are you trying to tell me that you *don't* think we're equal in the realm of desirability? Are you trying to imply that you're . . . um . . . superior to me, in some way?" Alan stared at Roland's locket, feeling sorry for whatever family member or sweetheart was in there. He pitied that relative for being associated with such a pompous ass.

Roland saw him look at his locket, guessed his thoughts precisely, and rolled his eyes. In his locket was not a family member or sweetheart, but cyanide, for the purpose of self-deliverance if the need ever arose. Wearing a cyanide-filled locket was a tradition in his family. The item had been passed down four generations. When Roland had turned fourteen, his father had taken him on a walk, "man to man." (*"D'homme à homme,"* is what he actually said, since they were French.)

"I want to give you this," his father had said, pulling out of his pocket a chain from which swung a locket just like the one hanging around his own neck, the inside of which had always remained a mystery to Roland and his sister.

The young Roland took the locket.

"C'est du cyanure," his father said. ("It's cyanide.")

Roland's innocent eyes opened wide. "To kill someone?"

"No!" the father said, shocked that his son's mind would jump to such vile conclusions. "To kill yourself."

Roland winced and looked up at his father to make sure he wasn't joking. "But I don't want to kill myself."

"One day you might."

"Why?"

"Sometimes in life, it happens," his father said, in his usual impatient tone that meant, "You are a moron, my son."

Roland tried not to cry, but couldn't hold back the tears. He threw the locket on the ground and kicked dirt over it.

His father hurriedly picked it up and wiped off the dust. *"Non mais, ça va pas la tête?"* ("Are you crazy?")

Roland's cheeks were like peaches in the rain.

"Why can't you ever act like a man?" his father said, pacing around him. "It's an honor, that I'm giving you this. I'm not giving one to your sister. Doesn't that make you happy?"

"That's because you don't want her to die!"

His father grabbed his arm and shook him. "I don't want you to die. Unless you want to."

Roland still pouted.

They resumed walking, and his father began a speech, which

Roland never forgot. His father said, "Life is a prison. Most of the time, it's a nice prison, and you want to be in it, but the prison is even nicer if the door is unlocked. Knowing that the door can be stepped through at any time makes your time in prison more relaxed, that's all. By giving you this locket, I am telling you, 'You are old enough, my son, to decide if you ever want to walk through that door.' I'm giving you freedom. Having quick and easy access to death makes us more elevated, more evolved than other men. Less like women. We're carrying around a bit of perspective at all times."

The young Roland reluctantly began wearing the locket. He would practice finding the idea of spontaneous self-destruction attractive.

After a few months, he always wore it and enjoyed what it meant, and now, as a grown man, he couldn't imagine what it must be like, psychologically, for the rest of the population, who didn't have this quick and easy access to death. Of course, they had certain means at their disposal—jumping out a window or hurling themselves in front of a subway train, for example—but those methods were inefficient and melodramatic.

"Well," Alan repeated, "are you trying to imply that you're superior to me in some way?"

"No, not in some way. In every way," Roland said. "I'm sorry, but I couldn't take it any longer. I didn't want to hear any more of your crap. I'm sure you understand." He got up and added, "We better call this game off. Maybe I'll see you next time." He walked away, dropping a small button.

Alan remained sitting for a long time. He had never been so insulted in his life. His skin prickled. There was not such a big difference between them. It bugged him that there was even a single soul on earth (Roland's soul) who thought there was.

Alan hated that soul.

He ordered a beer. The waitress asked him for ID. He could not believe it. "I'm thirty-four," he said to the waitress, who didn't seem to care. While searching for his driver's license in his bag, he thought, *Well, I may be short, fat, and balding, but at least I look under twenty-one.* He didn't find his license and wasn't given the beer.

The homeless man said to Roland, "They're still behind you. You're not alone."

To Lynn, he said, "You're being followed as well. Join a dating service, a choir. Take a break, an antidepressant. Get hold of yourself."

And to Alan, "Forget about her. Get a pet, a hobby, a makeover, dignity. Explore the world and gain perspective."

Roland felt guilty immediately. He regretted the things he had said to Alan and was surprised that Alan continued meeting with him for their racquetball games. When Roland tried to apologize, Alan didn't accept the apology and was not willing to forgive him.

Alan was smart enough to know that he was in an advantageous position. He would continue to sulk mildly, until he came up with a way to profit from Roland's guilt.

Alan liked hating Roland. In fact, he had wanted to hate him from the beginning, but it had been hard at first, Roland being nice, most of the time.

In an attempt to rekindle a semblance of friendliness between them, Roland brought up an old topic. "You know, it's a shame that we never came up with a plan to get back at Lynn. She toyed with us. We'll toy with her." Roland looked affectionately at Alan and managed the approximation of a smile, using his neck and eye muscles. "Whatever it is we'll do to her will be a lot of fun for us, I'm sure," he said. "So let's give it some thought, okay?"

Sitting on his beloved armless white easy chair at home, Alan did give it some thought. And he did come up with a plan. An excellent plan, for someone who hadn't gone to Harvard, he gloated.

Taking advantage of Roland's still-existing feelings of guilt, he told him the plan, and quickly pronounced it as the only way Roland could ever make up for the awful way he had treated him.

Resentfully, Roland said, "That's not the kind of plan I had in mind."

Firmly, Alan said, "I know it's not."

"Listen," Roland said, "you annoyed me so much when you pretended you couldn't see the differences between us, that I ended up saying those stupidities that made me feel remorseful. If it now amuses you to take advantage of that by forcing me to do this thing which you know will be a nightmare for me, fine. I will make this huge sacrifice for you. But then I'll be done with you."

Roland Dupont strolled into Lynn's gallery, casually dropping a button. He planted himself in front of Lynn and her assistant, who were standing in front of a blank wall, discussing it. They were stunned by Mr. Dupont's arrival.

"I need to speak with you. I have a proposition to make," he said to Lynn. "I propose that you spend a weekend with Alan, the gentleman who fancies you, and in return I will spend a weekend with you."

Lynn had no idea what he was talking about. She didn't know who "Alan" was. She knew lots of Alans, and it didn't occur to her that her stalker and stalkee could know each other. But regardless, she was already shocked by the repulsiveness of the offer.

"Who's Alan?" she asked.

"The gentleman who fancies you."

"Could you be a little more specific?"

"There are lots of gentlemen who fancy her," Patricia said.

"Alan is the gentleman you might have noticed walking behind you on occasion," Roland said. "He sent you a naked picture of himself, which you then kindly passed on to me. Am I jogging your memory? He sent you dozens of notes signed 'Alan,' which you covered in Wite-Out. You sent me the underwear he bought for you. You sent me the bonsai tree he gave you. And the flowers, and the cookies. It's always good to economize. Passion doesn't need to be expensive, nor does it need to use up mental energy or creativity."

Lynn was getting the sneaking suspicion she had picked a nutcase to stalk. "You know my stalker?" she asked.

"Yes. Your stalker, Alan, is my racquetball partner."

They stared at each other.

"So where are you from, anyway?" Roland asked. "If we're going to spend a weekend together, I'd like to know a little about you."

"Long Island," she said, and added nothing.

"So, are you interested in my weekend offer? Sex will not be expected, on either weekend, from any of the parties."

Since she didn't answer right away, he added, "I know that half of the deal is repulsive to you, but just think of the other half—the weekend with me."

"I am."

"She'd like to mull it over," Patricia said. "Wouldn't you, Lynn?"

"Yes," Lynn said.

They exchanged business cards, and her stalkee left, dropping a paper clip.

"I'm not sure my stalking therapy is working," Lynn said to Patricia. "My degree of revulsion is . . . phenomenal."

"You do look pale. But he's not so bad, Lynn," Patricia said. "He's pretty good-looking, and he could be intelligent. You never know, he might turn out to be the man of your dreams."

"No one is ever going to be the man of my dreams unless he utters my secret name," Lynn said.

"What secret name? You mean like Rumpelstiltskin?"

"I guess so."

"So what is it?"

"I can't tell anyone. That's part of the rules."

"What rules?"

"They're from my childhood," Lynn said, her head in her hands.

"I'm not surprised, it does sound rather childish."

"It's not childish, it's romantic."

"And what if no one ever utters your secret name?"

"Then I'll have boyfriends, maybe even a life partner or a husband, but not a man of my dreams."

"How sad."

"It may be sad, but that's the way it is."

"Your stalkers are still there," Ray the homeless man whispered to Roland, who was passing.

After accepting Lynn's coins, Ray tried to exercise his influence on her. "Do volunteer work, make new friends, learn an instrument, catch up on your reading."

He took Alan's money as well, and said, "Drink eight glasses of water a day. Wear sunblock. Endanger your life to gain perspective."

Lynn thought about the offer. Hoping that spending a few days with a man might revive her desire more effectively than following him down the street, she finally agreed to the deal, as long as she could do the weekend with Roland before the one with Alan. She wanted to get ready for maximum revulsion. The men accepted the order.

Lynn decided to go to Bloomingdale's to buy some cologne for Roland, cologne that she hoped would make her desire him.

In the perfume department, she approached a man behind a counter and asked him for the most widely proven men's cologne. He reached for a bottle. It annoyed her immeasurably that he didn't ask her what she meant by "widely proven." Clearly, he just wanted to sell her anything.

She sniffed the top of the open bottle. "And this will do what I want it to?"

"Yes, ma'am," he said, looking in the other direction, clearly bored.

"How do you know what I want it to do?" she asked.

"It doesn't matter what you want it to do, specifically. It makes all your dreams come true. And his, too."

"What if mine and his are not the same? What if they are mutually exclusive?"

"Then it finds a way to make them coexist without problems."

"Can I get my money back if it doesn't work?"

"If you haven't opened the package and you still have the receipt, yes."

"How can I test it out if I don't open the fucking package?"

"Excuse me?"

"How can I know if this perfume will make my dreams and his coexist without problems if I don't open the package?"

"You must have faith. If you open the package and it doesn't work, that means you didn't have faith, and your money's gone. But if you have faith, it will work."

Lynn felt a momentary twinge of desire. It was the desire to kill the sales assistant, so it didn't count.

Instead, she bought the cologne and walked home, hating the world and observing herself hating it. She always found it curious to be in a truly bad mood, a mood in which she got angry at her pocket, at the carpet, at the peephole, for all sorts of uninteresting reasons.

Four

In the car ride to the inn, Saturday morning, Lynn sat on the right edge of the passenger seat, as far from Roland as she could. She pressed herself against the door and looked out the window, disgusted and silent.

"You're not acting like a stalker," he said.

"I'm gathering my strength," she replied, not taking her eyes off the scenery while trying to want him.

"Boy, if you're so un-perky with me, I wonder what you'll be like during your weekend with your own stalker."

She became a shade paler. "Please let's not talk about him."

She tried to distract herself by meditating. She closed her eyes and in her mind focused on a large black dot—a giant period. And she tried to want. She opened herself up to desire, to desiring Roland, specifically. She tried to like the sound of his voice as he spoke to her. She waited for him to do something appealing. It seemed hopeless. Tears ran down her cheeks. Not wanting to draw attention to them, she didn't wipe them away. But soon Roland said, "Oh shit, what have I gotten myself into? A crying stalker." He sighed. "What's wrong?"

"Nothing at all. Please don't mind me."

"I'm sorry, but you can't cry and say 'please don't mind me.' It's rude."

"I was just meditating, and sometimes when I meditate my eyes tear."

Suddenly, she opened her bag and said, "I got you a present." She took out the cologne she had bought for him.

"Oh no," he groaned. "You're not going to shower me with gifts during the whole weekend, are you?"

"This is the only one I got." She opened the bottle and sprayed some on him.

A wave of nausea swept over her. "Pull over!" she screamed.

He did. She stumbled out of the car but was not able to throw up. She took deep breaths of fresh air and tried to calm herself.

Finally, she got back in the car. Roland had rolled down all the windows, for her sake. "I don't think it smells so bad," he said.

He started dialing a number on his cell phone, telling Lynn, "I have to call the hotel manager and let him know we're running late. He wanted the exact time we'd be arriving; otherwise, he said he might not be there to let us in."

Roland got the manager on the phone and told him they'd be there in an hour.

Lynn pondered the fact that Patricia thought Roland could turn out to be the man of Lynn's life. She smiled to herself when she recalled having told Patricia about her secret name.

Lynn, herself, didn't really believe the story, but she did find it romantic.

When Lynn was about six years old, she was at the birthday party of a friend of hers, on Long Island, whose wealthy family had the luxury of hiring a fairy, Miss Tuttle, to entertain.

"Are you real?" Lynn asked the fairy.

"No. I'm a fairy. Fairies are not as real as people."

"I mean are you a real fairy?" Lynn said, impatiently. "Can you prove to me that you're a real fairy?"

"How?"

"I don't know. You're the fairy. You should know how to prove it."

"Okay, I'll tell you something a real person would never tell you. Think of a secret name for yourself. This will be your real name. And one day, your Prince Charming will come along, and you will recognize him, because you'll hear him say your secret, real name."

"What's my secret real name?" Lynn asked.

"You have to decide for yourself. And it must be a name you've never heard before, a name you make up. And you must never say it to anyone."

"Can it be beautiful?"

"Yes."

Lynn thought about it for a while, and said, "Can it be Slittonia?"

"No," Miss Tuttle the fairy said, thinking it sounded vaguely pornographic. She didn't want to be accused of having a bad influence.

"Why not?"

"Because you just said it to me. I told you that you could not say it to anyone. Including me. In fact, never say it out loud, even to yourself, not even in a whisper. Only in your mind."

So Lynn chose "Airiella," in her mind.

It was only when Lynn got older that she realized Miss Tuttle the fairy must have been down on men, down on love, and that she had given Lynn a secret message, which was: there is no Prince Charming; Prince Charmings are as unreal as fairies.

For where, when, and how would Lynn come across a man who would, within her earshot, utter her secret name—a name she had made up when she was six?

Lynn later learned that Miss Tuttle, the grim fairy, also worked in the neighboring town of Cross as a hairdresser.

When Lynn and Roland entered the tiny lobby of the inn, no one was there. On the front desk were two keys, with a note that said, "For Roland Dupont and guest: In case I'm not back, you can go straight to your rooms.—Max the manager."

They went up. Lynn took the key to room six, and Roland the key to room seven. The door to room six did not have a number on it the way the other doors did, but since it was the only door between rooms five and seven, Lynn assumed it to be the right one.

As she pressed her key against the keyhole, the door gently swung open on its own.

Inside the room were two people having sex and talking about the weather. They did not notice Lynn right off, which was how she got to hear some of their talk.

The woman was lying on her back, on a desk, and the man was standing between her legs, thrusting. The man saw Lynn first and stopped. He turned red quickly, batted his eyes, but apart from that, was frozen. Lynn backed out, stammering.

The man pulled out of the woman and gushed with apologies. "Oh my God, I'm so sorry. Are you my new guests?"

Roland had joined Lynn in the doorway, and they were both speechless as the man grabbed his shirt off the floor and wrapped it around his waist. The naked woman had gotten off the desk and was crouching behind it, hiding.

"I'm really sorry," the man said to Lynn and Roland, "this is so excruciatingly, exquisitely embarrassing. But the fact is, you made a mistake. The number on your key is six. This is room eight."

"Room *eight*? But it's between five and seven! Where's room six?" Lynn said.

"Farther down the hall. The rooms aren't in order. This is only an inn," the man said.

"Who are you?" Roland asked.

"I'm Max, the manager. Why don't you go to your rooms and make yourselves comfortable, and I'll be with you after I wash up."

He found them in their rooms a few minutes later. "I'm glad you're here. Finally, some interesting people to rescue me! I have not been blessed by the guests here recently. They're so bourgeois."

Their eyes were focused on his codpiece. He took Lynn's hand, kissed it, said, "Charmed," and bowed low, his shirt ruffles sweeping the floor.

Lynn scrutinized him. He seemed to be in his late twenties. He was taller than Roland. He had better posture, was better-looking, and had long hair—a thing Lynn liked on men. And yet, somehow, through dress, mannerisms, and conversation, he was not as appealing as Roland, who was not that appealing himself.

"By the way, a Mr. Simon Peach called for you. He asked that you call him back," Max said to Roland. He then turned around and walked out, saying, "If you need anything, just think my name. I have ESP."

Simon Peach was Alan's code name. He had told Roland that the reason he'd be using a code name was that he wanted to reserve the right to call Roland at the inn as often as he liked without embarrassing himself in Lynn's eyes or having her suspect he was obsessive, or at least more obsessive than had already been revealed by his daily stalking.

Roland had promised Alan he'd call him as soon as they arrived at the hotel, but seeing Max naked had reminded Roland of Alan's naked photo, and now he no longer felt like calling him. After settling into their rooms, he and Lynn agreed to go for a walk. He would call Alan later.

Just as they were walking out their doors, a little man appeared saying he wanted to speak with them. They all three went into Roland's room.

"I'm Charles, the assistant manager, and I just wanted to apologize for what happened earlier when you unfortunately walked in on the manager having sex."

"Yeah, that was unfortunate," Roland said.

"It was no accident. It turns Max on tremendously to have people walk in on him. He absolutely relishes feeling embarrassed. He's sort of an exhibitionist. When he gets caught, he turns very red, really enjoying the sensation. The whole thing is painstakingly orchestrated. He doesn't allow himself to indulge in this favorite pleasure of his very often. It could be bad for business."

"Why are you telling us this?" Lynn asked.

"Because that's part of his pleasure, having it revealed to his guests, in case they hadn't figured it out on their own."

"But isn't he going to feel awkward dealing with us now?"

"No, he would love it if he did feel awkward, but embarrassment fades very quickly in him. That's why he treasures it so much. He experiences it so fleetingly."

"He's jaded?" Lynn asked.

"And calloused. And blasé," the little man said. "He has often described to me the pleasure he gets from embarrassment. It's a physical sensation, almost like being on drugs. As his face becomes red, he
feels the blood shooting up, prickling the roots of his hair. He feels
his pores opening. A warmth invades him. It's a rush. His aches and
pains go away momentarily. And he perceives himself as more attractive, both physically *and* personality-wise. He finds embarrassed people very, very charming. He envies them. He thinks that their
embarrassment reveals a kind of purity and innocence and often
even goodness."

"What if we feel dirty now?" Roland said. "And used? And sexually molested, sexually harassed? What if we sue him?"

"But I could be crazy. Everything I just said could be a lie. Don't
you think we've already arranged some evidence to attest to my insanity?" Charles said, and left.

Roland and Lynn debated whether they should stay on at this inn,
but they felt too lazy to find another one. They went to the garden
and looked at the pool, then they went on their walk.

They walked in silence down a sweet little dirt road. Roland
dropped a penny.

Since they had nothing to say to each other, Lynn decided to ask
him questions about her stalker, Alan. She asked him what type of
guy he was. In the process of describing him, Roland revealed that
Alan was from Long Island.

"So am I. Do you know what town?" Lynn asked.

"Of course not."

Tired of the topic, Roland asked, "What is it that you like
about me?"

This was a hard question for Lynn, who did not like anything about Roland.

She was saved from having to make up too many lies by a hare, running across the road. She took a few steps after it, exclaiming in a high voice, "Ooh, a rabbit!"

Roland was disgusted that she would display her stalking tendencies, even here in nature, and asked her to restrain herself. "Do you absolutely have to follow things?" he added.

She detected the revulsion in his tone, and this awakened an interesting feeling in her. She wasn't sure what the feeling was. Perhaps a twinge of excitement. She pounced on it.

"Aren't you a little bit flattered that I'm interested in you?" she asked.

"No. Not the least bit."

"Why not?"

"Because I don't find you appealing."

"Really?" she said. She had been so preoccupied by her own lack of attraction to him that she had forgotten that he was supposedly not attracted to her, either, and was forcing himself to be here this weekend as a favor to his friend Alan. He seemed more interesting now. She stared at his profile as they walked. "Are you sure, or are you just saying that?"

He looked at her, perplexed. "I'm sure. I could never, in a million years, be interested in you romantically. This weekend is a complete waste of time, I guarantee you."

She was scrutinizing him, as well as her feelings for him, and was on the lookout for any further shift.

"Can you be more specific?" she asked. "List the ways. And tell me how much."

"What?"

"The ways in which I don't do it for you. And just how much that's the case."

"Why? Are you a masochist?"

Good question. She would have to think about that. In the meantime, she said, "I don't think so. Just curious. Come on, tell me."

"Well, first of all, you stalk me."

"That doesn't count. I assume there are real reasons why you could never, ever be interested in me, even if I never stalked you."

He looked at her. "Yeah, sure."

"And what are they?"

"I can't explain it. You repulse me, that's it, in brief."

"Is there anything about me that doesn't repulse you?" she asked, trying to sound casual.

He laughed, which for him was something between a sneeze and convulsion, and said, as if only just realizing it himself, "No, actually." After a moment, he added, "Why are you looking at me like that?"

"You're not, actually, bad-looking."

"I assume you wouldn't be stalking me if you found me bad-looking."

Lynn fell into a long silence while they walked, and Roland did not break it. Lynn thought she detected twinges of her own desire. And yet she barely dared hope this could be true. It was just that it was so solid, his disgust. So refreshing and exhilarating. He began saying banalities about the scenery. It didn't matter how banal he was—he didn't want her and that mattered a lot. And what was more, he made it sound like there was nothing she could do about it.

"You look smug," he said.

She smiled broadly. How would she react if he made a pass at her, she wondered? But of course, there was no way he'd do that as long as he thought she was his stalker. She'd have to set him straight on that one, at some point. Or maybe not. Suddenly, inexplicably, she no longer felt the twinge of excitement. She looked at him. He had lost the slight appeal he had momentarily gained.

Back in the city, the thought of Roland and Lynn spending this time together was making Alan sick. Alan was grateful that Roland had agreed to talk to Lynn on his behalf and arranged this weekend exchange, but why wasn't Roland calling him as he had promised?

He tried to keep busy, went down the seventeen flights of his building verifying that all the stairwell doors were shut and went to a health food store to get some antistress herbs that might help him endure the weekend.

Lynn and Roland had lunch in the inn dining room. They were curious about the other guests. As they waited for menus, they glanced around and saw a man and a woman sitting together at a table, but could not detect any signs of unusually pronounced bourgeoisie or anything else out of the ordinary about them. Nevertheless, they could not help feeling flattered that Max had thought they were better than that couple, even if he was a madman, even if he was lying. It was always hard not to feel flattered by compliments, and doubly so if they involved being raised above other people, and triply so if the reason for the elevation was not at all apparent.

There were no menus. Max had no staff. He cooked mushroom omelettes for the diners.

He unexpectedly joined Lynn and Roland at their table. Stretching out in a chair, an elbow on the table, he asked, "So, who are you people, anyway?"

"Oh, just relaxing for the weekend," Roland answered.

Max leaned over and put his hands on both their shoulders. He said, "Children, are you lovebirds?"

"No," Roland said.

"I can rectify that. If you would like me to."

"Uh, we'll think about it," Lynn said.

"I have methods and instruments that can induce the shift, in case you change your minds. So, what's your connection?" Max asked, wiggling his finger between the two of them. "Are you relatives? Blind date?"

"No," Roland said. Lynn noticed him looking down modestly.

"Is she your secretary, your nurse?" Max asked.

Annoyed by his sexism, Lynn replied, "I'm his stalker. He kindly agreed to give me a chance."

"Really?" Max said. "I'm a scion. I think it's good to be blunt that way."

They just stared at him.

He went on. "My parents were friends of the Kennedys and Truman Capote. I grew up in splendor, but now work in this hellhole."

"Why?" Lynn asked.

"Oh, because my parents and I aren't getting along. It's one of those rich-family fights. You know, the kind that happens in dynasties."

Just then, Max was called away from the table by the other couple.

"This is the weekend from hell," Roland said, concentrating on his food.

"What do you mean?"

Roland chose his words carefully. "I am in the company of people I can barely tolerate."

"You mean him and me?"

"Mm-hm."

"Do I really turn you off that much?"

"Yes."

She smiled. She felt herself melting a little, and was suddenly reminded of the assistant manager's description of the pleasure Max got from feeling embarrassed. She felt the same way, her pores opening, a warmth invading her, her aches and pains leaving her momentarily. What else could this be but serious masochism? She knew she'd have to ask herself why she was finding rejection appealing and try to remember the last time she'd been rejected.

She said softly, "I have to confess something."

"What?"

"I'm not a stalker. I was forcing myself to stalk you."

"Good," he said, clearly not believing her. "Then, we can end this weekend right now and go home."

"No, it's not that simple. I no longer feel desire for anything or anyone, and so I picked you to practice on. I want to want you."

He sighed and put his napkin next to his plate. He said he was going to his room to rest.

Alan was in a state of awful anxiety. Roland still hadn't called. He tried not to think about it by busying himself with the preparations for his own weekend with Lynn. He looked for his lost driver's license, because he didn't want to seem unmanly in Lynn's eyes by asking her to drive. After searching for it for twenty minutes, he figured he had more important worries. He planned the weekend in great detail. He made a list of topics of conversation. He went shopping for attractive clothes. He researched hairdressers. He went to the gym.

But it all wasn't enough. He would not deserve her if he didn't do more to make up for his deficiencies. *Go to more trouble,* he told himself, but he wasn't sure there was any more trouble available.

Later, Roland suggested to Lynn that they go for another walk. She brought along some bread to feed the squirrels. The air was pleasantly cool at five-thirty. Their voices seemed unnaturally loud in the quiet of the country.

Lynn wore a cream shirt and brown suede skirt. She was a becoming woman, Roland thought. It didn't make sense that she would be stalking him, not that he was not becoming himself, or that becoming women didn't stalk, but there was just something that didn't fit.

He said, "You were putting me on, right, when you said you were forcing yourself to stalk me?"

"I so wish I was," Lynn said. "But no. Stalking you is an ordeal. I don't know how Alan manages to stalk me with so much energy."

"Listen, I have no idea if what you're saying is true, but it's certainly quirky. You know, I could have liked you if we had met some other way."

"I wish I could say the same to you, but I'm sorry, there's no manner in which we could have met that would have made me like you." After a pause, she added, "You, or anyone, of course. I don't always add that, because it gets wordy."

Softly, he said, "I think you should add it, even if it gets wordy."

"Oh, okay."

They came upon a bench and sat down. Lynn was on the lookout for squirrels.

Out of the bushes appeared a little pointy face. A raccoon. She threw bread at the raccoon, not quite far enough, in order to lure the animal closer. It worked.

"You should not feed this animal. It's vermin," Roland said.

"I strongly disagree." Lynn kept feeding it, bringing it closer.

"You're not even trying to like me. Why did you bother coming this weekend?"

"I am trying," she said.

Roland used another tactic. "I'm hungry. I want to eat your bread. Please give it to me."

"I don't have much left."

"Will you choose to give your bread to an animal rather than to a hungry man?"

"Yes."

Lynn continued feeding the raccoon. How much more she enjoyed taming than stalking. Perhaps the world was divided into two kinds of people: the tamers and the stalkers. She was clearly a tamer. Taming was a more evolved activity. Stalking was a more animalistic activity. Like eating. Like fucking.

"It might have rabies," Roland said, looking at the raccoon, who was a foot from Lynn's leg. "You better be careful."

By then the raccoon was eating out of Lynn's hand. It gave her a strange feeling of sadness that this was the level at which things could feel right and good. Roland better not move a hair and ruin this one sweet moment for her, or she would kill him.

He did not.

And the raccoon bit her.

She yanked her hand away, looking at the animal with shock as it ran into the bushes. He had bitten her out of the blue, the brute.

"Is it bleeding?" Roland asked.

"Yes."

As they walked back to the hotel to find the manager, Roland furtively dropped a button and said, "I told you that you should have fed me the bread. I wouldn't have bitten you."

"There has been one instance," Max said, "in these parts, of someone catching rabies from a raccoon. The only way you can tell if someone has it is to do an autopsy. If you're not sure, you have to get six shots over the course of a month. Was the raccoon aggressive? Or strangely forward? Did it approach you without fear? Sort of like . . . oh, I don't know . . . a stalker?"

"No, not without fear. It took a while for it to eat out of my hand."

"That's a good sign. But I still think you should see a doctor on Monday. Symptoms don't often appear before two weeks, but if you wait until they do appear, there's no treatment, you die."

"What are the symptoms?" Roland asked.

"Irritability, headaches, fever, spasms of the throat muscles, and, eventually, convulsions and delirium. The girl who died of rabies had everything going for her. It's a very painful death. And, obviously, it's contagious." Max looked at Lynn. "If you start acting strangely, I will have to put you down."

"You mean kill me?" Lynn said.

"If I see no alternative."

"That's ridiculous."

"Just don't act strangely."

All three stared at each other for a few seconds. Abruptly, Max said to Roland, "Simon Peach called for you again. He wondered if you had gotten his first message."

Lynn had an introspective, preoccupied look on her face during dinner. She was trying to detect rabid feelings in herself, feelings of aggressiveness. She worried that she might be salivating more than usual. And she felt strangely drawn to her knife.

She complained of these things to Roland, who tried to get her mind off them. To get one's mind off a worry, there's nothing like replacing it by another worry. So Roland talked to her about her desire for nothing and how unpleasant it must have been and must still be, and soon she was no longer complaining about strange attractions to knives.

Max had prepared them vegetable lasagna. He joined them for a few minutes, addressing Roland while looking at Lynn. "Earlier she mentioned being your stalker. I know it's probably wrong of me, but in my mind I tend to equate stalker with whore."

Lynn and Roland looked at Max, thinking he was completely insane.

Roland came to Lynn's defense. "Lynn stalks me not because she desires me, but because she doesn't."

"Whatever," Max said, nodding, and looked at Lynn. "I guess the reason I equate female stalkers with whores is that I assume they're desperate to have sex. So at some point if I happen to say to you, 'Do you want to sit on my cock?" please don't take it personally. I would say that to any female stalker who's not one of my own stalkers. Oh, and as you may have noticed, I wear a codpiece, which shouldn't frighten you. It's true I have a larger penis than most men, particularly in these parts, but it's not quite as big as the codpiece might lead you to believe."

"Is this some sort of show you put on to entertain your guests?" Roland asked.

"Now I'm offended."

"*You're* offended!"

Max nodded. No one spoke, so Max got up, and said, "It's okay, I'll get over it." He walked away.

Lynn wondered if her annoyance at Max was a sign of rabies or if a normal, healthy, nonrabid woman could have become equally annoyed.

Later, she mused to Roland, "Does the madness take hold of you suddenly or gradually? I mean, do you have time to realize what's happening?"

After dinner, they said good night and retired to their separate rooms. Roland dialed Alan, who picked up instantly.

"You didn't call me!" Alan wailed, his voice tinged with hysteria.

"I'm sorry, I was thinking about it all day," Roland said.

"Have you been unattractive?" Alan asked.

"I think so."

"Did you wear that hideous shirt you showed me?"

"Not yet."

"Oh, please wear it. Have you been offensive?"

"Uh, I think so."

"Like what? What did you say?"

"Um, well, when we took a walk, I criticized her for running after a hare. I told her to repress her stalking instincts."

"Ah! That's good. She ran after a hare? That's cute!"

"Yeah."

"What do you mean, 'Yeah'?"

"I'm just agreeing with you."

"You are?"

"Yes. What are you getting at?"

"You're agreeing with me that Lynn is cute to run after a hare."

"I guess I was, but I misspoke. I don't really think it's cute. It was just an automatic response."

"You don't really think it's cute. That's still more positive than how you felt about her before. You found her repulsive, before."

"You're being nitpicky."

"Are you falling for her?"

"No!" Roland said, emphatically and indignantly, which made Alan feel better.

"I wish I was in your shoes, man. I wish I was with her right now," Alan said.

They hung up, and Roland went to bed.

All through breakfast, Roland seemed sullen. Lynn didn't inquire about it. She had her own preoccupations. At the end of the meal Roland suddenly broke the silence with, "I'll help you to like me. We can both work toward that goal. Tell me what to do, I'll do it. What do you like in guys?"

Lynn turned her gaze out the dining room window. After a few seconds, she said, "I think we should hang out with the hotel manager."

"Max? Why?"

"Because you seem more appealing to me when he's nearby."

Roland frowned. "You mean by comparison?"

"Yes. You're enhanced by him." She said this because it was partly true, but also because she didn't want Roland to know the main quality that made him more appealing was his distaste for her.

They found Max and invited him to have tea and a snack with them in the sitting room. He made the tea, brought it to them with cookies, and seemed glad for their company. They were about to ask him questions in order to bring out his repulsiveness, but when they heard the words that came out of his mouth, they knew it would not be necessary.

Turning to Lynn, he said, "I don't think you'll ever see a woman who's properly fucked going around stalking anyone. Which leads me to my next thought, which might be advantageous to the both of us. You could service the men who stay at this hotel, and they would pay a moderate fee, which we would split. It's not a bad deal for you, since you wouldn't be getting just money, but sex, for free. The men wouldn't have to know that they were servicing you. Well, think about it." He turned to Roland and said, "I'm sure that with a little urging she'll accommodate any man in the hotel. Just a gentle prodding and poking."

Lynn glanced at Roland. He did seem improved by comparison. They smiled at each other with complicity. His smile looked like a squint.

The tea came to an end, and Roland believed he and Lynn had obtained what they had sought: Roland's increased attractiveness in Lynn's eyes. They quietly climbed the stairs to Lynn's room with this treasure. They were about to settle down and examine it, when Lynn broke the news to him that it was not there. It had, she said, vanished as soon as the manager had left their presence.

Roland was distressed. There had to be another solution. "What if we had a photograph of the manager, which you could glance at repeatedly while you and I talked?"

She remained silent.

"Or you could have photos of a lot of despicable people, and line them up beside me while we have a conversation," he said.

She liked him more, at that moment, than she ever had so far. It didn't quite make sense, though, for he was not exactly expressing his disgust in her. Nevertheless, she decided to follow her instinct. "Could you make more comments along those lines?" she said.

"Like what?"

"I don't know. But if you think of something similar, say it. It was endearing and generous and pathetic."

"Okay. I have to remember that. Endearing, generous, and pathetic."

"You're doing it again," Lynn said, puzzled.

"Doing what?"

"Being attractive. That's very likable, what you just did."

"You mean trying to remember the words?"

"And that, too!"

"What?"

"What you just said. When you said, 'You mean trying to remember the words?'"

"Did you say it was attractive?"

"And that, too, kind of!"

"DO YOU MEAN I'M BEING ATTRACTIVE?"

"You are."

"Wow."

"Yeah." She nodded.

They both felt sheepish.

"We may not need the photographs after all," he said.

"Let's not get ahead of ourselves."

She paused. "I hope this won't be too much of a . . . blow, but I'm afraid you've lost it. Or I've lost it. I don't see it anymore."

He blinked a few times. "That's okay. Maybe it'll come back."

"It has. I think."

He smiled, not with excitement this time, but with something almost like sadness. He achieved that smile by wrinkling his nose.

"Yes, it has," she said again, more firmly. "I see it."

"I don't dare move. I don't dare speak. I don't want it to go away."

"It's still there." She began advancing toward him slowly, as if approaching a wild animal. She didn't want to frighten the appeal away.

"Is it still here?" he whispered, barely moving his lips, as she got closer.

"Yes," she whispered back, almost inaudibly.

She just wanted to touch it before it fled. Just touch it. She extended her hand toward his face, but before she touched him, she stopped. It had retreated a bit, even though Roland had not moved. She was awed by this evidence of her madness. Was it rabies, she suddenly wondered? She doubted it—it seemed like her usual brand of madness.

When she regained the view of his attractiveness, she resumed her hand's progress. She touched it. It was there. She looked at him up close, from the side.

"You are attractive," she said.

He moved only his pupils.

"No, don't look," she said. "It was better before."

He took his eyes away.

"Yes, I see it now. I see it." She kissed his cheek. She felt it. She saw it.

It was best he not move. It minimized the chances of the appeal vanishing. She was taming the appeal. She kissed him closer to the lips, until she reached their corner. She was afraid of actually kissing them.

"It's there. And I don't know if I should risk scaring it away," she said.

He said nothing. She gathered her courage and kissed his lips lightly. She looked at his eyes. They were glazed, staring ahead. Good. And his hair was nice, too. She tilted her head, watching his face, basking in her faint but definite appreciation of him. Appreciation was almost desire. She wanted him to kiss her back, yet she did not dare ask, afraid the animal would flee.

He started returning her kisses of his own volition, and the appeal was still there; she could sense its presence even though her eyes were closed. And not only was it there, but it became clearer, unexpectedly. Their embraces became more passionate. They started taking off each other's clothes. Suddenly, he stopped kissing her and offered to tie her up.

"What?" she asked, having attained a sufficient degree of desire without needing more inducement.

"I mean, do you really think we should go further without tying you down?" Roland asked. "I don't want to catch rabies from you, in case you *are* rabid. I wonder if it's sexually transmittable."

"I think it's mostly through biting," Lynn said. "I could just not bite you."

"So you say now. But if you get gripped by the urge, you might do it anyway. Unless I keep my face and body away from your head and you're tied down."

She agreed. He tied her wrists to the railing of the headboard. He used a thin leather belt for one wrist and a terry-cloth belt for the other.

There was a knock on the door.

"Yes?" Lynn replied, from the bed.

"It's Max. I just wanted to find out if you were feeling okay and that possibility of rabies we discussed."

"Yes, thank you," Lynn said. "No rabies so far."

"Oh, good, good. Also, there's a call from that Mr. Simon Peach, for Roland, who doesn't seem to be in his room."

"He went out for a walk," Lynn said, having trouble uttering her words because of Roland's weight on her.

"Okay. I will relay the message to Mr. Peach. See you later."

"Yup!"

They heard the manager's footsteps fading away.

Lynn whispered, "What will you do if I start exhibiting rabid behavior while I'm tied up?"

Roland tightened her bonds a little more, and said, "I guess I'll have to call Max and have him shoot you."

"Just please don't mistake other things for rabies."

"Like what?"

"Oh, you know, like . . . ardor."

"Yes, that's a good point."

They began. They looked at each other and did not kiss. They found it curiously exciting. Their lovemaking felt so good that at one point Lynn thought it must be the rabies and got scared. She discovered that it was pleasurable to be afraid of herself, to know that at any moment she might no longer be able to trust herself and might lose control.

Afterward, when he was sleeping beside her, she managed to slip her wrists out of their bondage. She basked in her appreciation of him. She gazed at his resting body. His graceful legs. His hollow stomach. His locket. What was in his locket, anyway?

When he woke up, she asked him.

He stroked her hair. "It's personal."

That's what his father had said to his mother when they had begun dating, forty-two years ago. Except that he had added, "I need to have this one bit of privacy." But Roland didn't add that part. He needed a lot more than that one bit of privacy.

He retied her wrists, and they made love again. Her confidence grew stronger, her confidence that he had unblocked her, had allowed her to want again. She didn't care or worry about anything else. And he didn't either. He was handling her as if he didn't care what happened, had no more fear that anything would vanish—certainly not his attractiveness; maybe his interest, but that was a whole other story.

Alan had succeeded in coming up with another trouble he could go to. He had decided that he and Lynn should go riding on their weekend together. He took a riding lesson in order to be somewhat competent at it. He had a terrible time. It was a terrific trouble to go through, which made him feel that he was earning a positive outcome for the weekend. He fell twice. But he got right back on the horse, even though he was a bit hurt.

When he got home, he was gripped once again by anxiety when he saw there was no message from Roland on his answering machine. Despite his aching, bruised right butt cheek, Alan performed his daily check of the stairwell doors in his building.

He then sat sideways on his armless white easy chair, pressing his facial cheek against its plush back.

Roland was alone in his room on Sunday evening after a whole day of lovemaking. It was almost time for dinner, and he was famished. He had just taken off his clothes to jump in the shower, when he heard the knock at his door.

"Hi, it's Max. There's a call for you. It's that Mr. Simon Peach. He called earlier, I don't know if your stalker told you."

"Yes, she did."

"Do you want to take the call?"

"Hmm. Okay," Roland said, wondering why Max delivered these messages in person rather than by phone.

Roland picked up the phone and said hello.

"It's me," Alan said. "Did you get the message that I called, earlier?"

"Yeah, um, listen, I'm very sorry to tell you this, but there's been an unexpected twist. I'm afraid you won't be able to get your weekend with Lynn. You see . . . she and I ended up hitting it off."

"Did you fuck?"

Roland could not bear to answer that question, so he chose to misunderstand it. "Did I fuck up? I guess so."

"NO! DID YOU FUCK *HER*?"

Roland sighed and lay down on his bed to try to think of a loophole. He held the base of his mostly limp penis between his thumb and forefinger and swung it from side to side, slapping his thigh with it. The light came in through the window in a lovely manner.

Alan waited for an answer, staring fixedly at the stiff and erect riding boots he had bought for his weekend with the woman of his dreams, his queen, his goddess, his little bird. He could not accept the idea that he might have to return the boots.

Roland searched for a way merely to mislead. Lynn had been tied up. Did that make it any less fucking? No. How about the fact that she was possibly rabid and might die soon? That didn't do it either. If *only* he had been the one tied up, then he could have gotten away with saying that no, he had not fucked her, and have a clear conscience knowing that she had fucked him.

"I guess I did," Roland finally said.

He could hear Alan breathing.

"Was it nice?" Alan asked, quietly.

"I'm sorry, Alan. I didn't mean for this to happen, but when she told me she had been stalking me insincerely, in order to try to want me, it changed things for me."

"Whatever. I still think I should get my weekend with her."

"No. I wouldn't be able to take it. It's too late. She and I are involved."

"Traitor," Alan whispered. "My whole life revolved around this woman. I would do anything to have a chance with her. Do you understand? Anything."

"Is that . . . some kind of a . . . threat?"

"Think what you want. I have nothing to live for if she's out of my life. And that also means I've got nothing to lose."

Roland stopped swinging his penis and sat up a little. "Correct me if I'm wrong, but I'm getting the impression you're threatening me."

Alan snorted, kicked his boots. He could still return them, even if he kicked them.

"Come on, man, be realistic," Roland said. "It's not that big a betrayal. I don't even know you that well. It's not as if we're old friends. Or even much of friends at all. Listen, I've got to go, okay? But if you want, call me tomorrow when I'm back in the city."

Alan didn't answer, so Roland said good-bye and hung up. The room felt cold. Roland put on some clothes and sat back down on his bed.

Five

Patricia felt guilty about having forced Lynn to go away on that weekend, even though Lynn had forced her to force her to go. Patricia didn't have to obey Lynn's orders. Some orders in life were best not obeyed. And had Patricia really believed the weekend would help Lynn? No. She had pressured Lynn to go partly for her own entertainment. It was as gruesome as that.

Which was why, when Lynn arrived at the gallery Monday afternoon, after having gotten her first rabies vaccination that morning, Patricia said, "I will not force you to go away next weekend with your stalker. I don't care if you fire me. You can't force me to force you."

"I'm glad you won't force me, because I won't go," Lynn said.

After Lynn amazed Patricia by telling her all about the weekend, Patricia asked, "But why would your desire be awakened by Roland not wanting you? Hasn't anyone not wanted you before?"

"Not in a while. Or at least not that I noticed. I haven't been rejected by anyone or anything in the past year or two."

"Lucky you."

"How can you say that after you've witnessed the ordeal I've suffered?" Lynn said, with a scandalized frown. "It's not lucky, especially for someone like me, who thrives on resistance. I've succeeded, perhaps too consistently, too well, at everything I've set out to do. I've gotten everything I've wanted."

"But what about when Roland started wanting you? Why didn't your desire disappear then?"

"Maybe because it just had to be reawakened, and once it's awake, it's awake."

"But what if it happens again, one day?"

"It will never happen again."

"How can you know?"

"Because I won't let it. I have a method I'll use."

"What is it?"

"To make sure I'm rejected on a regular basis."

"But what if you're not?"

"I'll make sure I am! I'll apply to clubs which would never, in a million years, have me as a member."

"But what if there aren't any?"

"That's impossible. I'll apply to men's clubs, children's clubs, Mensa, if I have to. And I'll find other ways of being rejected."

"You might get *into* Mensa."

"I'm very flattered you think so, but I doubt it."

"How often do you think you need to be rejected to maintain optimal health?"

"I don't know. I'll play it conservatively and make sure I get rejected at least twice a month."

Lynn was right. She would never again lose her desire. Whether that was because of her rejection method was another question.

Finally getting rid of a plaguing problem tends to make one lose sight of the fact that other problems are usually waiting in the wings.

"Let's look at some slides!" Lynn said.

They went through hundreds of slides sent by artists over the past few months. Lynn wanted to see if her desire had been restored in areas of her life other than romance, particularly that area in which she made her living.

It didn't take long for her to feel certain that it had. She had regained her taste and judgment in art. She felt smart and confident, like her old self.

Patricia asked a delicate question. "Do you think you can fix things with all those artists you've alienated?"

Lynn thought about it.

Patricia added, "Do you think you can lure back the ones who've joined other galleries?"

Alan sat on his white chair for hours after Roland told him of his betrayal.

His love for Lynn was the only thing that had given his life meaning. His father had died a year ago. His cat had died soon after. His ex-girlfriend, who had been his best friend, had become a successful secretary and apparently gotten bored with him, because she no longer called and rarely returned his calls.

Roland had been wrong when he had said, "It's not that big a betrayal. It's not as if we're even much of friends at all."

Roland was Alan's only friend. And, therefore, his best friend.

Alan asked himself what would it matter if he had a friend to talk to, anyway. He couldn't talk to him about his thoughts of murder. Maybe he should get a pet. He could tell a pet about his thoughts of murder.

He went to a pet store and looked at the various animals, trying to imagine himself talking to them about murder and seeing what kind of expression they'd have on their faces. He did this little exercise with the kittens and puppies first, but they were too cute and floppy. The snakes and lizards were not bad, but he felt they were mocking the mildness of his evil, which gave him a feeling of inferiority. The rabbits posed the opposite problem. The fish just turned their backs to him. And the mice were oblivious.

He was sure he would never murder anyone, but thinking about it was helping him get through this tough period.

As Alan walked out of Petland petless and looked down at the curb, he thought of the ideal animal to confide in. He went back and asked, "Do you have any rats?"

A rat would be perfect. He could send it murderous thoughts for hours on end and get satisfying vibes back. He was certain of it.

"We have just one."

It didn't look like the ideal type of rat to receive murderous thoughts, for it was mostly white with a few brown patches, but the mere knowledge that it was a rat would more than make up for its prim coloration. If he ever felt uncertain, he'd just stare at its eyes and nose and repeat the word "rat" in his mind, and he'd get a metaphorical hard-on. He just knew it.

He bought the rat. The love affair began immediately. It was torrid. That evening, they watched TV together, the rat lying spread-eagle, flat like a pancake, on Alan's stomach. Alan was stroking its back while the rat practically purred with contentment and fell asleep. When it woke up, Alan fed it chocolate pound cake, and they checked the stairwell doors together.

Alan took a bath with the rat. Then he combed it and talked to it and named it Pancake. The rat's small abrupt movements were

slightly annoying, and Alan thought Pancake would look more intelligent if only he didn't move so jerkily. That was really the pet's only
flaw: bad body language.

Alan held Pancake on his chest, his hand over the rat's back, his
fingers around the rat's face, to hold it in place and prevent it from
making those movements that made Pancake look as though he had
Parkinson's disease. Alan stared into the rat's eyes and said, "What
do you think? Should I kill them? Should I?" He stared deeper into
the little black eyes that reminded Alan of periods.

Lynn called Charlie Santi and asked him to bring over all his new
work.

"You mean all that stuff you called crap?" he asked.

"I didn't say it was crap, I just didn't . . . But yeah, bring it over,
would you?"

A half hour later, Lynn was staring at Charlie's work. "Oh,
Charlie."

"What?" he said, coldly.

Her hand was over her heart as she kept staring at the little shape
that was either strangling or hugging the other in the midst of all the
white. "I'm so sorry," she said.

He waited for her to elaborate.

But all she said was, again, "I'm so sorry."

"That's what you said the last time I was here."

"I was sick. These are magnificent. Your best work yet, by far.
You're now my best artist. I hope I haven't lost you."

After a long moment, he said, "I guess not. But I don't want to go
through that nightmare again."

"Me neither."

"I felt like I had lost you."

"You haven't," she said, hugging him. She noticed Patricia giving her a little smile and raising one eyebrow.

The following day, thanks to the rat's company, Alan felt slightly better and was able to eat. He skipped work again, and by the end of the afternoon, he felt strong enough to get started on a little stalking of Lynn and Roland: the couple.

Alan intended to quit stalking soon. He knew it wasn't healthy for him. He would stop it, cold turkey. He already had an idea of how he would do it. But before reforming, he wanted to sink into the most gross behavior he could manage.

"Traitors!" he shouted at them, when Roland picked Lynn up at her gallery after work.

Carrying a small white basket, he followed them down the street. He didn't even try to make the stalking good. "You stink, you pretentious asshole. And you, Lynn, you're ugly! And what is this crap about you trying to want him! And about you stalking him insincerely! You sicko! You are both fucked-up sickos!"

They walked more briskly. Roland dropped a button on the sly. He and Lynn gave change to Ray. Alan did, too. The redheaded, ex-psychologist, homeless man scrutinized them and tried to repress his curiosity. He restrained himself from throwing the change at their backs.

He heard Alan scream at the two others, "And look what I have here!" He saw Alan take a squirming animal out of his basket, and say, "It's a rat!"

Pancake was on a leash and halter, so there was no risk of his running into the gutter to join the other rats. "He wants to kiss you,

Lynn! Won't you give him a little kiss? I know you like kissing vermin." As was often the case with people who intended soon to quit something cold turkey, Alan was binging on his addiction.

Roland suddenly stopped in front of a fabric shop and said, "I need to go in here for a second."

"Why?" Lynn asked.

"I'm out of buttons."

Alan did not follow them into the store. Roland picked out some buttons and paid for them.

Lynn examined the buttons and couldn't think which of his clothes they would suit. Some were red, some yellow, some were suede, some were tiger's eye, and some were covered in fabric. They were all small. "What are these buttons for?" she asked.

"For nothing. I just need them."

"Do you collect them?"

"No, I lose them. I don't know what's wrong with me."

"Why does something have to be wrong with you? Everybody loses buttons."

"But not as many as I do."

Alan stalked the couple again the next day, after work. Roland begged him to stop, and promised he'd go out with him to help him meet women. But Alan wanted Lynn. The couple decided to endure the stalking. They didn't think Alan was dangerous, and they felt sorry for him.

Alan was frustrated by their newfound indifference to his stalking. After what they had done to him, they could at least do him the courtesy of acting annoyed. He toned down his stalking to make them nervous. When neither subtle nor obvious stalking was unsettling them, Alan shut himself up in his apartment and didn't go to work or eat for days. He sat facing his window hour after hour. Sometimes he held Pancake on his lap. Finally, one afternoon, weak from not having eaten, and yet not hungry, he put on his boots and went to a meeting of Stalkaholics Anonymous.

Most of Lynn's fifteen artists came back to her. A couple of them even cried from joy that she wanted them. She only lost two, who were by then committed to other galleries, but even they were disappointed that their ties were severed.

Opening Lynn's mail one morning, Patricia saw that Lynn had not lost time in using her rejection method to prevent the future loss of her desire.

Patricia popped her head in Lynn's office and said, "You just received your rejection from the Over Seventies Club in southern Florida."

Six

During the next seven months, something extraordinary happened. With the help of Stalkaholics Anonymous in conjunction with the emotional support he was getting from Pancake, Alan began to believe that perhaps he could turn his life around, improve it drastically.

The beginning of Alan's transformation happened on the subway one day, when he was thinking about an article he had read that morning entitled "Looking for Alternatives to the Rat Race." He had recently realized that he was not, at this point in his life, interested in climbing the corporate ladder and making lots of money. He wanted to be happy, sane, and not stalk. But happiness could be expensive. Not to mention sanity. He had therefore followed the article's advice and checked out the Web site FrugalLifestyle.com, but had been turned off by the method called Alternative Acquisition Methods, or Dumpster Diving, which translated as rummaging through garbage.

Nevertheless, he would seek out fullness in his life, even if that meant decreasing his chances for a promotion. He would do things that were enriching. Perhaps he would even try to demand three-day weekends. He wanted to balance work and personal life.

He was standing in the middle of the subway car, holding on to the pole, letting his body sway gently to the movements of his train of thoughts. Feeling uplifted, his eyes naturally lifted, and happened to land upon an advertisement for NYU's continuing education program. The timing could not have been more perfect for either Alan or the advertisers. Alan got off at the next stop and took the subway to NYU and got their course catalog. He then got catalogs at Parsons, the New School, and the YWCA. And then he got more catalogs from bins on the street for the Learning Annex and the Seminar Center. He went home and stretched out on his couch with Pancake and his catalogs.

He was immediately drawn to classes like, How to Get Anyone to Return Your Phone Call, and Create Your Ideal Life, and The Confidence Course.

But he was also extremely attracted to a section in the NYU catalog entitled "Fire Safety and Security in Buildings," and particularly to the class called Disaster Management for High-rise Office and Residential Buildings. He dwelled on its description: "This intensive workshop surveys the appropriate and necessary procedures to minimize injury and avoid loss of life in the event of major fires and explosions, bomb threats, terrorist actions and hostage situations, earthquakes, toxic accidents, and nuclear attacks."

Building safety and getting his phone calls returned were not his only interests. There was a third. He envied artistic people and had a great desire to explore his artistic side, which, as far as he knew, did not exist. He just wanted to poke it gently and see if it moved. He didn't want to take an art class that was too difficult and would highlight his incompetence. He was therefore delighted to find a fair number of classes that would probably not put too much pressure on him: Tin Decorating, How to Create a Tabletop Fountain Garden, Puppetry, and Potpourri for Beginners, to name but a few.

Alan read the catalogs for so many hours that he began coming across classes that sounded even more intriguing—downright fascinating—and he was always disappointed when, on second glance, he'd realize he had misread the classes' names, and that the school did not offer courses called Internship in Poverty, Be a Maggot to Money, How to Tempt Your Way to the Top, Decorative Yoga, and Intuitive Poisoning for Beginners. The schools did, however, offer pale versions of those classes, such as: Internship in Property Management, Be a Magnet to Money, How to Temp Your Way to the Top, Restorative Yoga, and Intuitive Positioning for Beginners (also Yoga). *Reality is so dull,* Alan thought. *Any mistake in one's perception of it is inevitably more interesting than the real thing, and lucky are those who remain uninformed of their error.*

When Alan's bloodshot eyes finally made contact with How to Access the Goodness Within You, in the Seminar Center catalog, he was stunned. Goodness: what an idea. He suddenly felt that goodness was the way to go. What was more, the class met just one time and took place the very next day, which was perfect for Alan, who was eager to begin his transformative journey.

Alan slept well that night and arrived early Saturday morning for class, held at the Hungarian Church, in a room containing a large table around which the students sat. He was the only man. He hoped the women appreciated how rare it was to find a man who had any interest in accessing the goodness within him, and therefore how special a man he was.

The teacher arrived. She was middle-aged, heavyset, nunlike. Her gray hair was pulled back in a tight bun. He could easily picture her helping him access his inner goodness.

She stood at the head of the table, and began: "I will show you how the knowledge, passion, and nurturing of the goddesses can help transform your life."

Alan didn't really understand why the teacher was referring to goddesses. He glanced down at his school catalog, which he had brought along. His pupils constricted when he saw that he had mis-read the title of the class.

He rose and began tiptoeing out.

"Where are you going!" the teacher exclaimed.

"I'm sorry, I thought this class was, How to Access the Goodness Within You, not the Goddess." He chuckled sheepishly.

"If you leave, you are doing a disservice to the women in this room. You are creating negative energy—the energy of with-drawal—which men love creating, and which is why we need classes like these. And you will certainly *not* have achieved your goal of ac-cessing the goodness within you."

"But isn't this a class for women?"

"Look at your bulletin. It says, 'A Workshop for Men and Women.'"

Alan found it easier to sit back down than to create the energy of withdrawal.

Everyone was then told that during this seminar they were to ad-dress each other by their first names, preceded by the words "Sister Goddess."

Alan thought they might make an exception in his case and call him "Brother God Alan." But they didn't. The teacher said that since gods, in our sexist world, were still considered more important and powerful than goddesses, it would be unfair toward the others if Alan got to be a god. He would therefore be Sister Goddess Alan. No special treatment.

After embarking on a short lecture regarding the Greek goddesses, Sister Goddess Jane (the teacher) said, "Part of accepting who you are as a woman is your crotch. Those confident about their crotches are happy. By the end of this seminar, you all will be."

The students were then each given a lump of Play-Doh and ordered to make a sculpture of their vaginas, from a gynecologist's perspective.

Alan sat staring at his clump of pink clay, stunned. He tried to imagine what his vagina would have looked like had he had one. The other women began sculpting theirs right away, and Alan, wanting to fit in, began kneading. When he could no longer look natural kneading, he placed his lump of clay down on the table and, with a trembling finger, poked a hole in it and left it at that.

He sat on his hands, to make it clear he was done. Sister Goddess Jane immediately told him he had to make his vagina more detailed.

So he added a fish tail to the back of the ball of clay.

The teacher loomed over him. "What is that creature?"

"My vagina. If I had one," Alan mumbled.

"It's very offensive!"

Alan quickly collapsed the tail against the body and smoothed it out, which shrank the hole, which upset Sister Goddess Jane. She found it offensive that he had made the hole so small. She said it was a typical sign of men wanting to hurt women, of being excited by women's pain. She added, "You probably wish there was no hole at all, right? Or just a pinprick of a hole, so that you could go in there and rip it open, and have it be tight, tight, because that's all you really care about, your pleasure." She walked away.

He applied his fingers to the clay, trying to feel as cool as a gynecologist. In his mind, he told the chunk of clay to relax, to take a deep breath. He even placed a little Kleenex over the back part of it. The goddess came back and pointed to the Kleenex. "Sister Goddess Alan. What is that?"

"It makes me feel more comfortable that way. It's more . . . clinical, impersonal."

She snorted and let him be, for the moment.

He made the hole big. Like a grotto. So big that having sex with it would be like having sex with air. But he had to be careful, for if he made it too big, Goddess Jane would say something. He knew she would say it was offensive. So he shrank it slightly, but still left it quite big.

"Sister Goddess Alan?"

"Yes, mistress," he replied, meekly.

"Goddess! Not mistress," she said, looking shocked.

"Sorry! I mean Goddess. Yes, Goddess. Sister Goddess Jane."

"You couldn't leave it big, could you? You had to make it smaller. You just couldn't make it a big vagina. You couldn't bear the sight of a big vagina."

It sounded to Alan as if she had a Japanese accent when she uttered that word, "vagina." Her teeth sliced the air like guillotines, coming down three times on "va-gi-na."

"No, I thought you wouldn't like it too big," Alan said.

"Don't you think mine is big?"

"I'm sure yours is big. No! I don't know," Alan said, traumatized, enlarging the opening with his thumbs.

. . .

Following the dictum that you should get right back on the horse from which you have just fallen, Alan immediately signed up for another class, making sure to read it correctly this time. He took Acupressure for Your Pet: Alternative Health Care for Your Dog or Cat. *Or rat,* he thought to himself. The course description was, "Acupressure consists of gentle massage techniques that can be used by any pet owner in the treatment of various illnesses and behavioral disturbances. Bring Your Pet to Class."

Alan and Pancake went to class and enjoyed it very much. They were popular among the traditional pet owners, except for one or two hysterical types.

Through tremendous willpower, Alan succeeded in not thinking too much about Lynn. He attended Stalkaholics Anonymous regularly. People talked about their itch to stalk. He embraced Step One of their twelve-step recovery program, which was: "I admit I am powerless over my stalking compulsion and my life has become unmanageable." And he adopted their belief that "once an addict always an addict." He knew he would probably have to attend those meetings for the rest of his life, just like the alcoholics.

Alan's new life went well. He wasn't absent from work as much anymore.

Alan tried to improve himself in certain ways. Pancake's nervous body language had made Alan acutely aware of his own. He practiced moving in a calm and confident manner. He edited his movements, eliminating all the unnecessary gestures that cluttered his image.

He also developed a personal philosophy of mental health. After spending hours trying to figure out the one thing that could be responsible for stalking tendencies, he concluded that it came down to a difficulty in letting go. Stalkers had trouble letting go of the person they were obsessed with.

So he practiced letting go. He bought a rope, tied it to his bathroom's doorknob, and pulled on the rope regularly, for many minutes at a time, until his muscles hurt and his face was red and the tendons in his neck were taut. Then he slowly let go of the rope, trying to appreciate the pleasures of letting go.

He came to believe that stress-related health problems were caused by not letting go, by clenching one's muscles, being afraid of releasing them. So he got massages and forced his muscles to unclench, to let go.

Alan slowly changed. The change was internal, mostly, but sometimes internal things emanate.

He took more classes. He made friends. Some were recovering stalkaholics, like himself. He went out with them and met more new people. Before he knew it, and to his astonishment, he believed he didn't care about Lynn anymore.

He met Jessica, a woman with a gun license, who became his girlfriend and moved in with him after three weeks. Alan marveled at how making just a few changes in one's life, like taking a class, or getting massages to relax, could bring about a whole positive chain reaction. They were happy, the three of them. She and his rat got along well.

Ray the homeless man noticed the change in Alan and whispered little reinforcing tidbits whenever he passed, such as, "I'm proud of you," and "You've come a long way, baby," and "Super new girl-friend."

During those same several months, Lynn and Roland sublet their apartments in the city and moved into Roland's country house.

Lynn was taking a break from managing her gallery full-time, leaving it to Patricia, except on Tuesdays and Fridays, when she drove in with Roland, who commuted every day. Patricia would update her on everything, including the recent rejections Lynn had received in the mail.

Lynn had diligently gotten the five follow-up shots against rabies and had been fortunate to get no side effects.

She spent most of her week in the country, painting, not because she had a passion for it or any ambition to develop as an artist, but because she found it enjoyable.

As long as there was still uncertainty about whether Lynn's desire for Roland would remain, the excitement and chemistry continued. Things changed the day Lynn finally felt confident enough to say, "Your appeal and my desire are here to stay. I know it. I can feel it."

A few days later, Roland told Lynn, "Listen, I think you should have your weekend with Alan."

She just stared at him, stunned, and finally said, "Are you insane?"

Roland sighed. "For my sake. I just feel that it wasn't right, what I did. It wasn't right what we did."

"Forget it. It's out of the question." She got up and left the room.

He followed her. "I believe it's important to act decently."

"Why now? What's going on?" she asked.

He threw up his hands and went outside to his lounge chair to tan. He liked to get tan, she didn't, said it was dangerous, that he might develop a melanoma. The more she urged him not to tan, the more he did, until his face was all crispy.

The truth was that now that Lynn's desire for Roland appeared permanent, their romance was less appealing to him. Alan's no longer wanting Lynn also made it hard for Roland to keep wanting her. The couple fought all the time. Roland became verbally abusive, frequently putting Lynn down.

To make matters worse, Lynn got a call from Patricia saying that Judy had been run over by a truck and died. Patricia and Lynn speculated whether Judy had done it on purpose, to "refreshen her zest," as she had put it, all those months ago. In any case, the news hit Lynn hard.

"As far as I'm concerned," Roland said, "all her friends should feel responsible for her death."

"I'm one of her friends," Lynn said, staring at him.

"I know," he said, staring back at her.

"You think it was my fault?"

"Absolutely. But no use crying over spilt milk."

"You call the death of a friend spilt milk?"

"I call it what it must have been to you. If she had meant more to you, you wouldn't have let her get to this state."

He knew he wasn't being nice, but he couldn't stop. He wasn't happy and didn't want her to be either. Anytime she seemed happy, it irritated him.

She told him she was thinking of ending their relationship. He said she couldn't because he had booked a surprise weekend for them at a pleasure camp he had read about in *Hedonism* magazine.

They went to the retreat. They were pampered, washed, and groomed by three staff members. Their room had a giant crib filled with pillows for lovemaking, which enhanced the delights of sex. But sex was one of the few things they had no problems with. Lynn had always been impressed by Roland as a lover.

After the weekend, Lynn tried being nice, bought Roland attractive buttons.

When Roland unwrapped the package, he said, "Oh, good, I was out of buttons."

"You were? But you bought some the other day."

"If you thought I still had those, then why did you buy me these?"

"For your collection."

"What collection? I don't collect buttons. I lose them. I told you that already. If you expect me to collect these, you're going to be disappointed, because I'm going to lose them. You better return them. They look expensive."

"Maybe you don't sew them on well enough. Maybe next time I should try sewing them on."

"It doesn't matter how tightly you'll sew them on. I'll still lose them."

"Why?"

"I would give much to know that. I guess I can't help it."

Roland made efforts to be a better boyfriend. He tried to show concern and give compliments. The concern came in the form of—

"Does it bother you that your friends don't really like you?"

"What are you talking about?" she said. "My friends love me."

"No, not really. I'm good at sensing these things."

The compliments came in the form of—

"It's really great that you often read fashion magazines."

"Why?"

"Because it shows you're interested in the outside world. It's better than sitting on the couch, staring at the wall."

Roland would play pranks on Lynn. Mean jokes. He'd tell her to meet him at a restaurant, and he'd be waiting at another restaurant.

They fought about orange juice.

Occasionally, when he was annoyed, his hand would fly up, as if to slap her, but then it would stay frozen in the air. One time, after his hand had been frozen in the air for a second, it came down against his own face. He slapped himself instead.

Lynn's self-esteem started to suffer. When she expressed doubts about their relationship, Roland said that despite all her weaknesses and shortcomings, he loved her. He was helpless in his love for her.

Lynn hung on, hoping things would get better.

They discussed the problems in their relationship, tried to come up with solutions. As they talked, Lynn was painting his portrait while he ate grapes and dangled his leg off the arm of his chair.

"We are discontent," he announced. "We find no pleasure in our life or in each other."

"Yes, I know," Lynn said, mixing black with blue to get just the right shade for his eyes—a blue she loved, a blue so black his eyes looked almost dead.

"The reason we're not happy," Roland said, "is that in leaving the city, we lost perspective."

"What do you mean?" she asked, adding a little more black.

"We need to expose ourselves to people whose lives suck more than ours, to remind us of how lucky we are. In brief, I think we need a meeting with Alan."

She thought about it. It was true that exposing themselves to such a grand degree of wretchedness as Alan's could be nothing but beneficial. They would no longer take for granted what little good was in their relationship.

And perhaps they could also, while they were at it, try to help Alan, thereby filling their hearts with a pleasant feeling of benevolence.

Roland decided to call Alan immediately and request a meeting.

Seven

At the same moment, Alan had a painful erection, as he had had every afternoon that week, because an excessively sexy woman at whose apartment a film was being made in which Alan was acting, was doing everything she could to seduce him.

Alan was taking a few days off from his job to do a favor for one of his new friends, Bob, who had begged him to play a part in a highbrow independent feature film he was making. It was quite a big favor indeed, because it was tax season, and Alan had on average forty tax returns to prepare each week. Bob had succeeded in luring Alan by being very honest with him, telling him that even though he knew Alan was not a professional actor, he had wanted someone exactly like him—someone with a noble air. Flattered, Alan modestly proclaimed that was not him, even though he knew it was now, and acquiesced.

The filming was taking place in a luxurious apartment on Fifth Avenue and Eleventh Street. Alan tried to take advantage of the time between takes to prepare tax returns, but the seductive owner of the apartment had taken a liking to him and was driving him to distraction. His penis was annoyingly erect, a condition that shocked him and of which he disapproved, since he had a wonderful girlfriend, Jessica, and would never cheat on her. A month earlier, they had officially decided to make their relationship monogamous, not that it had not always been.

The day before, Alan had discovered a fun-filled solution to his tormenting lust. The apartment had very large, very private, comically lush bathrooms, and when his erection got in the way of his concentration, he would politely excuse himself with his cell phone, retreat to one of the far bathrooms, and call his girlfriend, who fortunately was spending her afternoons in his apartment, which made it convenient for them to engage in phone sex. They had done this before, on occasion, but it was particularly helpful this week.

"Why are you out of breath?" he asked, when she answered the phone.

"I'm exercising for you," she said, and suddenly he heard an exercise video in the background.

Alan asked her to take off her clothes. She was always up for phone sex. As well as real sex.

"I'm taking off my underwear now," she said, while moving up and down over a man, who had his penis in her.

"Are they off?" Alan asked, lying on the floor, on a giant, plump, pink mat, his own underwear and pants lowered to his thighs.

"Yeah, oops, hang on, they're caught on my heel. There," she said, easing herself down more slowly onto the penis of her afternoon lover, who knew not to say a word when Alan called. His hands were on her butt, trying to speed up the pace, but she liked it slow, particularly during phone sex with Alan, which she had engaged in before while cheating on him. The afternoon lover was not averse to this. He was sprawled on Alan's white easy chair, the chair with no arms, which made it ideal for Jessica to straddle him in the way they both liked. The white chair had gotten gradually more stained with each passing day, but Jessica diligently scrubbed the stains after each ride, succeeding only, of course, in making them paler and larger.

Midway through the phone sex, which was even more real than Alan imagined, Jessica's call waiting beeped. Not wanting to miss a call from her morning lover, she checked, but it was some guy with a French accent, asking for Alan, claiming to be an old friend. He said his name was Roland. She gave him Alan's cell phone number, and added, "But I'm actually talking with him on the other line right now, so please wait a bit before calling."

Thirty seconds back into the phone sex, it was Alan's turn to announce he had another call coming in.

"Fuck that guy, I told him to wait," Jessica said.

"Fuck who?" Alan asked.

"This jerk who just called and interrupted us. Just don't answer it."

"I have to. It could be my friend John, who's in a terrible mess."

"No, that wasn't the name he gave me. I can't remember it, but it wasn't John."

"It could be someone else in need. Hang on."

Alan switched lines, and this time it was indeed his friend John, sounding very depressed.

Alan apologized to Jessica for having to stop things in the middle like this.

"Suit yourself, honey. It'll be harder for you than for me," she said.

Alan laughed. "Why?"

"Because I can finish. And you have to talk to John."

"Have fun." Alan zipped up his pants and switched back to his friend in need: a full-fledged stalkaholic from an SA meeting.

John was crying, saying he was on the verge of following the woman he had been trying not to follow for months.

Alan attempted yet again to persuade him to forget about the dumb woman. And he added, "Did you use the gift certificate I gave you for that massage?"

"No."

"Well, use it, man, please. It helps."

"I want to follow her."

"She's gonna call the cops on you again."

John sniffled.

"Or just come here," Alan said. "Come to the set. There's a nice woman here, who owns this apartment. She's very sexy, very hot. I'll introduce you."

"No one else interests me."

"I know what it's like. You don't have to tell me. Go get the massage."

There was a loud knock on the bathroom door. It was the director, calling him for the scene. Alan was sorry to have to make the crew wait, but he felt it was his responsibility to talk to his friend until his obsession to stalk passed.

Roland paced, unsure how long he was supposed to wait before calling Alan's cell phone. Sitting on their bed, Lynn was watching him.

"I think this is going to be good," he said. "A chick answered the phone at his apartment. It could be a friend or relative, but even if it's a girlfriend, it doesn't mean his life is good. She was panting,

and I could hear an exercise video in the background, which probably means she's fat, trying to burn calories, which would explain
why she's going out with a guy like Alan: She couldn't find anyone
better."

Lynn flipped through a magazine.

Roland glanced at his watch. Half an hour had passed. Enough.
He dialed Alan's cell phone. Alan himself, once again, did not answer. It was a man, asking Roland to hold on. Roland listened,
straining his ear for signs of pathos. Suddenly he heard "Cut!" He
frowned. Then he heard people clapping and saying, "Wow, that was
great, Alan," and a sexy female voice, "Alan, that was amazing," then
someone else, "There's a call for you, Alan!"

Four days later, Alan was sitting with Lynn and Roland in a coffee
shop. Roland had not said much about their reason for inviting him,
claiming only that it would be nice to see him. When Alan had
lightly pressed him for a more plausible explanation, mentioning he
had forty-two tax returns to prepare that week plus a movie role,
Roland had replied, enigmatically, "It would be good for all of us."

Sensing Alan's hesitation, Roland had handed the phone to Lynn,
urging her to say something encouraging. Not knowing what to say,
she blurted that she was from Long Island, too, and asked him what
town he was from. He said Cross. She said she was from Stanton, the
next town over. They chuckled politely.

After taking a day to think about it, Alan had accepted their invitation.

He was starting to wonder if he had not made a mistake, because
their questions were getting strange. At first they had asked him simple things, like the plot of the movie he was in.

"A married woman falls in love with another man," Alan had replied.

"What's your part?"

"The other man."

They asked him how he was doing, and he answered, "I'm doing well, thanks," and they said, "It must have been hard for you, what we did."

Alan couldn't quite figure out what their intention was—to revive his murderous thoughts?

"Yes, it was hard."

"Oh, boy, I can just imagine," Lynn said. "Did you have to go into therapy?"

"Yes."

"Hmm," Roland said. "Did you ever have suicidal thoughts?"

"Yes." Alan saw a twinkle in their eyes. So he added, "I also had murderous thoughts."

They were visibly less interested in those. Misery seemed to be what they wanted to hear about. Less so the anger.

"And now? How is your life now? Are you lonely? Depressed? Unmotivated?" they asked, with an air of hopeful concern.

"No," Alan said.

Roland scratched his cheek. After a time, Lynn said, "It must be hard for you to see us now. I mean, painful."

"No. It's almost the opposite. It helps me realize how much better I feel now. How much better my life is. You know, in a way, I should even be grateful to you both for what you did to me. If you hadn't helped me reach bottom, I might not have kicked back up."

It was nauseating how he was going on and on about himself, the little self-centered prick, Roland thought.

"That's a very generous way of looking at it," Lynn muttered. She was watching Alan closely. Within a few months, his body language had completely changed. He was calm, that was a big part of it. And he didn't seem to hold a grudge, which was remarkable. He had risen above it. Wait. Was he on Prozac, or something?

"How's your job?" Roland asked.

"Good."

"Have you made partner yet?"

"No."

"Supervisor?"

"No."

"Still doing all the grunt work, huh?"

"Yes, but it's fine."

"Are you on any antidepressants?" Lynn asked.

"No."

"But you've changed so much!" she said. "You don't even move the same way. You seem less agitated, and you no longer make those silly facial expressions that were too drastic and too frequent."

Alan was so well-adjusted that he barely felt the sting of that remark. Nevertheless, he did flag down the waiter, knowing there was a 25 percent chance of getting the result he wanted.

"Could you bring me a beer?" he said to the waiter.

"Could I see some ID?" the waiter asked.

Bingo. Alan glanced at Roland slyly, who already had a beer in front of him and hadn't gotten carded.

Roland said to the waiter, "You think he looks under twenty-one?"

"You never know," the waiter said.

"I'm sorry, I've lost my driver's license," Alan said. "Can I have the beer anyway? I'm thirty-four, a year older than this man, and you didn't ask him for his ID."

"I'm instructed to follow my judgment," the waiter said. "I shouldn't sell you the beer without ID."

"That's fine, no problem," Alan said. "I'll have a Coke."

When the waiter had left, Roland asked Alan, "Do you still have that rat?"

Alan smiled. "Yes, Pancake is a wonderful pet."

"You know," Roland said, smiling and stroking Lynn's hand resting on the table, "I was telling Lynn the other day that I thought perhaps we should let you have that weekend with her."

Lynn stared at Roland in shock.

"I'm . . . flattered," Alan said, looking uncomfortable, "but I'm in a relationship now."

"Lucky her. Or him?" Roland said.

"Her," Alan said.

"Is it that girl who answered the phone when I called your apartment?"

"Yes."

"Is she fat?"

"No, why would you ask that?"

"Oh, because she was clearly exercising, you know, aerobics video in the background, panting, so I figured, hey . . . she must be fat, trying to shed the pounds."

"When you called, she was actually on the phone with me—as she told you—and the reason she was panting was that we were having phone sex."

Roland and Lynn looked slapped.

"What does she do for a living? Does she have some kind of sex phone line, or something?" Roland asked.

"No. She's a private detective."

"Are you serious?"

"Yes. And she owns a gun."

Alan could see them absorbing this information.

"So she's a professional stalker . . ." Roland mused. "What a perfect match for you. How did you meet her?"

Alan hesitated, and finally confessed, "I was coming out of an SA meeting . . . that stands for Stalkaholics Anonymous . . . and she was coming out of her meeting in the next room, and we met in the hallway."

"What kind of meeting was hers?"

Alan was reluctant to disclose so much to these problematic people. But finally, he did, because he was not entirely ashamed of the information. "Sex Addicts Anonymous."

Roland's eyes were like Ping-Pong balls released underwater. "She's a sex addict?"

"Was."

"Aren't you afraid she'll cheat on you?"

"No. She's doing much better now. Just as I am."

"She must be pretty freaked out by your rat."

Alan frowned and shook his head. "No, women with guns don't usually mind rats."

"You mean because they can shoot them?"

"No, it's just a gutsier category of women."

They asked him more questions about his life, and they began sounding to Alan as if they were trying to guess the answer to a riddle. And it was clear to Alan that the riddle was: What, in Alan's life, still sucks? They were having such a hard time coming up with the answer that Alan decided to give them a hint, in the form of another riddle. He clasped his hands on the table, and said, "What is greater than God, more evil than the Devil, the rich need it, and the poor have it?"

"I've got no clue," Roland said.

"That was the clue," Alan said.

"What was the clue?"

"The riddle I just told you."

"The clue to what?"

"To the larger riddle."

"What larger riddle?"

"The one you have both been trying to guess since we sat down."

"And what is this larger riddle?"

"I don't need to tell you. We all three know what it is," Alan said.

"Well what's the answer to it?" Roland asked.

"The same as the answer to this smaller riddle. I'll let you figure it out. Supposedly, third-graders more often guess this little riddle than do graduate students."

On the drive back to the country, Roland was in a bad mood trying to guess the riddle. He was repeating it to himself out loud while driving. Lynn was looking out her window quietly, lost in thought. Softly, she finally said, "It's nothing."

"What?" he said, turning toward her angrily. "What are you saying? Speak up!"

"Nothing."

"You said something. Have the courtesy to tell me this thing which you impolitely mumbled, *nom de merde!*"

"Nothing, that's—"

He raised his hand to hit her. She raised her arm to shield her face. The car swerved. She screamed. Horns honked. He pulled over on the side of the road.

"Now tell me what the fuck you were saying," he said in a quiet, chilling voice.

Eyes wide with fear, she chose her words carefully, making sure not to begin her reply with the word "nothing."

"The answer to the riddle," she said, "is the word 'nothing.' That's what I was trying to tell you." She waited, still worried he might hit her. But instead, he looked at the steering wheel and made little sounds as he went over the riddle in his head. "Hmph," he finally said.

Lynn quietly added, "And what is wrong with Alan's life? Nothing."

"Oh, he thinks he's so clever, the little prick, with his *ri-dull*."

Lynn stared at Roland.

He started the car, muttering, "His stupid riddle that's so dumb only third-graders can guess it. Third-graders and Lynn."

Three weeks later, Alan was making love with his girlfriend when the phone rang.

"Don't answer," she mumbled, her mouth full.

"I have to. It could be my friend Martin, who's been feeling suicidal lately."

Alan answered the phone, and Jessica stopped what she was doing, out of respect for this suicidal Martin, in case it was him.

But instead, Alan said, "Lynn?" with surprise. He sat up a little.

Jessica immediately resumed what she was doing. Alan tried to push her away, but he knew it was futile.

"Yes, it's me," Lynn said. "How are you?"

"Fine, and you?"

"Um, not so great. That's why I'm calling. I just wanted to ask a little favor. Um . . ." and she began to talk to him about Roland, and how she didn't think he was doing very well.

Alan felt awkward being on the phone while Jessica was tending to him so devotedly and exquisitely, but he didn't see how he could interrupt the call with Lynn, who sounded quite upset.

He found an opening and said, "I'm sorry to hear things aren't going so well. You said you had a favor to ask?"

"Yes, you see, um, I was really impressed by how much you've changed, how much happier you seem to be. It's miraculous, the way you've turned your life around, except I'm sure it's the furthest thing from a miracle, considering all the work you've probably put into it. And so I thought to myself, if Alan can do it, anyone can do it. No offense, Alan."

"None taken," Alan said. He started playing with Jessica's gun, which she had discarded with her clothes in a heap on the floor. After taking out the bullets, he twirled the gun around his finger. Jessica was still occupied with him.

"Anyway," Lynn said, "I was wondering if you would mind having a meeting with Roland, but this time one-on-one, where you could perhaps advise him, or I don't know, just do some good."

At first Alan wondered if this was a practical joke, but he had become good at recognizing genuine misery.

"Does Roland know about this?" he asked.

"No."

"And you think he'd be interested?"

"No. Never. You'd have to trick him into it, make it sound like you're having some problems and want to confide in him. Make him feel like he's doing you the favor, not that you are doing me a favor. Then I think he'd go for it."

"Hmm. Listen, I'm flattered that you think I've changed so much, but you know, I really have a lot of work. I wish I could help, but I just don't have the time."

There was silence on her end. And then, softly, she said, "You were my last hope. I'll have to end it with him."

"Is it really that bad?"

"It's worse," she said, and he could hear her cry. "He's verbally abusive. Sometimes almost physically, too."

"Well you should leave him, then! Get outa there!" Alan said, aiming the gun at the clock on the wall as if it were a head.

"I can't . . . quite. I keep thinking it will get better," she said. "If only there were some beneficial influence on him."

Apparently fed up, Jessica got off him and walked away.

"Okay. I'll do it," Alan said, eager to get off the phone and recapture his girlfriend.

"Thank you so much," Lynn said.

"Sure. Oh, but what type of problem should I say I'm having?"

"Anything. Like, that . . . you're afraid your girlfriend might be cheating on you, or something."

The next day, as Lynn walked into the house carrying bags of groceries, Roland pranced into the kitchen in his boxer shorts and said, "Guess who called?"

She hadn't seen him this cheerful in a long time. "Who?"

"Alan."

"Really?"

"Yup." Roland plucked a grape from a bag, popped it in his mouth.

"Why?"

"It seems that I was right. No one's life is perfect. His is not, despite that little show he put on for us, and his stupid riddle. He's having some problems."

"What are they?"

"Wants to meet up with me, man to man, to confide. What a loser."

Lynn placed the milk in the fridge sadly.

Roland went on. "And so I very cleverly thought of something we could get out of it."

"What do you mean?"

"Well, in exchange for doing him this favor, I asked that he let us see his apartment."

"Why?"

"So that we'll have something to amuse us afterward. In case his problems aren't enough."

"But if he wants to see you man to man, I can't go with you."

"We can still meet him at his place, then you can go off and do something else while I have lunch with him."

"I don't feel like going into the city."

"You're such a drag. I want you to come. I did this for you."

"Did what for me?"

"Got him to agree to let us see his apartment! I did it for the sake of our relationship, so that you and I could hopefully have a little *rapprochement,* through laughter. If you don't come with me, I'll take it as a sign that you have no interest in our relationship."

Lynn sighed. "Okay, I'll go."

He leaned his body against hers, pressing her against the fridge, and lifted her skirt. The magnets squeaked, digging into her back. She tried to resist him, slightly. He persevered. There was really only one type of occasion left in their daily lives when she didn't find him repulsive, and that was when he pretended to force himself on her. But the appeal of even that was fading.

"Not a bad little place you've got here," Roland said, standing in Alan's living room, as Lynn looked on. "This white chair seems out of place here, though. It's dirty."

"I know," Alan said. "It's my white elephant. I keep meaning to get rid of it, but I can't stand the thought of just throwing it away. Do you know anyone who might want it?"

"Lord, no. Just dump it. And that rat, too, in my opinion. Okay, shall we go to lunch?"

"Yes," Alan said. "Lynn, will you be all right on your own? Feel free to stay here while we're out, if you want to rest. There's plenty of food in the fridge."

Lynn started objecting, but Roland cut her off. "That's so nice of you. I'm sure she'd like to rest a little before walking the streets."

Lynn rolled her eyes at Roland's fondness for incorporating lame insulting double meanings in his comments about her.

"Okay then. Let me just go to the bathroom, and we can go." Alan left the living room.

Roland whispered to Lynn, "When we're gone, rummage around a little. Try to find stuff we can laugh about later. Believe me, we need it."

The two men left Lynn alone in the apartment. Roland dropped a button on his way out.

Ray the homeless man had been surprised to see Lynn and Roland entering Alan's apartment building and was even more stunned to see Alan and Roland leaving together with Lynn still inside. He wondered what it all meant, but he suppressed his curiosity, telling himself that whatever the explanation, it was bound to contain a core of triviality. Strange people were just trying to tantalize him, and he was determined to resist.

"So, what's your problem, little buddy?" Roland asked, biting into a cheeseburger.

That French accent didn't mix well with his Americanisms.

"I'm afraid my girlfriend might be cheating on me," Alan said, not having had the time to come up with a better pretext for the meeting.

"Hmm. I'm sorry to hear it. But before we get into that, I've always wondered, why is being a sex addict a problem?"

"It gets in the way of work and relationships."

"How did it get in the way of her work as a private detective?" Roland snickered. He was capable of snickering in a normal fashion.

"For example, she was hired to follow a man to find out if he was having an affair. And even though he was not, he ended up having one with her."

"Oh, I see. And you said you met her when she was in a Sex Addicts meeting next to your Stalkaholics meeting? How did you start dating?"

"The two meetings let out at the same time, and you can often see the stalkers and the sex addicts eyeing each other. It's not uncommon for members of one group to start dating members of the other."

"Please go on."

"There's a lot of tension when the stalkers and sex addicts mingle in the hallway. Many of them scurry away like criminals, trying to resist their temptations. She, being a professional stalker, liked the fact that I didn't seem ashamed of my addiction. That was important to her, since my addiction is her profession, and she didn't want to be with someone who was ashamed of what she did for a living. It's kind of ironic since she's ashamed of her addiction."

"She's ashamed of being a sex addict?"

"Oh, horribly. In fact, she's in complete denial of it. Not at first, she wasn't. Later, when she started getting her addiction under control, she no longer wanted to think of herself as a sex addict and became convinced she no longer was. I had to constantly remind her of the twelve-step belief that an addict is always an addict."

"Well, maybe she isn't one, any longer," Roland said.

Alan gave him an exasperated look. "One of our ongoing battles is she wants me to dress up as a pink rabbit and go to Central Park and have sex with her in public."

"Is she nuts?"

"No. She's a sex addict."

"For everyone to see? In the middle of the crowds?"

"Yes, but hidden by the costume I'd be wearing, so it wouldn't be obvious what we were doing."

"Do you guys have sex a lot?"

"A fair amount. She's like a very lovely patient who needs to be administered to. The Sex Addicts Anonymous meetings have helped her a lot, though. She's doing so much better. She's had relapses in the past, but not since I've met her, and I don't think there's much chance of one happening at this point. I really trust her." Alan caught himself just in time. "Except, of course, that I don't."

Roland nodded. "So what makes you think she's cheating on you?"

"Oh, nothing. It's just my paranoia."

"You brought me all the way over here for your paranoia? No, man, tell me the truth."

"It's just a feeling I have. But I'm probably wrong."

"Give me some facts."

Not having expected Roland to be so pushy, Alan had not prepared any facts. So he had to improvise. "Oh, there's that chair. My white chair. It has some spots on it."

"Damn you, I can't believe you dragged me to the city for this."

"Well, how do you explain the spots?" Alan stabbed at his spinach salad. "They look as though they've been washed."

"So? Do people only scrub off sex spots, not food spots? What makes you think they're sex spots and not food spots?"

"I don't know. It's just a feeling I have. I told you it was my paranoia."

"What else?"

"Hmm. The fact that sometimes when I call her, she's out of breath and when I ask her why, she says she's exercising, and only *then* does the aerobics tape start playing in the background."

"Maybe she turned off the volume to answer the phone, then turned it back on when she heard it was you. What else have you got?"

"Actually, once when she said she was exercising, I told her to undress so we could have phone sex, and she said something like, 'Hang on, my underwear is caught on my heel.' Her *heel*? She was wearing *heels* while exercising?"

"Maybe she meant the heel of her sneaker or the heel of her foot."

"Right. Or maybe she meant the heel of her red pumps, which she only wears while having sex. Or maybe she lied and was already naked, already having sex, with someone else, on my spotted white easy chair."

"Too bad you can't ask the rat. He probably saw it all."

Alan didn't answer. He was looking down at his food, playing with his spinach salad.

Roland said, "Jeez, man, I'm sorry. It sounds like she probably is cheating on you."

"No, I'm sure she's not. It's all in my head." Abruptly, Alan raised his hand, flagged down the waitress, and ordered a beer, hoping to get carded, but he wasn't.

Finally, he said to Roland, "So anyway, how are things with you and Lynn?"

"Hmm. Not so well. My problem with Lynn is that I can't get over the fact that she used to stalk me. It's hard for me to respect her. Scratch that. It's impossible for me to respect her."

"That's a shame. You may lose her."

"Pff! Where do you get off?"

"I don't mean to sound presumptuous, but isn't it the same story with lots of folks? If only you hadn't succeeded in winning her over so thoroughly, you'd probably still be crazy about her?"

"It's not just that. It's also what I said. I don't have a problem with people, like your girlfriend, who stalk for a living, who stalk for profit. But when people stalk for pleasure, that bugs me. It's the same as with hunting. Hunting for pleasure is sick. Hunting for food is fine. And it's the opposite of sex. Sex for pleasure is fine. Sex for profit is wrong."

"But she was only fake-stalking you. She was forcing herself."

"I don't buy it anymore. I think that was her ploy to get me."

"That was her ploy to want you. Not to get you."

"I said I don't buy it anymore! Also, this will probably sound sick to you, but the fact that you wanted her . . ."

"What?"

"Well, that added some spice for me."

Alan just stared.

Roland added, "Now that you don't want her anymore, it's not the same. You don't want her, right?"

Alan hesitated. "She's . . . a very desirable woman."

Roland snorted. "That answers my question."

Alan tried to reason with him, sang Lynn's praises, but it didn't seem to do much good. He gave up and drank his beer.

Back at the apartment, Lynn did not rummage or snoop. She sat on the armless white easy chair, flipped through some fashion magazines she had brought with her, made a few phone calls from her cell phone. And then she thought.

When the two men returned to the apartment, Lynn raised her eyes, but not herself, from the white chair, and said, "I'm sorry, but it's over, Roland. I'm not going back to the country with you. I want out of this relationship. I called Patricia. I'll be staying with her."

"Lynn, are you sure about this?" Alan asked. "We talked at lunch."

"Very constructive, I'm sure," she said.

Alan could not, in all good conscience, tell her that it had been very constructive. "I don't know," he replied.

"Well I do," she said. "It's better this way."

Roland's pride did not allow him to show that he was stunned, did not allow him to say much more than, "Okay, then, if that's what you want. I'm off."

When the door closed behind him, Lynn cried. She cried in Alan's arms. "I don't know why I'm crying. I'm not really sad."

"It's okay," Alan said, holding her nobly.

When Ray saw Roland leaving alone, he didn't know what to think. He tried not to think. He distracted himself by thrusting his cup at passersby more vigorously than usual.

Eight

After Roland left, Lynn and Alan talked all afternoon. Alan canceled his plans to meet up with friends in the park, so that he could stay and comfort Lynn.

They drank herb tea on the couch, facing the empty white easy chair, and talked about her problems. She apologized for the way she and Roland had treated Alan, and also for never having given him a chance romantically. She again expressed admiration for the way he had turned his life around and said she wanted to do the same with hers. Would he teach her?

He told her that one good way was to meet new people and that she might like to come on the set of the movie he was acting in, the filming of which was continuing tomorrow at the miniature boat pond in Central Park.

Lynn was noticing how even his voice had changed. It had become more relaxed, less tight, deeper. It was as if he had let go of his voice.

They continued talking until Jessica, done with her day's work, came home. The two women were introduced and Lynn, intimidated by the idea of a private detective sex addict and not wanting to stand in the way of Jessica's addiction, promptly departed.

That night Roland called Lynn, threatening that if she didn't come home immediately it would be over between them. Not bothering to remind him that it already was over, Lynn said fine.

What gall, he thought.

The shooting of the scene set in Central Park ended up taking three days, because the director was a perfectionist when it came to filming kisses, and there happened to be two in this scene.

Many people came to watch the filming, including six recovering stalkers from Stalkaholics Anonymous who had come to support Alan. Outings were a big deal for these men, who ventured out rarely and only in groups in order to be stronger in case the need to fight temptation arose.

They arrived carrying folding chairs and checked out their surroundings to make sure they were relatively free of temptation. To their consternation they spotted, three benches away, a group of people equipped with binoculars and telescopes, which were pointed at a tall building across Fifth Avenue.

One of the stalkers grabbed a crew member's arm. "What in God's name are those people doing?"

"They're bird watchers."

"Why are they looking at a building?"

"There's a huge hawk's nest up there, on top of a window. In it is a red-tailed hawk family. The birders come here every day of every spring to watch the babies."

The stalker grimly turned to his associates. "They're stalking the hawk. They're stalking the whole damn hawk family, even the babies."

The stalkers slumped, defeated. They had not counted on running into bird watchers.

"Jesus, they've got five, no six, telescopes, and what, ten, twelve binoculars!"

They debated whether they should risk staying anyway. They decided that they would, as long as they positioned their folding chairs so that their backs would be to the birders.

The informative crew member walked by again and leaned over them. "And in the building next to the one with the nest is the apartment of Woody Allen and Soon Yi, who sometimes come out on their balcony to stretch, and when that happens, all the telescopes change direction."

The stalkers glanced at each other, alarmed, and shook their heads with disapproval, but they stayed. They wanted to see their friend Alan perform.

As did Lynn, who was also there and very curious to see how much Alan had changed. She immediately noticed she was not the only one fascinated by him. There was a very sexy woman watching him, alternating between looking riveted and just sitting there looking at him suggestively.

Alan introduced Lynn to the crew and to the sexy woman at whose gorgeous apartment he said they had shot much of the movie. After the introductions he went back to makeup.

Lynn's cell phone rang. It was Patricia telling her a curator wanted to have lunch with her next week. Lynn set a date. Before hanging up, Patricia said, "Oh, and I keep forgetting to tell you that you've been rejected by the World Wrestling Entertainment Training Camp."

"I see," Lynn said softly, absorbing this information, giving it time to seep into her emotional bloodstream and work its preventative magic.

They hung up.

Lynn observed Alan perform the kissing scene numerous times. She was particularly absorbed by the pause just before their lips met. She was also captivated by the way he had his fingers threaded through his scene partner's hair, and the way he held the back of her head so tenderly. Lynn admired the fact that he repeated the kissing scene with endless patience and goodwill. And the fact that his scene partner didn't seem at all bothered to kiss him. The actress was even kidding around with him, treating him totally respectfully, and she was quite attractive.

The sexy woman came and sat next to Lynn. They both watched Alan and his scene partner.

"He told me he used to be a stalker," the sexy woman said to Lynn, not taking her eyes off Alan. "You wouldn't think so, would you?"

"No," Lynn said.

"I wouldn't mind being stalked by him."

Lynn laughed. "I was," she couldn't resist revealing.

The woman looked at her. "You were?"

Lynn just smiled.

"Did you go for him?"

"No."

"How come?"

"I was messed up, then. And he was, too."

They watched the filming in silence for a few minutes. And then the sexy woman said, "Look at the way she flirts with him. Shameless. She has no pride."

It was between takes, and Alan's scene partner was showing him her bra strap and giggling. Then she mussed up his hair.

"Uh-huh," Lynn agreed.

"I guess I don't blame her," the sexy woman said. "There's something about him."

Lynn began flipping through a fashion magazine. The sexy woman leaned over and whispered to her, "If you could pick only one of those guys to stalk you, which one would it be? Not counting Alan, of course." She was pointing to the six recovering stalkers.

"None."

"Me neither." She paused. "Although maybe that one at the end, just for the hell of it." She licked her lower lip. "But it wouldn't bring me much pleasure." After a few seconds, she said, "I'm very naughty," and got up. She walked over to the recovering stalkers and said, breathily, "You boys stalkers?"

They nodded; one uttered, "Yes," and another specified, "Recovering."

She slowly walked to the one sitting at the end, and said to him, "But, what if a girl wants to be stalked? Would you make an exception?"

To their embarrassment, the stalkers noticed they were breathing in unison, which they immediately tried to stop doing, causing some of them to hyperventilate and others to suffocate. And then they glanced at their buddy at the end, who could not bring himself to look up at her; he was staring down at her feet.

Finally, one of them asked the others, "Do you know the answer? Are exceptions allowed in cases of women who want to be stalked?"

"I seriously doubt it," said the one at the end, still staring at her feet but jiggling his leg nervously.

"Are you sure?" the woman said. "I'd really like to be stalked by you. It would be so . . . titillating."

Lynn listened, while pretending to be absorbed in her magazine.

"Just say no," they whispered to the one at the end. They nudged him. "Recite the anthem."

"Okay." He shifted in his seat, cleared his throat, continued bouncing his leg, and began to recite, "Stalking is not for me, not my thing. That's not to say I won't ask a woman or man on a date. I'd say, 'Would you like to go to the park? Stroll about? People watch, not stalk? Would you like to give me your number? Or would you prefer to take mine? I respect women's privacy, men's, too. I would never do anything you don't want me to. Especially I wouldn't stalk you.'"

He finally glanced up at her with apprehension.

"But I *want* you to do something I don't want you to. I want you to stalk me. *Stalk* me," she exhaled.

"OKAY!" he exploded, shooting up out of his chair. "I will stalk you! I will stalk you day and night, whether you want me to or not. Move! You have to move for me to stalk you. If you just stand there, I can't. So move. Take a step, then another." He was shouting in her face, so she took a step back, and he took a step forward.

The other five stalkers gasped and shielded their eyes from this tempting display of stalking.

Alan heard the commotion and came over. "What's going on?"

The five stalkers couldn't answer, as they were too busy protecting themselves from the bad influence. The sexy woman took another step back, and the man a step forward.

"Tom," Alan said, shocked, "are you . . . stalking her?"

"You know I am!"

"How did this happen?"

The five stalkers pointed their fingers at her with their faces still averted from the spectacle. "She did it! Horrible woman!"

"Everyone here is insane," Alan said. "Lynn, tell me what happened."

Not wanting to get the sexy woman into trouble, Lynn said, "I didn't really see. I was . . . reading." She slightly lifted her fashion magazine.

"It's true what they say," the sexy woman said, throwing her head back defiantly, reminding Lynn of Kathleen Turner. "I did it, and I don't regret it."

"Not yet anyway," Alan said.

"I like it, I tell you."

"You like it so far. You've been stalked exactly two steps. Wait till it's been a thousand."

"I look forward to it," she said.

Alan next addressed Tom, the relapsing stalker. "Just turn away. It's not too late. You can still turn away."

"No," the stalker growled. "Don't touch me. I've never been happier in my life."

"You shouldn't be hearing this," Alan shouted to the five stalkers.

They all stuck their fingers in their ears.

"If this is what you both want, please go and do it somewhere else. I shouldn't be exposed to this either," Alan said. "I feel my resistance weakening."

But they did not go somewhere else. They were too absorbed with each other, she taking one tiny step back, and he responding with

one small step forward. It was a beautiful, enticing dance in the eyes
of the stalkers.

One of them suddenly remembered he had an antistalking moti-
vational tape—a tape especially made for stalkers faced with temptation. He yanked his Walkman out of his knapsack and shared half
of his headphones with one of his buddies. They listened to the tape
for a few seconds, then allowed the three others to hear some of it for
a few seconds, like scuba divers sharing one mouthpiece connected
to one air tank, to survive. The headphones ended up breaking in
half, because of the hysterical energy with which they were handled,
but they still worked.

The stalkers calmed down. The commotion was over. The fallen
stalker was finally gone with his prey, and the only bothersome thing
left in their surroundings were the birders, from whom they occasionally heard distracting exclamations, like, "They're both on the
railing!" and "It's been a very busy birdy day."

Although the stalkers bad-mouthed the birders, they repositioned
their chairs in order to hear the annoying things the birders were saying, such as: "I like the way the pigeons fly in that direction, then see
the hawk and they go, 'Uh-oh, uh-oh, never mind!'"

But most of all the stalkers heard talk of the babies. Whenever
anyone caught a glimpse of a fuzzy white head in the nest, the birder
shrieked, then the rest of them shrieked.

The stalkers rolled their eyes and shifted in their seats uncom-
fortably.

One of them seemed more nervous than the others, less cavalier.
He began to repeat, while perspiring, "I will be the next one, I just
know it."

"Don't think so negatively. Here, use the tape." They thrust the

Walkman into his sweaty palms. He pressed a broken half of headphone to his ear, but he could still hear the dangerous birding chatter in his other ear. His frustration increased. His desire to see the hawk's babies was becoming intolerable.

Suddenly, there was a great commotion at the birding benches. Many of the birders exclaimed, "Soon Yi just came out on her balcony! Look! There's Soon Yi!"

The pent-up stalker threw the Walkman at his compatriots, leapt out of his chair, and ran to the birders, tripping over the leg of a tripod, almost knocking over the expensive telescope. Not wasting a moment, he grabbed someone's binoculars without bothering to remove the strap from her neck, and shouted, "I want to see the babies and Soon Yi!"

Nine

That evening, Lynn received another call from Roland. He sounded softer, contrite. He apologized for the way he had treated her, and said, "Come on now, hop on a bus and come home."

"No."

"Fine, but don't come crawling back in two days then!" He hung up.

Lynn attended three more days of filming. And then it was over. It was time for Alan to get back to work at the accounting firm. When Lynn made little hints that she'd be depressed without his company to fill her days, he just chuckled and didn't know what to say—he couldn't very well invite her to the office to watch him work. Little did he suspect that she probably would have accepted the invitation, so fascinated was she by his new self. Since he had not extended the invitation, she settled for secretly following him to his job and "accidentally" bumping into him when he came out for lunch. She then suggested they have lunch, but he couldn't because he had to have lunch with a client. He added, "You can walk with me there, if you want." So they walked together, and when they arrived at the restaurant and he said good-bye to her, she said, "Well, I've got to have lunch, too. This looks like a nice place. I often come here myself. I'll just sit at another table, if you don't mind."

He couldn't very well say no. So they both went in, he a bit puzzled, and she picking out a table with a good view of him. During lunch, she watched him while pretending to read a fashion magazine. It was hard for her to pinpoint what enchanted her so much about him. Maybe it was simply the contrast between what he had been and what he was now. She remembered having been seduced by contrast before—the contrast between Roland and the hotel manager, and contrast within the same person was even more provocative.

As for Alan, he was dismayed, not only that Lynn had come into the same restaurant, but that she was sitting there, staring at him. What was wrong with her? He wondered why he found her so puzzling, having himself engaged in her type of behavior once or twice. He recognized the symptoms. She was stalking him! It broke his heart.

He was still nice to her when she called him on the phone, knowing too well the anguish of stalkers.

As Lynn did not come crawling back in two days, nor in six, Roland called again, sounding sorrier. For the first time, she was a mystery to him.

"I miss you," he said. "Let me come and get you. I could drive in, right now, and pick you up, and we could drive back and start things over."

"I'm sorry, Roland, I'm not interested anymore. I'm in love with Alan."

"What! The bastard! What has he said to you? What has he promised you?"

"Nothing. He doesn't even know I love him. Or maybe he suspects, but not because I told him. Good-bye now, Roland. Take care." She hung up.

He called back. "You little bitch! You get your ass on a bus this second and come back, do you hear? Or I'll come and get you myself, and you don't want that!"

"Please leave me alone. Get on with your life." She hung up.

Oh! Indignation and outrage burned the roots of Roland's recently thinning hair.

He called back. "You were the one stalking me! You were the one humiliating yourself, degrading yourself, like a little whore, following me down the street, panting, and now you have the gall to—"
She hung up on him. He slammed down the receiver and screamed. He picked up the phone with both hands and shook it, and squeezed it hard. *"Putain d'bordel de merde!"* he said. He placed the phone down and redialed her number, breathing deeply.

"Please do not hang up on me," he said to her. "Please let me finish my sentence, that's all I ask. As I was saying, you were the one following me down the street, and now you have the gall to play Miss Hard-to-get, Miss I'm-gonna-go-and-be-a-whore-for-someone-else-now!" he screamed. "You are a fucking slut!"

"I'm going to hang up now."

"Don't you dare! Don't—you—dare."

He was silent. She hung up.

He did not call back. He drove to New York and checked into a hotel. He bought her flowers. He bought her a ring. He followed her down the street, dropping a penny.

"I'm sorry. I love you," he said, walking next to her, holding out the little black box.

She eyed it without moving her head. "It's over, Roland. I don't want anything from you."

"Oh, please just take this gift. Then my heart will be at ease."

She stopped, opened the box. Inside was a diamond ring, as she had expected. She snapped the box shut, handed it back to him, and resumed walking. "Thanks. Lovely gesture. But I'm finished with you, Roland."

Roland sniffed. Tears were running down his high cheekbones. "I love you, Lynn. I need you. I need you for now at least. I don't think I can live without you. If you're sure you don't want to spend the rest of your life with me, can't you at least wean me gradually, not so abruptly? Please. It's too cruel otherwise."

Lynn rolled her eyes. "You are ridiculous. Why don't you look into Stalkaholics Anonymous? Alan said it was very helpful." She hailed a cab, hopped in, and left him standing on the sidewalk with his flowers and ring.

Lynn was headed for the restaurant where she knew Alan was having dinner with his girlfriend.

When she got there she sat at a table away from theirs, and watched them.

The next day, Lynn followed Alan down the street. He went to have a massage. When he came out, forty-five minutes later, she went in and asked to be massaged by the same person who had just massaged Alan.

She asked the masseuse to massage her exactly the way she had massaged Alan with all of Alan's preferences. Lynn tried to imagine being Alan, receiving the massage.

. . .

Following Alan and being near him made Lynn feel warm and comfortable. Watching him gave her pleasure. She wondered if Alan had truly changed as much as she thought he had, or if the change had taken place in her, instead. To find out, she dragged Patricia on one of her stalking outings.

They sat at a table with a good view of Alan while he was having lunch with someone.

Lynn asked her assistant, "So, is it me or is it him? Do you see a big difference in him or not?"

Under her bushy eyebrows, Patricia gazed at Alan. "Yes," she said, "the difference is that he's not stalking you anymore."

"No! I'm not talking about that. Doesn't he seem . . . normal?"

"Yes, but why does that excite you so much? You know a lot of normal people. Or maybe you don't, actually. Maybe you've been hanging out too long in the art world. Perhaps you should frequent some bankers or lawyers or something."

"But isn't it impressive how normal he seems now, considering how weird he was before?"

"Lynn, what are you doing with yourself, with your life?" Patricia said, leaning toward her boss emphatically, her long hair dangerously close to dipping in the olive oil. "You can't go around following this guy. What do you want from him? Do you want to date him? If so, ask him out on a date. Don't follow him."

"I can't, he has a girlfriend." Lynn paused. "Look at him, it's not a change in superficial things like clothes or even body weight or muscle tone or hairdo. It's a change in the core, and it radiates outward. The people I've seen him with seem to like him more. No one used to like him. Now, even his clothes like him. They embrace him in a more loving way, as if they're proud to be associated with such a great guy. Their pride is evident in the way they hang on him."

Patricia was no longer observing Alan, but Lynn. "Why have you become obsessed with him?"

Lynn thought about it. "I guess because I assume that if someone can change that much, he must be an extraordinary person."

Day after day, Lynn followed Alan down the street, and Roland followed her. Ray the homeless man was becoming tormented, tempted. He had noticed the change in the stalking direction, the stalking order. His curiosity twitched. He was afraid he might lose his faculties. He still wanted to resist the lure and tried to downplay the situation in his mind. *They're always enticing at first, but I shouldn't be fooled. Sure, they do things like change their stalking order, but it doesn't mean anything. They inevitably disappoint.*

The summer semester was approaching, and Alan tried to decide what classes he would take. He was drawn to a class called How to Say No Without Feeling Guilty (And Yes! to More Time). He marveled at how far he had come, because two semesters ago he considered signing up for practically the opposite class, called How to Get Anyone to Return Your Phone Call.

In the end he signed up for map-reading, swimming, and beading.

Alan went to the first class of his map-reading course in high spirits. He arrived at 6:45 P.M., fifteen minutes early. To his horror, Lynn followed him into the classroom. She sat two chairs away, and he stared at her in amazement.

"You can't take this class," he said.

"Why not?"

"Because this is my class."

"But you're sharing it with these other people," she said, motioning toward the seated students.

"You're not interested in this class," Alan said.

"Yes I am."

At that moment, Roland entered the classroom and sat between them.

Alan and Lynn looked at him, horrified. Alan said, "You guys should not take this class. It's very bad for you."

"Why?" they both asked.

"You don't even know what class this is, do you?"

"No, what class is it?" Roland asked, suddenly alarmed.

"It's called Lost in Space: Map-reading for the Geographically Bewildered."

Roland laughed and blushed on Alan's behalf. His laugh, this time, came out as a long "Nnnn" sound, with only a little bit of jiggling and wavering to indicate it was a laugh. "I see what you mean. We might die of boredom or embarrassment."

"No. You guys are stalkers. Not even in recovery, like me. This class is just going to stimulate your stalking urges even more." Alan was trying to speak in a low voice, which a quick look at the other students assured him was not low enough. They were glancing at each other with curious expressions on their faces.

"Why would it stimulate our stalking urges?" Lynn asked, like a rapt student.

"Because this class has to do with space, geography, destination, traveling, which are all elements of stalking. Not to mention the element of following. Following a map."

Roland was midway through an eye roll when the teacher walked in, saying loudly, "What is a map? A map is an overview of something. It allows you to see things in perspective. Don't you wish everything in life were as easy as following a map?"

"No," Alan said. "I wish following a map was as easy as everything else in life, or I wouldn't be in this class." There were some chuckles.

"I want each of you to tell us about a time when you were lost. If you cannot recall a time when you were lost, I want you out of this class."

When it was Alan's turn to speak, he said, "It's hard for me to recall a time when I was not lost. I've been lost my whole life. I'm a recovered stalker, you see, and most stalkers become stalkers because of what psychologists call an 'attachment disorder,' stemming from the childhood absence of a caring and consistent parent or guardian, usually in the first six years of life. But that wasn't the case with me. What caused me to become a stalker was my poor sense of direction. The first time I was lost, as a young child, was traumatizing. It was in Central Park, and I finally just started following someone, hoping she knew where she was going and that her knowledge would rub off on me. Well, it didn't, but it introduced me to the sick pleasure of following. Ironically, having a poor sense of direction is very inconvenient for a stalker, because it makes it hard for him to find his way home."

The teacher raised his eyebrows and turned his attention to Roland. "What about you?"

Roland decided to call the teacher's bluff. "I've never been lost."

"Think harder," the teacher said. "I'm sure there was a time when you were lost. Otherwise, I want you out of this class."

"Well," Roland said, softly dropping a paper clip under his desk, "I don't know if it counts, but I'm lost now. I'm lost as to what I'm doing in this class."

The teacher stared hard at Roland and suddenly turned away, saying, "Yeah, it counts." He paused. "Now, let's talk about the map-reading personality, people who have an easy time reading maps versus those who don't, and what it means. As one may suspect, people who have a hard time reading maps are often more creative."

Alan realized he must be the exception to that rule.

"And the ones who are good at reading maps," resumed the teacher, looking at Roland and Lynn, "are often more analytical, more orderly, more anal, everything you would expect."

"Less loved?" Alan asked.

"No, not less loved," the teacher said.

"More loved?" Roland asked.

"No, I wouldn't say that either," the teacher said. He then opened a small suitcase and took out various maps. He placed them on his desk one by one, saying, "I've brought a lot of maps. Here's a map of a department store. And this is one of your psyche. And this one helps you find your way around in life. This little green map helps you find out what you really want."

Alan stood up, relieved that he had an excuse not to take this class with his stalker and his stalker's stalker. "I'm sorry," he said to the teacher, picking up his shoulder bag, "I made a mistake. I thought this was going to be a class about how to read real maps."

"Oh no, please don't leave," the instructor said. "I can teach you to read any kind of map you want. I have astrological maps, cooking maps, maps of the heart, body, and soul. Sexual maps, athletic maps, morality maps, antique maps."

Alan shook his head. "I'm sorry, that's not at all what I had in mind when I signed up for this class."

He was about to take a step toward the door when the teacher exclaimed, "Sit down! I was kidding."

Alan was too stunned to sit back down, so the teacher told the whole class to get up, and announced that they would all be going into the subway and begin the course by learning how to read subway maps.

The teacher locked arms with Alan, to prevent him from slipping away, and led him toward the door. As Alan passed the teacher's desk, he glanced at the maps scattered on top of it. The titles of the maps were, "Map of the Mind," "Map of the Heart," "Athletic Map," and "Sexual Map."

Once they were down in the subway station, they stood on the platform facing a large map of New York City. The teacher, whose arm was still locked with Alan's, said to him loudly, "Why don't you tell us what train we should take to go to . . . let's say Union Square."

Alan felt mildly insulted at the ease of it. He told them the Number 6, they all took it, and when they came out the exit the teacher asked him which way was north and which way was south. Alan didn't know, and when he guessed, he got it wrong.

Secretly on the verge of tears, but hiding it well, Alan said, "I'd rather we go back to reading the maps of the heart and of the mind."

The professor seemed pleased and said, "Fine. What's the quickest way to make someone love you?"

"Not by stalking them, that's for sure," Alan muttered, glaring at Lynn and Roland.

"To treat them well?" a student volunteered.

"What are you talking about? This is a map-reading class, not a psychology class. I need facts, concrete information," the teacher said.

They were all stumped.

"Through the stomach?" Lynn ventured.

The teacher snorted and took the students back down into the subway. "We will now learn how to ask people for directions. Roland, you begin. Ask the first person who walks by how to get to Times Square."

Roland categorically refused, saying he would never, under any circumstance, ask anyone for directions. "I always know where I'm going."

"And where are you going now?" the teacher asked.

"I'm not going anywhere. I'm sitting on this bench."

"That's exactly right. Your life is going nowhere, and when you do move, you are headed toward a life of misery. You gotta know where you wanna go." He turned to Alan. "Let me ask you, Alan. Where do you want to go?"

Alan was thinking furiously, when the teacher added, "In life."

Alan sighed with relief and said, "I want to have a well-balanced life and be completely free from stalking urges."

The teacher nodded. "And you?" he addressed Lynn.

"I want to be loved by this man," she said, pointing to Alan.

"And you?" the teacher asked Roland.

"I want to be loved by her," Roland said, pointing to Lynn.

"Fine. I'll bring you maps next week that will show you the ways to those places."

Roland grunted.

"Do you have a problem?" the teacher asked him.

"What kind of class is this?"

"THIS IS A MAP-READING CLASS!" the teacher screamed. "Goals are in places. I will give you maps to reach your goals. I will teach you how to read those maps. What more do you want from me? Isn't that enough?"

"That is a lot," Roland said. "I just have a slight quibble with your notion that goals are in places."

"In life," the teacher explained, "you can reach your goals through various means, and one of many means is physically. There is a place for everything. Haven't you heard that before?"

"Yes, but generally for cleaning," someone said.

"There is a place, and time, for everything. Unfortunately, in some of your cases, the time has passed. Once the time passes, you can still get to where you want to go by knowing where it is."

"Hi, Lynn," Lynn heard someone say, who she feared was not from the class. Lynn was sitting on the back of the bench, her feet on the bench, with the rest of the students. She turned in the direction of the voice. It was a very competitive gallery owner with her co-owner husband.

"Hi, Tracy, hi, John," Lynn said wearily, not getting up.

"What are you doing?" Tracy asked.

Lynn looked at them without answering right away, just nodding her head slightly. "I'm with some friends, just hangin' out."

"In the subway?" Tracy smiled. "Your gang?"

"Yup."

"I'm sorry to interrupt," the teacher said to the couple, "but you are interrupting my class."

"Oh. What kind of class?"

"Map-reading," the teacher said, bowing his head slightly.

The couple tried to hide only their amusement, not their surprise. "Sorry," they said, and waved Lynn good-bye.

At the next class, the professor said he had found the maps they wanted.

On Lynn's map was an arrow pointing to a town in Westchester, with a handwritten street address and the words, "Intersection of Alan's love" written underneath.

On Roland's map was an arrow pointing to a town in Long Island and a handwritten name of a road and of a field called Simple Plain Field, followed by the words, "Deserted field of Lynn's love," in parenthesis.

On Alan's map was an arrow pointing to a town in New Jersey with a handwritten street address followed by the words, "Restaurant of balance and freedom from stalking urges for Alan."

The teacher said, "All you have to do is go to these places, and you will have those things you want."

"What is this, some kind of magic?" Roland asked.

"No. Have you ever noticed in life how sometimes you get what you want unexpectedly, for no apparent reason, and long after you've given up hope of getting that thing you wanted? Well, that's usually because you've accidentally, unwittingly, stumbled upon the place where that thing can be gotten. For example, if you want a great job that has always eluded you, and let's say your getting that job happens to be located under a certain tree in Central Park, and one day you're strolling about, and by chance you happen to pass under that tree, well, you know what happens next."

"You get the job?" a student asked.

"Yeah," the teacher said. "I'm sure none of you believes me. And if you ever go to those places, and you don't get what you want, it doesn't mean this method is wrong, it just means the maps are wrong, or inaccurate. You can't always trust your sources."

Despite their passionate desire to get what they wanted, neither Lynn, Alan, nor Roland believed in the maps one bit or had any intention of going to those locations.

Alan was upset that Lynn and Roland were admitted into his Deep-Water Confidence class. They swam extremely well. It wasn't fair they got in.

The previous semester, Alan had taken the class called Petrified People Don't Sink. The course catalog had described it as "A special class for those with a deep-seated fear of water. Talk about the cause of your fear and gently make the necessary adjustments and acclimation to the water." When it had been Alan's turn to talk about the cause of his fear, he had said he was afraid of what might be in the deep, to which someone had answered, "More chlorine."

Alan's dream was to eventually pass the Lifeguard Training Pretest, the description of which was: "500-yard continuous swim using front crawl, sidestroke, and breaststroke. Surface dive and retrieve a ten-pound brick, return to surface. Tread water for two minutes using legs only. Must be 15 years of age on or before course end." Ahh. Self-improvement was wonderful, but passing the Lifeguard Training Pretest was a long way away. Alan still could barely swim, and he was starting to suspect that what kept people afloat was not doing the right strokes but having the right personality.

He followed the strokes very precisely, like people who followed cooking recipes more closely than was necessary. One, two, three. As he swam, he was much more concerned with moving upward than forward. The result was that he didn't advance very rapidly. He felt like a bug in a toilet and had the uneasy sensation someone was about to flush. He could feel himself sweating in the water. It didn't help that Roland was swimming next to him, taunting him, trying to make him seem ridiculous in Lynn's eyes, or that Lynn was swimming on his other side, staring at him lovingly, telling him to relax.

"You're sinking," said Roland.

"No, you're not," Lynn said. "I'll save you if you are."

A Japanese woman in the class told him he might be a hammer, that in Japan people whose bones were so heavy that they had trouble staying afloat were called hammers. Alan loved that concept; he was undoubtedly a hammer. He hoped she would tell the swimming instructor.

"So, Alan, let me ask you a question," Roland said.

Alan scowled, trying not to be distracted from the strokes.

"Why didn't you learn how to swim before now?"

"Just never did," Alan said.

"Did you have some traumatic experience as a child, drifting in shark-infested waters for days, clinging to an inner tube?" Roland said, flipping onto his back and leisurely doing the backstroke alongside Alan. "I mean, you must have some pretty bad water memories, right?"

"Wrong. I have just one, and it's fond."

"Really. What is it?"

"Nothing."

"Aw, come on, tell me."

"No." The passion with which he uttered that word made him momentarily lose track of where he was in the stroke pattern, and the water came up to his mouth, which unnerved him. He steadied himself.

"Come on!" Roland said, loudly.

"Shh," Alan said.

"Tell me!" Roland said, again loudly.

"Damn you. I was in the ocean, lying on a floating raft, when I was five or six, and a woman helped me pet a mangofish. Are you happy?"

Roland's eyes opened wide. He switched to sidestroke, staring at Alan. "A mangofish."

"Yes, it's a gentle fish that lets people pet it sometimes."

"And did you pet the fish?"

"Yes."

Alan, Roland, and Lynn reached the end of the pool, turned around, and began the next lap.

"What does a mangofish look like?" Roland asked.

"I didn't see it. It doesn't like to be seen."

"But it likes to be petted. Hmm. What did it feel like?"

"The way you would imagine a fish to feel."

"Which is?"

"Soft and slippery."

"That woman didn't, by any chance, say, 'This is a perfect day for mangofish,' did she?" Roland asked.

Alan blanched, and chills coursed through his body, causing him to lose track of the stroke pattern again. The water came up to his nose, and he flailed and doggie-paddled up to the edge. Lynn was grabbing him around the waist, pressing the length of her whole body against his. She did not promptly let go of him when he was holding on to the edge. He had to push her away and say, "That's enough, I'm fine."

Alan turned to Roland. "There is no way you could have known that. How did you know she said that?"

"Lucky guess, I guess," Roland said, treading water using legs only. Alan was annoyed because treading water using legs only was a feat that was attained only in the most difficult class, the class Alan was dreaming to be in one day, the Lifeguard Training Pretest class. Alan knew Roland knew that and was showing off.

Roland said, "But listen, maybe one day you should tell a therapist that little story. Even though it's a lovely memory, I'm sure a therapist would be able to whip up some explanation as to how it might be related to your avoidance of water." Roland arched his back and did a backward somersault under the water.

When Roland came back up, Alan repeated, "How did you know the woman said that?"

Roland glanced at Lynn to see if she was impressed by his knowledge. His face sagged when he saw she was smiling at Alan beatifically.

"Relax," he said to Alan. "I went to Harvard, remember? Nothing beats a good education."

Alan blinked, awed by Roland's vast and mysterious knowledge that had endowed him with such acute psychological insight that he was able to speculate as to what someone had said thirty years ago.

"I suggest you read a short story called, 'A Perfect Day for Bananafish,' by J. D. Salinger," Roland said. "You might gain some insight into why you never learned how to swim. Then again you might not."

"Yeah, whatever." Alan carefully let go of the edge and resumed the breaststroke. Lynn and Roland flanked him like pilot fish.

The instructor told the class that the next week they would be learning how to turn over front to back to front, and how to perform deep-water bobs, and that in three weeks they might try some beginner synchronized figures.

Two days later, Lynn was hosting an art opening at her gallery, looking at her watch. She knew Alan's yoga class finished at seven o'clock, and she wanted to be there when it ended, so that she could stalk him for a few hours.

At ten to seven, she walked over to Patricia, who was standing with a glass of white wine, talking to two artists. Lynn told her she was leaving.

"You can't leave now," Patricia said. "Look who just walked in."

It was Aaron Golding, the senior curator of contemporary painting at the Met.

"I can, and I will," Lynn said.

Patricia grabbed her arm hysterically. "Now Aggie just got here."

"I don't care," Lynn said, yanking her arm away. She walked out of her crowded gallery, avoiding eye contact with Aggie Slinger, the president of the Museum of Modern Art, and a very wealthy collector herself.

A few months ago, Lynn would have considered any gallery owner who left her opening as Aggie arrived to be completely deranged. But now, Lynn ran to the gym and got there not a minute too soon. She followed Alan down the street. She checked behind her. Roland was following her.

Alan tried to ditch his stalkers before going to his beading class.

Alan was improved, but not perfect; he still had his insecurities. Last semester he hadn't wanted his girlfriend to know he was taking a beading class, and this semester he didn't want her to know he was continuing his beading studies. Jessica, being a detective, knew everything he did, and when he gave her some odd, beaded necklaces and said he had bought them for her, she knew he had actually made them.

Alan thought he had succeeded in derailing his stalkers before arriving at his class, but he was wrong. They joined the class.

They all got immersed in the beading and were quiet. You could hear Roland, faintly humming the song, "*Ne me quitte pas.*" Finally, he said to Lynn, "I'd be a lot happier if you weren't so obsessed with Alan. I read maps better than he does. Or rather, I can read them, and he can't. I sing better. I swim better, or rather, he can't. And I bead better."

Alan didn't say anything. He nobly continued stringing his inferior bracelet.

Roland asked him, "Why did you decide to take this class, anyway?"

"I thought I would enjoy it," Alan said.

"It's always about you, isn't it?" Roland said. "You thought you would enjoy it. What about us? I just don't understand why you can't pick more fun things to do, out of consideration for us poor stalkers who follow you. I mean, you knew we'd follow you. You know we can't help it. If you were truly considerate, you would consult us as to which activities we could all enjoy."

"I'm enjoying all Alan's classes," Lynn said to Roland.

"I think Alan does it on purpose," Roland said, dropping a paper clip. "He chooses deadly boring activities to torture me."

Alan ignored them and tried to concentrate on his beads. He had a feeling he had already screwed up the pattern. It was one blue, one red, one white. Or was it one red, one blue, one white? He couldn't remember the order.

The teacher took out some new beads, made of crystals. They were all the size of small peas, and she said each type of crystal had special metaphysical properties. She described those properties as she held each one up for the class to see.

"Citrine is sometimes called the 'success' stone. It strengthens your willpower and lessens your mood swings." She then held up a pale pink bead and said, "You probably all know that rose quartz is the 'love stone.' Dumortierite enhances organizational abilities, self-discipline, orderliness. Amethyst," she said, holding up a translucent purple bead, "has been called the 'addicts' stone,' because of its metaphysical property of diminishing addictions. Calcite helps you if you have a sense of being lost in spirit and if you have memory problems. Golden topaz increases creativity. Peridot lessens jealousy. Sugilite, also known as luvulite, helps you deal with shock and disappointment. Tourmaline enhances happiness. As for tektites, they are a type of glassy mineral believed to be of extraterrestrial origin. They increase your wisdom."

After only fifteen minutes of beading, Alan got irritated that Roland had hoarded all the creative beads—the golden topaz. Alan had only three of them. Roland had maybe forty. Alan watched as gorgeous beaded strings trickled from Roland's fingers. And this was only his first semester. Alan tried to trade him the love beads for the creative beads. Roland declined.

Then the teacher made the mistake of stepping out of the classroom for a few minutes. Roland still refused to trade beads. Alan's sense of injustice mounted. In a moment of frustration, he secretly, discreetly, placed his three golden topaz beads, one by one, in his mouth, and swallowed them. He figured their creative powers would be more effective absorbed into his bloodstream.

Lynn saw what he was doing, was at first disturbed, but when she realized the logic, thought it was clever, and began swallowing the love beads.

Roland saw her, was horrified, and a moment later was doing the same, guzzling down pink quartz to win Lynn's love, as well as golden topaz to bug Alan.

The beads were rolling around on the table, as the three bead-eaters made a grab for them.

Lynn's cell phone rang. She was reluctant to interrupt her quest for beads, but on the third ring, she answered her phone. It was Arthur Crackalicci, one of her very rich clients. A year ago he had bought a painting for a hundred thousand dollars, which was her biggest sale.

"Patricia is being very secretive as to your whereabouts, Lynn," he said to her now.

"That's because she doesn't know where I am," Lynn said, antsily eyeing Alan, who was devouring the wisdom beads of extraterrestrial origin in hopes of improving his map-reading.

"Great art opening, but you disappeared before I could say hello. Of course, I can't be offended since you did the same to Aggie. My God, Lynn, Aggie of all people. Everyone was quite impressed. Now they think you're more mysterious than ever. Who are you fucking? Who is more important than Aggie? I can't think of anyone. Wait, is it the White House? Is that where you went? Where are you now?"

"I'm in beading class, Arthur."

"Say again?"

"Beading class," she enunciated.

"Why should you be embarrassed? Beading is a fine activity, I'm sure."

"I'm not embarrassed."

"Then why all the secrecy?"

"I didn't know I was going to beading class until I got here."

"Is this a new lifestyle you're trying out? The Don't-know-where-I'm-going-until-I-get-there lifestyle? The Walk-out-on-the-president-of-the-MoMA-for-an-unknown-destination-which-could-turn-out-to-be-beading-class lifestyle?"

"Sort of," Lynn said.

"Well, I don't want to keep you," Arthur Crackalicci said, sighing. "I also wanted to know if you currently have some of Charlie Santi's work, because a friend of mine wants to drop by your gallery next week to see some."

"I sure do. Great stuff. You should see his recent work. Tell your friend to come over, and you should come, too. I'll talk to you soon." She hung up.

Interestingly, the tourmalines were left largely untouched, undoubtedly because the bead-eaters thought they could reach nirvana faster by eating specific facets of happiness. They also didn't partake of the addicts' beads, the memory beads, the success beads, the organizational beads, or the antijealousy beads, except one or two, by accident.

Once all the most useful beads were in their stomachs, the bead-eaters resumed their beading.

"I feel even more creative than before," Roland said, glancing at Alan slyly. "It's all that golden topaz I ate."

When the teacher came back, she wondered aloud where all the rose quartz and golden topaz had gone.

One of the other students said, "They ate them."

More of the students confirmed this, and one added, "They're nuts."

Roland and Lynn did not feel the need to explain or deny anything. They remained silent, staring down at the table. Alan, however, apologized, tried to make the teacher forgive him, feel sorry for him, not kick him out of the class. He gave her a sob story about being so artistically disinclined, and how he desperately wanted to try to squeeze some tiny drop of artistic ability out of himself, or into himself, or whatever, and he couldn't stand the fact that Roland was better at it than he was.

"Do any of you see a therapist?" the teacher asked.

"I see a massage therapist," Alan said.

That night, the bead-eaters had stomachaches, particularly Alan. Jessica asked him whether he had eaten anything bad. He wouldn't have minded confessing to the bead-eating part, because that was merely deranged, but he didn't want to confess to the taking-a-beading-class part, because that was embarrassing, and he'd rather seem deranged than pathetic.

So finally, he said, "I bought you a necklace, and I put it in a bag of candy I had bought for myself, and somehow the necklace broke in the bag, and all the beads were loose, mixed in with the candy, so of course, I ate many of them, thinking they were the candy."

"You didn't notice you were eating rocks? That's very strange," Jessica said, looking at him as he sat on his white easy chair holding his stomach.

"No, I didn't notice," Alan said. "They were round, and polished. How could I know?"

"Hmm," Jessica said, petting Pancake. She knew very well that Alan had made the necklace and not bought it, but as to why he had eaten it, she had no idea.

"Oh, by the way," Alan said, "they were golden topaz beads, supposed to increase creativity, according to that New Age crap. I wonder if eating them is more potent than wearing them."

So now she knew. "Who knows. You may feel very creative later, while defecating your golden topaz."

At the attorney general's office, Roland's office manager took Roland aside and said, "You know, it's a little disturbing that you said you were going to be at a meeting at Marty Bernstein's office, but then when we tried to reach you there, he said there was no meeting." He paused. "Is there some problem we can help you with? You've been out during the day a lot lately."

Ten

Weeks passed. Summer classes ended. After a great deal of thought, Alan decided not to register for the fall semester. First, he knew his stalkers would follow him, and he wanted to minimize their interactions. Second, he felt he had improved himself and his life enough, and he wanted to devote more time to his girlfriend. Third, he had always looked at the classes as a crutch, and he wanted to prove to himself he no longer needed them to be happy.

He realized his stalkers, particularly Lynn, must be feeling frustrated now that the classes were over. He wondered why she never tried to follow him into a Stalkaholics Anonymous meeting. Little did he know she was always there, in disguise. But Alan's sense of observation was no better than his sense of direction, so he never noticed. Plus, he was very trusting and unsuspicious by nature.

At his SA meeting, he talked to the group about how annoying it was to be stalked. The group complained that he was drifting away from the topic of the meetings. The topic was: how distressing it was to stalk, not to be stalked. Alan apologized and said they were right. So then he talked about how he sometimes had the urge to stalk his girlfriend. Or even just stalk strangers walking down the street. "It's been a big help, though, being stalked by Lynn. It's been helping me see how unattractive it is, how much I don't want to be like that. And it really decreases my temptation to stalk again. The best thing that could happen to any of you is to have someone stalk you."

As he was talking, Lynn discreetly began to cry. No one thought it was strange, because people sometimes cried during the meetings.

As time passed, Ray the homeless man was having more and more difficulty handling the change in the stalking order. The mystery of it was hard to bear. But he would not give in to his curiosity, would not ask them questions. When they passed, he closed his eyes and held his breath, to minimize his sensory contact with such tempting creatures. But in his mind, he screamed, *Why have you changed direction? Why have you changed your order? WHYYYYYYYYY?????*

One afternoon, when Alan was walking to his doctor's office, followed by Lynn and, therefore, by Roland, his cell phone rang. He had grown to dread answering the phone while walking down the street because it was sometimes one of his stalkers, usually Roland, complaining about how long they had been walking. Roland would whine into Alan's ear, "Are we almost there yet, wherever the fuck there is?"

This time, when Alan answered his phone, Roland said, "Let's talk."

Alan was supremely annoyed. "What do you mean let's stalk? I've given that up, and you're already in the middle of it!"

"I said let's *talk*," enunciated Roland. "As in chat. As in, over lunch."

"Not interested," Alan answered.

"I need to talk to you about something."

"So talk."

"In person."

"Then catch up with me right now and tell me."

"No, because then Lynn will do the same, and she mustn't hear."

Alan sighed. "I'm on my way to a doctor's appointment. I can tell the doorman to let you in, and not Lynn. We can talk in the waiting room. It's Dr. Reilly, third floor." Alan turned off his phone.

In the waiting room, Alan read a magazine. There were two other people in the office: a young woman and a man in his fifties, arms crossed, legs not, staring straight in front of him, which happened to be at Alan.

Roland arrived. "Why are you seeing a dermatologist? Acne?"

Alan sighed. "No."

"Melanoma?"

"No. My skin is dry."

"You're here because your skin is dry?" Roland said, sitting in the chair next to Alan's.

"It's very dry," Alan said. "From the chlorine. What did you want to talk to me about?"

"I assume you would like it if Lynn, and therefore I, too, stopped stalking you."

"No. 'Like' doesn't describe how I would feel. I would love it. Which reminds me, shouldn't you be at work? What excuse did you give them?"

"I said I had something to do in court. And you? What did *you* tell your boss?"

"That I had a doctor's appointment," Alan answered, looking at

Roland with meaning. "I think you're missing even more work than I used to when I was stalking."

Lynn waited outside patiently for the two men. A passerby noticed her standing there and stopped.

"Well, hello, Lynn." It was Maria Stanley, a social-climbing artist.

"Hi there," Lynn said.

"I heard you didn't attend Jania and Peter Collin's party. They didn't invite you?"

"Yes, they did. I had something else to do," Lynn said, trying to remember what had prevented her from going. She suddenly remembered she had been attending a Stalkaholics Anonymous meeting.

"Oh," Maria said, sounding disappointed. "They didn't invite me. I felt excluded."

"Yeah, I know how you feel."

"But you were invited."

"Yeah, but exclusion can come in all shapes and sizes."

"I doubt you get excluded very often."

"Not true. Just last week I was excluded by a club I tried to join."

"What kind of club?"

"A club for people who want nice hair," Lynn said, stretching the truth a little bit—it was actually a club for people who wanted hair. It was the Hair Club for Men.

Maria gazed at Lynn's lustrous, dark blond hair. "You already have nice hair. Is that why they rejected you?"

"No," Lynn said, self-consciously pushing a bunch of hair behind her ear. "But anyway, you shouldn't get upset about not being invited to parties. Exclusion is like an apple. Getting a regular dose of it is healthy and keeps the doctor away." She was suddenly reminding herself of poor dead Judy, with her extravagant theories on happiness.

Maria didn't seem comforted by Lynn's words. Lynn took pity on her and gently added, "Your invitation probably got lost in the mail."

The artist smiled feebly. "What are you doing here? Are you waiting for someone?"

"Yes."

Maria said good-bye and walked away.

"Let's get back to my topic," Roland said to Alan in the waiting room. "There is one way to make Lynn and me stop stalking you."

"And what is that?"

"If I win her back."

"You've been failing miserably."

"I need your help."

"I've already spoken highly of you to her. I don't see what more I can do."

"Redo the weekend deal," Roland said.

"You're insane."

"I'm sure I can win her back if I just have one weekend with her."

"But *I* don't want to spend a weekend with her," Alan said.

"I did it for you." Roland looked as though he suddenly realized the extreme ineptitude of that argument. After all, he had ended up keeping Lynn for himself on that famous weekend. He quickly added, "I'll do the weekend with her first, and I'll win her over, like the last time. Then you won't have to do the weekend with her, and she'll be off your back."

"But what if she still wants to do the weekend with me afterward? If I give her my word, I can't back out. I'm not like you. Or like her."

"I thought of that, and if it comes to that, maybe you should do it. It would give you a terrific opportunity to make her fall out of love with you. It's a lot easier to be unappealing during a weekend than while walking down the street."

Roland had a point. And made another. "And then you would be free of her, free of me, free of your stalkers."

"Okay. It's worth a shot. I'll talk to Jessica about it. I think I can persuade her to trust me."

When they were all back on the street, Lynn said to her stalker and stalkee, "I felt excluded just now. I know you guys were plotting something. It disrupts the stalking order, what you did, and that's wrong. You two have nothing to discuss without me." After a moment she said, "So what were you plotting?"

"Nothing," they answered, one walking ahead of her and one behind her.

Alan and his girlfriend had a special day planned for the coming Saturday. Jessica had persuaded Alan to fulfill her rabbit suit/Central Park sexual fantasy. It had taken her months to talk him into it (she'd been trying since Easter).

A small part of him could see the appeal of it. After all, he had enjoyed himself at Halloween, when he and Jessica kept repeating "We really shouldn't," while having sex dressed as a priest and a nun.

But the reason he had finally agreed was that afterward might be a good time for him to ask Jessica if he could go on the weekend with Lynn.

When they woke up on Saturday, Jessica said, "It's not too hot. It's a perfect day for wearing a rabbit suit."

Alan sighed, remembering Roland had guessed that the woman in the ocean had said, "It's a perfect day for mangofish."

Alan and Jessica went to a children's playground in Central Park. They were being followed by Lynn, and therefore also by Roland, who were wondering why Alan was dressed like a big pink rabbit. Roland suddenly remembered Alan telling him months ago that this was one of Jessica's fantasies and an ongoing point of tension between them. Roland chuckled to himself.

Alan was able to walk comfortably in the suit. It was not as heavy and hot and itchy as Alan had feared. Jessica headed for the jungle gym. She jumped, gripping an overhead bar. Her thin form lengthened and narrowed a little more. Alan glanced nervously at the hem of her very short plaid skirt. He knew she wasn't wearing panties, and the elongated position she was in had caused her hem to rise. Luckily, no one was around, except for Lynn hiding in the bushes, and, therefore, Roland not far away either, but they didn't really count.

Jessica hung there, swaying gently, and said, "Frisk me."

"Frisk you?" Alan said.

Her "Yeah" was a cavernous exhale.

Sometimes when he frisked her he found her gun.

He placed his rabbit head on a seesaw and approached Jessica. He pressed his palms against her ribs, against her back. He searched and came upon some very small, hard bumps, and he took them out, and they were pink foil-wrapped chocolate Easter eggs. He continued searching her body and he pressed his chest against her hips, and his face against her stomach, and he was turned on, not only sexually but romantically, and he loved her. She let go of the bar and slowly sank into his fluffy pink rabbit arms, wrapping her legs around his soft rabbit hips, crossing her ankles over his fuzzy white tail, and kissing him deeply.

Lynn sighed painfully in the bushes.

Alan was happy, but would have been even happier if Lynn weren't hiding in the bushes. Hopefully, his weekend with her would be the solution to the problem. He had to bring it up with Jessica that afternoon.

But first, Alan and Jessica had sex on a bench. Jessica was sitting on his lap, facing him. There was a special opening in Alan's rabbit suit.

Then they had sex on the grass.

Lynn and Roland knew exactly what they were doing, but not many other people did. It looked as though Jessica was just straddling the rabbit man lying on his back. She was barely moving.

She and Alan then went to the Ramble, and walked on the path holding hands. Alan brought up his possible weekend with Lynn.

No sooner had he explained the idea to Jessica than she started fleeing from him. She ran through the woods like a gazelle. Alan ran after her. Lynn and Roland ran after him, staring at his fluffy white tail bouncing crookedly behind him. It was poorly sewn on but cute anyway, Lynn thought.

When Alan caught up with Jessica, she said breezily, "Let's go downtown."

He couldn't tell if her breeziness was benign or the type of breeze that turns into a hurricane.

"Okay," he said.

Walking downtown, Alan kept his rabbit head on, hoping it would make her feel more kindly toward him. He finally, cautiously, asked, "So, how do you feel about this idea of my spending a week-end with Lynn?"

Abruptly, Jessica turned right, walking into a clothing store. Alan frowned. He had a feeling she was upset. Part of him was flattered that she might be jealous.

He followed her into the store, taking off his rabbit head like a gentleman taking off his hat upon entering a church.

Neither of them realized they had just entered a store for larger-sized women.

Jessica began compulsively trying on outfit after outfit, distraught and preoccupied by her own thoughts. There were no tags on the clothes indicating sizes, the store not believing in numerical sizes, so Jessica assumed the gigantic proportions were just a different, loose style.

Alan thought the clothes really didn't look very good on her, and they were not at all her usual style of dress. He couldn't quite pin-point what was wrong with them, because his sense of style was not much better than his sense of direction or observation, but then again, he wasn't giving it much thought either; he was trying to read his girlfriend's mind through her gestures. His best guess was that she was fuming with jealousy and trying unsuccessfully to hide it.

Alan couldn't have been further from the truth. Jessica was indeed very upset, but the one thought that kept running through her mind since Central Park was "I'll try not to be too bad." She was horrified at the prospect of being left to her own devices for a whole weekend. She was trying to bring herself to tell him not to go away with Lynn, so that she, Jessica, wouldn't be able to indulge in all the fun she would be powerless to resist. Unable to make herself tell him, she decided not to think about it, hoping to gather willpower by finding an outfit that fit. None of the clothes suited her, which was weird; usually everything looked great on her. She was too perturbed to notice the reason.

Jessica did not consider herself a sex addict. She knew she used to be one, but believed she no longer was. Yes, she had affairs. Yes, she had a morning lover and an afternoon lover, but so did lots of women, and that didn't mean they were sex addicts. Even though she was not a sex addict, she knew that because she used to be one, she was vulnerable to temptation. Temptation had to be avoided at all costs. Alan should know that. Especially since he was a strong proponent of the ridiculous notion "Once an addict always an addict."

Outside, Lynn spied. She couldn't understand why skinny Jessica was trying on large sizes in a store for heavy women. Suddenly, a chilling thought occurred to her: Perhaps Jessica was shopping for maternity clothes! Maybe she was pregnant!

Jessica continued trying on outfits, drowning in them, as the war within her still raged.

Alan thought she clearly seemed ill at ease with the weekend idea.

"Jessica," he said, "you're not answering me. I need to know if it's okay with you if I go on this weekend. I need you to tell me how you feel about it."

"Hang on, I want to find an outfit."

"We can go somewhere else if none of these fit you."

"No! I love these. The colors are gorgeous, and the material is soft and there is so much of it. I've never worn clothes this great. They're unrestraining, I feel naked in them. I can feel my own flesh, it's very sexy. Look, the armpits are so low, they come all the way down to the waist, practically. So the skin of my upper arm can feel the skin of my rib cage. It's really fun and secretive. It feels like I'm my own lover."

She was restraining herself from screaming to Alan, "Go for it! Fuck her brains out! And I will do the same with my own lovers. Leave me to my fun!"

The two large saleswomen sat there, watching Jessica.

Alan saw their perplexed expressions, went up to them, and said, "Can you be honest with her and tell her these outfits just don't look right?"

One of the saleswomen exhaled, heaved herself up, and made her way to Jessica. "May I help you?"

"Yeah, is this how it's supposed to fit?" Jessica asked.

"No."

"Oh, good, I had a feeling I hadn't put it on right. How does it go?" she said, turning to the woman and holding her arms out, offering her body for modification.

"These outfits don't look good on you," the woman said, without moving to help her.

"I realize that. Could you make them look good?"

"I can't do it for you, but I can give you instructions."

"Okay," Jessica said, thinking this woman must have some sort of phobia about touching people.

"Go home, eat a box of cookies, a pint of ice cream, and six slices of pizza. Repeat every day. Come back in three months."

"Oh." Jessica looked around her and finally understood. To save face, and also because it was true, she said, "That's pretty much what I eat every day anyway. So I guess I should just give up hope that these clothes will ever fit."

The saleswoman nodded, and said, "Some things in life are unfair. It's best just to accept defeat. Move on."

Jessica chose to take those words as military advice regarding her inner war. She nodded to the woman knowingly. "Thank you for your help."

They walked down the street without talking for a while, Alan carrying the rabbit head under his arm like a motorcycle helmet. Finally, he said, "I understand if you're uncomfortable with this weekend idea. I just want to know your thoughts on it."

She was trying to persuade herself that maybe she'd have enough willpower not to engage in the mock-bordello scenario she always fantasized about. In the fantasy, she was in a bedroom, and there was a line of twenty men outside, taking their turns with her.

"The foods that saleswoman mentioned made me hungry," she said, and headed for an ice-cream store across the street.

The ice-cream store only served those perverted European cones where the two scoops of ice cream were positioned side by side, like testicles. She always avoided getting those cones because they aggravated her problem. Sick, those Europeans, to make an innocent ice cream look like a penis.

She considered not getting an ice cream at all, but she was afraid Alan would suspect her problem.

Or maybe he wouldn't suspect anything—she could never tell how obvious sex imageries were, to other people. Nevertheless, not wanting to risk arousing his suspicion, she took the cone and gave the testicles a tentative lick, just to look natural. She tried to be relaxed, but her tongue came out pointy and tense. It jabbed at the balls in a manner that might not have pleased them had they been alive.

"So, what do you think about this weekend idea? Is it okay with you?" Alan asked.

She looked at the ground, holding the edible penis guiltily. "Yes, it's okay with me." She was disappointed that she didn't have enough willpower to tell him not to leave her to her orgiastic fun.

Alan laughed. "Don't seem so sad! You trust me, don't you?"

She sighed and nodded. He wrapped his arm around her and pulled her close, kissing her temple and squashing her creamy testicles between his furry pink chest and her breast.

"Oops." He grinned. They wiped themselves.

A few blocks later, they passed a bookstore, and Alan wanted to stop in.

"Why?" asked Jessica. It had already been four hours since their last sexual intercourse, and today, on her day off, she expected more sex. Plus, the ice cream got her hot.

"I want to check out a short story called 'A Perfect Day for Bananafish,' that Roland told me to read," Alan said. "Have you heard of it?"

She didn't answer. Alan looked at her and saw a curious expression on her face. He had no idea how to interpret it, so he repeated, "Do you know it?"

"Yes. There's no reason you should read it. Roland is a fool and an asshole. Let's go."

"Aren't you curious to know why he wanted me to read it?"

"No."

"Because you already know?"

"Yes."

"So why?"

"You obviously told him that story about when you were little and the woman said it's a perfect day for mangofish and she helped you pet one. I don't know why you open up to that bastard. You shouldn't tell him personal stuff."

"It's not very personal."

"Yes it is, as a matter of fact. It's very personal."

"Well, I don't agree," Alan said, swinging open the door to the bookstore and heading toward the literature section.

"Alan," Jessica said, in a small voice behind him.

"What?"

"I'm sorry, I didn't mean to sound harsh." She stroked his neck affectionately and gave him a kiss. She looked sad.

"Are you okay?" he asked.

She nodded, smiled reassuringly.

He found the book. He skimmed the story and suddenly dropped his rabbit head, which went rolling down the isle. He sank to the floor. Jessica ran to his side, hugging him, kissing his cheek.

"Say something," she said.

"Why didn't you tell me?"

"Because you can't change the past. There was no need for you to know."

"No need to know I was sexually molested as a child?"

"What's done is done."

Later that evening, Alan said, "I wish I had known years ago. My life could have been different."

He didn't say anything more about it.

But he thought about it. And thought about it. And thought about it.

His abuser was his mother's neighbor, Miss Tuttle, and she had given him to pet what she claimed was a mangofish, but what he now learned was her vagina. He had been floating on her yellow raft. She had brought his hand under the water, his view blocked by the raft. She said the mangofish was shy and didn't like to be seen. He remembered what it had felt like. It was mushy and it had folds. And yet, in all the years since, it had not occurred to him that he had touched the woman's genitals.

Maybe he would pay her a visit one day and confront her about what she had done.

Over the years, Alan had frequently asked his mother how Miss Tuttle was doing. His mother had always told him Miss Tuttle was the same as ever, that she hadn't moved and still earned her living mostly as a hairdresser, and occasionally entertaining children at birthday parties. He never understood why he inquired about Miss Tuttle. He didn't care one way or the other about her. Now he recognized this neutrality was his repressed shame, his disgust, his hatred of her.

In awe, he thought, *I am actually a normal person, who happened to have been abused. Deep down, I am normal. I was not born defective—I was damaged a little later.*

Alan had always felt inferior to the other stalkaholics in SA meetings, who seemed more sane than he, because they talked about their childhood abusers, on which they blamed their stalking addiction. Alan had a happy, sound childhood, which made him feel like an outsider, a freak, a truer criminal than the stalkers with excuses.

Now that Alan had discovered he had not had a wholesome childhood, things were different. His sexual abuse was like religion. It explained his deficiencies, his problems, even his lack of artistic talent. All of it was the fault of that abuser. He almost felt grateful to her. Grateful that he could dump it all on her. His stalking habit—her fault. His poor sense of direction, of style, of observation—her fault. His facial expressions that were formerly too drastic and too frequent—her fault. His poor singing, poor dancing, weight problem, hair loss, poor muscle tone—her fault. Life made sense. Finally.

He pondered his problems with swimming. He wondered if there were swimming lessons made for survivors of aquatic sexual abuse. He thought of himself as a completely different person now: a victim. It was liberating and empowering. It raised his self-esteem. He marveled at how his life just kept getting better and better: First he had conquered his stalking addiction, then he had embarked on self-improvement and improved himself, then he had found a great girlfriend, and now he had just learned he was a victim of childhood sexual molestation!

Patricia informed Lynn, "The British Transport and General Workers' Union has rejected your application for membership on the grounds that you are not British and not a transportation or general worker."

Lynn nodded slowly, a look of concentration on her face.

Patricia admired Lynn's devotion to her rejection method, her perseverance in applying it despite getting rejected by Alan on a daily basis anyway.

Alan and Roland told Lynn about their idea of redoing the weekend deal. They gave her no choice as to the order—she'd first be going with Roland, then with Alan.

She agreed.

Ray the homeless man still closed his eyes and held his breath when the stalking chain passed. He had long ago stopped his therapeutic comments. These beguiling crazy people.

. . .

When Roland and Lynn arrived at the inn, Max exclaimed warmly, "Ah, Roland and his stalker!"

"Not quite," Lynn said. "Things have changed. Roland is now my stalker, and next week I'll be coming with the man I'm currently stalking."

Lynn scrutinized Max. He hadn't changed at all. He still had his long curly hair, his ruffles, his codpiece. For some reason, Lynn suddenly wondered how Max and the sex addict Jessica would have hit it off if they had met. After all, he was the guy who thought female stalkers were whores and wanted to be fucked. Jessica would probably have no problem with that. If he were to say to her, "Come and sit on my cock," she'd probably say, "Are you sure you don't mind?" It could free up Alan.

When Roland was carrying their bags up to their rooms, Lynn said to Max, "The girlfriend of the guy I'm stalking is a very pretty sex addict. And in complete denial of her addiction. I think you guys would really hit it off. If I succeed in winning him over, she'll be free. She forced her boyfriend to dress up as a big pink rabbit and have sex with her in Central Park."

"That seems a little tame," Max said.

Lynn coldly replied, "I think she would like you. That's not tame. And neither is the fact that she has a gun."

When Lynn was unpacking, Roland found Max and asked him if he could speak to him privately. They went into Max's office.

Roland discreetly dropped a button. "I need you to help me win Lynn back."

"Sure, man. How?"

"Make yourself as unattractive as possible."

"Why? You don't need to worry about her being interested in me."

"I know. What I'm looking for is the contrast."

"Contrast?"

"Between you and me. We need to increase the contrast. Even more."

"Why?"

"So I'll shine by comparison."

Max produced an amazed chuckle. "You think that would work?"

"Yes. It did the last time."

"What do you mean? I wasn't trying to be unattractive the last time."

"No, but it worked anyway. So it should work even better when you're actually trying." Roland realized he was being mildly insulting, and he didn't know how to get himself out of it. So he tried this tack: "Lynn thinks that you and I are a perfect match, that you are my most sublime enhancer. You know, like a precious stone and its most perfect setting."

"You mean you shine, next to me, by contrast?"

"Yes," Roland said, as if this were a good thing.

Max was silent. His mood had undergone a shift. He gazed at Roland fixedly. "Do you really think I can make myself even more unappealing than I already am? I mean, do you think there's room for me to get worse?"

"I don't know. I would be at a loss how to do it. You would know."

"I guess I would. I'm honored that you have confidence in my judgment."

"Well, it worked the last time, and you weren't even trying."

"No, I wasn't trying to be unappealing. On the contrary, I was trying to be charming and entertaining. So you can just imagine how gross I'll be when I'm actually trying to be repulsive."

He waited to see if Roland would say anything, object in any way, but he didn't. Roland just nodded. And that's when Max's heart, which had gradually been sinking, finally hit bottom and broke. But he didn't let on.

Back in the city, Alan was sitting on his spotted white easy chair, stroking Pancake, who was sprawled on his lap, and dwelling on his abuse. He was relishing it and cursing it in turns, but he didn't want it to take over his life, so he tried to distract himself by perusing some of his continuing education catalogs, even though it was too late to register for fall classes. In one of the catalogs, he came upon a particular swimming class he had not seen before. The name of it was, Swimming: For Adults Afraid in Water. There was a picture of a woman with a dolphin, and it said, "You can learn how to swim quickly and painlessly—and to love the water and the spectacular creatures in it!"

Spectacular indeed, those creatures! He slammed the catalog shut. He felt mocked. How naïve he was. Or had he, in fact, known, deep down? That was the question that haunted him. Why else would he have attached a fish tail to the vagina he had sculpted in Goddess class, producing a vaginafish?

He opened the catalog again and read the rest of the class description: "A variety of swimming aids are used, from swim noodles to floating devices."

Again, he felt mocked. Was the catalog implying he was a noodle? In his own swimming classes they hadn't used noodles. Maybe that's why he hadn't made more progress. Maybe the noodles were necessary for noodles like him, dense noodles abused in water.

Alan went to check the stairwell doors in his building. He hadn't been as good about checking them every day these past few months and had taken that as a sign of his increased mental health. He also knew that neglecting the doors was dangerous.

As he walked down the seventeen flights of stairs, making sure the doors were all closed, he wondered if he would ever actually visit Miss Tuttle. He wondered what he would say to her and how she would react.

The next time Lynn and Roland saw Max was at breakfast the following morning in the dining room. They were stunned. Max was barely recognizable. He was gorgeous. He had cut his hair, gotten rid of his ruffles and codpiece. He was dressed for the twenty-first century.

Roland was confused. He looked at Lynn. She looked dazzled.

Max said to both of them, "I hope my music didn't keep you up last night. I was listening to Maria Callas sing an aria from *Il Trovatore* . . . wonderful. You should get a disc of her arias, if you don't have one already. Or I'll make a copy for you." After a pause, he said, "By the way, I can suggest lovely spots around here if you'd like to picnic. The kitchen can prepare you a basket."

"When you say 'the kitchen,' what do you mean?" Lynn asked, knowing he didn't have any staff.

"I mean me, of course," he said, smiling. "I could prepare you a picnic."

Roland was outraged. It was obvious to him that Lynn was charmed by the transformation. He could kill Max.

. . .

After breakfast, Roland sought out Max.

"What have you done! I asked you to make yourself worse!"

"I did. I got rid of my few attributes. I cut off my luscious locks. Do you know how many years it took me to grow that hair? And I put away my wonderful ruffled shirts, and my manly codpiece, and now I'm wearing these wimpy pants."

"You look marvelous!" Roland said, giving him a fierce push in the chest. "You've ruined it. And what the hell did you do to your personality? It's even more changed than your appearance!"

"I'm glad you noticed. I turned myself into a clean-cut, anal prick, for you! So that you could shine in contrast!"

Roland decided he had to take matters into his own hands. He tried to be charming all day. He even offered to feed the squirrels and raccoons and any other wild animals there might be, like rats and skunks and snakes and bears, anything at all. It was all to no avail. Lynn was cold and uninterested in him. He bad-mouthed Alan. He warned her that they would have ugly children. But nothing seemed to soften her up.

As a last resort, he made a feeble attempt at forcing himself on Lynn physically, something she had enjoyed in the past. This time she sprayed him with Mace.

As Lynn sprayed him, she felt as though she were spraying a giant mosquito. It was a tired and weak mosquito that seemed almost at the end of its life. It buzzed around her heavily, unnervingly slowly, not aware of its own sluggishness, which made it perfect for killing.

She hoped that spraying him would make him so mad that he

would leave her alone for good and give up all hope of a reconcilia-
tion. Instead, he wailed and made her feel so guilty that she had to
nurse him.

The weekend was turning out to be a fiasco.

Just before leaving the inn, Roland privately gave Max instructions.

"When Lynn and Alan come on their weekend, I want you to stay
exactly the way you are now. Don't change a hair. Alan will pale by
comparison."

"Sure."

Roland concluded with, "You and I will be in contact via cell
phone the entire weekend. I'll want constant reports."

The next day, Roland was called in to see his boss, the solicitor general.

She said to Roland, "You told me you were going to review David
Lester's brief of the Garcia case and take out that shitty First
Amendment argument."

"I thought I told him to take it out," Roland said.

"Also, you missed the deadline for filing a notice of appeal in the
Freestone Industries case."

"Yes, I know, I'm sorry."

"What's the excuse this time?"

Roland considered saying, "I've been stalking somebody, and my
job has been interfering." What he said was, "I've had some personal problems. Health issues. I'm sorry. I've got things under control now."

Eleven

After Lynn's weekend with Roland, she received a phone call from Alan. He invited her to join him and his girlfriend for dinner at his place.

Alan said, "I want to reassure Jessica that my upcoming weekend with you isn't a big deal and that you're not a threat to her."

"What do you mean I'm not a threat?" Lynn asked, offended. "Why would having dinner with me convince your girlfriend I'm not a threat? Is it the way I look?"

Alan sighed. "No, just our interaction."

The real reason Alan wanted Lynn to come over was for her to see that he and Jessica were very happy together and would not be torn apart by anyone.

Jessica was seated on the armless white easy chair, staring sullenly at Lynn and Alan, who were sitting across from her on the couch, talking to each other politely. Jessica was not participating much in the conversation, even though she was hosting the dinner.

Jessica resented Alan for planning to go on that weekend and leaving her in a position to be tempted. He was so blind that way. Like the times he'd given her gift certificates for massage appointments, insisting that she ask for "Roman," who was supposedly the best, not suspecting for one instant that of course—of course—she would seduce this Roman dude, whoever he was. Poor little Alan. And who could blame her, in such an intimate setting? It had nothing to do with being a sex addict, which she was not.

She would have to negotiate the timing properly in order to maximize the use of that brief weekend. She had written out a list of men she would invite over. There were twelve. She was trying to show some restraint, even though, after much ruminating, she had decided that there was actually no limit to how many men she could have sex with on this particular weekend and still not have it mean she was a sex addict. Any self-respecting woman would be sure to stay home and have affairs if her boyfriend was spending a weekend with another woman. That was abusive treatment on his part. Twelve men did not signify sex addiction. They merely signified that she was a spurned, jealous, normal woman.

As she sat watching Lynn and Alan chat, Jessica realized she should force herself to make some displays of discontentment, just to put on a good show of jealousy and normalcy.

"So, you're going to try to seduce Alan and steal him from me," she said to Lynn, while sipping her tea. She hadn't managed to convey the right tone of repressed hysteria or even edginess. This shortcoming in her delivery made her a little uneasy, until she realized no one had noticed her monotone, her words having been potent enough. Lynn and Alan looked very uncomfortable. This reassured her, and she was able to relax again. She stretched, arching over the back of the spotted white easy chair.

Jessica was lithe, Lynn noted.

"I'm really grateful that you're so understanding, so . . . accommodating," Lynn said to Jessica.

Lynn attempted to entertain her hosts with descriptions of Max the hotel manager. A troubled expression came over Jessica's features. She softly asked, "He really says, 'Come and sit on my cock'? And he really has a codpiece?"

"Yes!" Lynn said. "He's quite a character. He took it off recently—his codpiece—and was just wearing normal pants, but I'm sure anyone could ask him to put it back on. And he says he has a very big penis. Bigger than most penises in those parts."

Jessica looked preoccupied for the rest of the evening.

Lynn knew that what she had done, tempting and tormenting Jessica that way, was cruel. She didn't care.

The truth was, Jessica was even more perturbed than Lynn imagined. Jessica had to use all her willpower to restrain herself from jumping into a car and going to the hotel manager.

God, how badly she wanted to hop on his penis.

But she was not a sex addict.

She was a normal woman, having affairs.

The problem was that now her mock-bordello fantasy seemed pallid compared to that hotel manager.

Suddenly, she realized that a normal woman would be too jealous to stay home having affairs and would instead secretly follow her boyfriend to that hotel, in order to spy on him, and would do her damnedest not to get caught by that sleazy hotel manager; otherwise, she'd have to beg him, no bribe him—with all sorts of off-color means—not to tell her boyfriend she was spying on him.

. . .

Roland had certainly had urges to beat up Alan since the first day he had met him, but never as much as now. He had just told Alan on the phone that Lynn had sprayed him with Mace, and Alan, the little jerk, still intended to go on the weekend with her.

"You should back out," Roland said. "Out of loyalty to me."

"I'm sorry," Alan said. "I'm not like you. I stick to my word. We promised Lynn that if she went with you, then I would go with her."

Roland promised himself that as soon as Alan came back from the weekend, he'd beat him to a pulp. But for now, he contented himself with hissing into the phone, "You want Lynn."

Alan felt sorry for Roland. He said, "You should try to do something fun . . . and distracting during that weekend. I can tell you from experience that it's not pleasant to wait a whole weekend while the person you love is with the person she loves."

"When are you going to stop rubbing it in my face that she loves you?"

On Friday, Patricia came waltzing into Lynn's office, waving a letter. "I have some strange news to relate."

"What?"

"Disney World has accepted your application to play one of the seven dwarfs in their summer production."

"But I'm not very short!" Lynn said, slapping her desk and rising out of her chair.

"No, not very."

"That's really insulting of them to accept me!"

"Calm down. You shouldn't have applied if you thought you might get in."

"I obviously didn't think I would get in, Patricia. I'm not short!"

"Yeah, but height is relative. Maybe they'll make you act on your knees."

"Well, write back and tell them I've already committed to playing Mini-Me in a touring Austin Powers production."

Early Saturday morning, as they had agreed with Roland, Alan and Lynn were driving Roland's Jeep to the inn. The leaves were brilliant, red and yellow.

Jessica, in a rented car, followed them. She had brought all her equipment—binoculars, disguises, Kleenexes—as a spurned woman would. Her radio was blasting as she bounced in her seat, and she occasionally grabbed her big binoculars and looked through them at their car to reassure herself that she was normal.

She couldn't wait to get to the hotel and was tempted to tailgate Alan to make him move faster. He was so unobservant, he'd never notice it was her.

As soon as they arrived, she would waste no time in trying not to get caught by Max. The mere words "get caught" made her let go of the steering wheel and wave her arms in the air to the beat of the disco music.

Max greeted Lynn and Alan warmly when they arrived. Lynn was surprised that Max had gone back to his old self. His codpiece was on as well as his ruffles. His long hair, of course, could not grow back immediately, and he had not resorted to a wig.

Lynn made the introductions.

"Max, this is Alan, the man whose girlfriend I told you about."

Alan looked at Lynn. "You told him about Jessica? What did you say?"

"That she's a very pretty private detective," Lynn said.

Max had been greatly looking forward to Alan's arrival and the opportunity of doing the opposite of what despicable Roland had ordered him to do. Max had put beautiful satin sheets on Alan's bed and the most expensive bath products in his bathroom. And the most luscious towels. And flowers and bowls of candy. He did everything possible to put Alan in the most flattering light, figuratively as well as literally. He even had someone come in to give him a massage and a facial. Alan was certainly not averse to the massage. Max explained that it was included in the price of the room. Why Lynn didn't get all those amenities was a mystery. When asked, Max said the luxuries happened to be included in Alan's particular room— room 5—not in any other. If you were lucky enough to happen to be the occupant of that room, which was not more expensive than the others, then you got those advantages.

Max had no desire to give Lynn any luxuries, because even though he had not been as offended by her as he had been by Roland, it hadn't delighted him to hear that she thought Roland shone next to him in contrast.

Alan offered to switch rooms with Lynn so that she could get the luxuries, since she was the one truly in need, the stalkaholic. He felt that sensual pleasures would do Lynn good. They always helped stalkers. Alan thought to himself that he should one day write a self-help book for stalkers. The number one advice he would give them was pamper yourself. Stalkers usually didn't pamper themselves enough. There were, of course, exceptions—cases of stalkers who pampered themselves too much, which increased the severity of their stalking. One needed a perfect amount of self-pampering in order to lessen stalking. Too much worsened it. Too little worsened it. But too little pampering worsened it more than too much did.

So they switched all their belongings and went out for a walk. By the time they returned, they were astonished to see that the satin sheets, the fancy bath products, and other luxuries, had switched rooms and were in Alan's new room. There was a note that said, "The management frowns upon guests switching rooms. Switching rooms will do no good. The room will follow him wherever he goes, for the remainder of his days. Unless he is discovered to be a prick."

Alan stared at the note, shrugged, and said, "Whatever" to himself, intent on not letting the manager's quirkiness sidetrack him from the purpose of this weekend. Alan had a plan to be unattractive. Bad clothes, bad cologne. He tried once again to make facial expressions that were "too drastic," as Lynn had put it long ago. He tried to recapture his nervous body language, but he found it just too disturbing, too frightening, like being repossessed by the Devil. He decided his body language was the only thing he would not mess with, for that was too dearly earned. Instead, he focused on speaking well of Roland. "He's energetic. He has a great metabolism. He's tan. He's French. Oh! And he used to beat me at racquetball every single time!"

During lunch, Max sat with Lynn and Alan while they ate the grilled salmon he had prepared for them. Max praised Alan incessantly, pointing things out to Lynn about Alan that he thought were wonderful. Lynn agreed completely.

. . .

As for Jessica, she roamed the hotel, spying. She kept trying not to get caught by Max, and he kept not catching her. She tried spying more vigorously, but she still didn't get caught. So she spied so fervently that she barely hid. And Max finally caught a glimpse of her at 3:00 P.M. in the sitting room, wearing a black miniskirt and two pairs of binoculars dangling around her neck. She fled behind the sitting room's heavy door.

Max approached her and asked, "Why are you hiding?"

"I'm spying on my boyfriend."

"Do you want me to help you?"

"No. I just really, really don't want you to tell him about it. I would do anything so that you not tell him."

After a few seconds, he said, "Oh." Not sure what to say, he finally just said, "Anything?"

"Yes. That's how much I don't want you to tell him."

It was only then that Max realized this woman might be Alan's girlfriend, the terrific sex addict whom Lynn had raved about. "You wouldn't, by any chance, be Alan's girlfriend, would you?"

"Yes, I am."

He frowned. He appreciated the situation she had set up for him.

"I highly disapprove of spying. So the price may be high."

"I know," she said, lowering her eyes bashfully and even managing to blush a little.

He was impressed.

"You may not be ready for what I have in mind," he said.

She kept her eyes lowered.

"It may involve bringing my repulsive person near you." He took a step forward.

"You are not repulsive," she said, softly.

"Oh no? Flattery will not lighten your sentence, you know."

"I know."

His body was now very close to hers, and he dared to bring his hand under her skirt.

"Where is your underwear?" he asked.

"I lost it."

"Where?"

"In the garden. It fell off when I was spying. I didn't have time to retrieve it."

"How unfortunate for you. That will not help your case."

He pressed her back against the wall, behind the door, and un-hooked his codpiece. He whipped a condom out of his pocket and slipped it on.

He slid his erection under her skirt, between her legs, and pushed himself into her.

She had a startled, helpless expression on her face. Her eyes were open wide; her eyebrows downward slopes of sorrow. Her lovely lips were parted, looking innocently shocked. He moved himself in and out of her. Slowly. Every time he pushed himself in, there was a sharp intake of breath on her part. Dismay. He appreciated her acting.

They could hear people talking in the hallway, right outside the sitting room. He slowed his movements even more, but did not stop them completely. Her legs were barely parted.

"I am far from done with you," Max whispered in Jessica's ear, and pulled himself out.

He took her to an empty bedroom and told her to stay there. He said he had some work to do, that he'd be back.

Roland couldn't take it anymore. Getting reports from Max by phone was no longer placating. Roland needed reports every half hour, or an average of twelve times in six hours, and Max had agreed to this, and despite having agreed, Max only answered his cell phone half the time. So Roland decided he had to come to the inn and see for himself how things were going. He would see if Alan was trustworthy, making himself disgusting to Lynn.

At 4:00 P.M. Roland rented a car and started his journey.

When Lynn mentioned having fed the raccoons her first time at the inn, Alan got excited and said he wanted to go and feed them, too.

"But one bit me," she warned. "They can have rabies. I had to get six shots over the course of a month."

His desire to feed raccoons was greater than his fear of rabies and greater than his desire to seem unappealing.

"I don't care," he said. "I'm going to feed some raccoons. You don't have to come with me."

They had fun feeding raccoons, and Lynn found him very appealing.

Jessica waited in the room for Max. Finally, he opened the door. She found him surprisingly handsome at that moment.

She was sitting at the desk. He sat on another chair, near the bed.

"Have you seen any good movies lately?" he asked.

And he asked her where she wanted to travel and what hobbies she had. She didn't understand why he was toying with her. He knew why she was here.

She got up, walked over to him, leaned down, and gently kissed him on the lips. They liked each other quite a lot. He got up and said he had to leave again to tend to something in the hotel.

She remained in the room, perplexed, wondering what she should do.

Ten minutes later he came back, took off his codpiece, donned a condom, lifted Jessica in the air, and impaled her with his erection.

"Life is too short not to have sex all the time, don't you think?" he said.

"Yes," she agreed.

Alan and Lynn, seated next to an open window, were eating dinner while Max buzzed around their table, being friendly, serving steak and baked potatoes to them and the two other couples. The air was unusually warm and pleasant for an October evening. Hiding right outside, in the darkness, dropping a penny, was Roland. He could hear every word they said.

Roland was stunned when he saw Max sit at their table and say, "You guys really make an excellent couple."

Roland yanked out his cell phone and dialed Max's cell number. He saw Max look at his ringing phone, sigh, and say to them, "It's him again."

"Hello?" Max answered the phone, kindly.

"Are you with them right now?" Roland asked, as he always did, except now his voice was a tight whisper.

"Yes," Max said.

"Okay, so I'll only ask you yes or no questions."

"Okay. Why are you whispering?"

"Because I'm . . . in a public place . . . in a bookstore."

"Ah, I see," Max said, then placed his hand over the mouthpiece and said to Alan and Lynn, "Roland is hounding me with questions about you guys. So pathhhhhetic."

Roland heard him through the open window.

"Hello? Are you still there?" Max asked into the receiver.

"Yes," Roland whispered.

"What else do you want to know?"

"Are you treating them badly?" Roland asked, feeling weak.

"Oh, yes!" Max replied, pouring Alan more wine.

Roland winced in the darkness. After a pause, he asked, "Are they having fun?"

"No," Max answered.

"Does Lynn . . . seem to like him?"

"Lord, no." Max put his hand over the mouthpiece again and said to Alan and Lynn, "Can you believe it? He's asking me if you guys have had sex yet!"

Outside, Roland felt faint. "Okay, thank you," he said.

"That's it?" Max asked, sounding almost disappointed.

"Yes, thank you for all your help." Roland hung up. He had known for most of his life that he was probably not the nicest sort of person. Nevertheless, he never thought he'd have an urge to kill anyone other than himself. But suddenly, to his dismay, nothing seemed more important than to kill Max. The necessity and certainty of the act made him feel helpless, and he resigned himself to it.

. . .

Sunday afternoon, Lynn and Alan were lying by the pool.

Flipping through a fashion magazine, Lynn asked him, "If you didn't have a girlfriend, would you be interested in me?"

"Romantically?"

"Yes."

"No."

"Why?" she asked, shocked.

"Because that would be taking advantage of you. You are not lucid. You're a stalker now."

"Cut the bullshit! If I were lucid, would you be interested?"

"Stalkers are not appealing."

"But you stalked me. And first! You used to want me so badly! Don't you remember?"

"People change."

"But I haven't. I'm still the same person you wanted before."

"No, you're not. You are creepier now. But I've been there. I don't blame you."

Lynn's voice was becoming strained. "Okay, okay, what if I were not a stalker, but just . . . reasonably interested in you, would you . . . could you then be interested in me romantically?"

"Hmm, no, it would never work, with our history of me having stalked you and humiliated myself so much."

"Not half as much as I'm humiliating myself!"

"First of all, that's arguable, and second of all, that's not a good argument."

It meant nothing to her what happened after that. "I don't want to drive back with you. I'm taking the train home." She marched into the hotel and packed her things. Within a half hour, she was gone.

Having done everything he could to help Lynn and Roland get back together, Alan decided to stay one more night at the inn to relax and enjoy his newfound freedom from his stalker.

Early the next morning he would drive back to the city. He called his apartment to tell Jessica his plans, but his girlfriend wasn't answering. He left a message. He hadn't been able to reach her since he'd left the city. He hoped she was doing okay and not overly jealous, but he wasn't too worried, because she'd told him she might spend the weekend with her friend Mary.

He called Roland's cell phone to give him a report of how the weekend had ended. Roland was in his rented car, parked on the side of the road, right at the end of the driveway that led to the inn. He was waiting for the few guests to check out, as they were bound to do on a Sunday night, so that he could be alone with Max and put an end to him. One couple had already left, and he saw Lynn leave in a taxi.

When Roland answered his cell phone, Alan said, "Lynn left without me. She's mad at me." Alan thought this would please Roland.

"And you? Are you leaving now?" Roland asked.

"Uh, no, I'm going to stay one more night."

That was very inconvenient for Roland, who didn't want to have to sleep in his car overnight waiting for Max to be alone. "Why?" he said.

"To unwind."

"Don't you have to be at work tomorrow?"

"I'll go in late."

"Can't you unwind at home with your girlfriend?"

"I don't think my girlfriend's at home. I'm here, I might as well unwind here. Why do you ask?"

"I want my car back."

"Is it urgent?" Alan asked.

"Yes! I want it back now."

"I'm really not up for driving back right now, after all this stress with Lynn. I'm afraid I'd have an accident."

"I need my car back now."

"Why is it so urgent?"

Roland couldn't come up with a good reason. "Because the deal was you could have the car until Sunday night. That's it. I want my car back tonight. Stick to your word, as you say."

"I'm tired. You're being unreasonable. I'll drive back in the morning."

Roland sighed. "God, you're such a jerk." He could not wait for an opportunity to beat up Alan. He came up with a way he could treat himself to it after visiting Max. "Okay, I want my car back tomorrow morning. I'll be going to the field of Lynn's love, because, you never know, maybe that map-reading professor was right and it'll increase my chances of Lynn falling back in love with me. The field is on your way back into Manhattan. You can pick me up there, and we can drive together."

He gave Alan directions to the field and told him to meet him there at eight-thirty the following morning. He added, "Do you think you'll find it, with your poor sense of direction?"

"I'll find it," Alan said.

"By the way, Max is kind of a jerk, isn't he?" Roland asked.

"Yeah, he goes a bit overboard with the preferential treatment and the luxuries and the compliments."

Roland was reassured that he had neither misunderstood nor misinterpreted what he had heard through the window.

Alan was still lying by the pool. Max came up to him and said, "I'm sorry Lynn left in such a huff."

"Oh, I know, it's a shame, but probably unavoidable. Maybe for the best."

"What time will you be checking out?"

"Seven o'clock tomorrow morning."

"You're welcome to help yourself to anything you want in the kitchen when you wake, in case I'm not up yet."

Alan squinted up at him, at his kindness. The descending sun shone behind him.

"Thanks."

Max planned to have sex with Jessica in the sitting room at about 7:00 A.M. He didn't tell her that was when her boyfriend would be coming down. What he said, as he lured her down from her room, was that the public aspect would add tremendous excitement to the situation. The truth was that he was smitten with her and wouldn't mind having her for himself. He was hoping Alan would break up with her.

At 7:00 A.M., Alan caught them.

He pushed Max off his girlfriend, screaming, "What have you done to her! She's ill! You are fucking with an ill person!"

Max screamed back, "Shit! What does she have? Herpes, gonor-
rhea, HIV? Please don't tell me it's HIV!"

"She's a sex addict," Alan hissed.

Jessica said, "I'm sorry, but it's over, Alan. I can't be with anyone
for very long. Being with you this long was my record, and I thank
you for it, but it was becoming too hard for me."

"You're dumping me for him?"

"No. I'm not interested in having a relationship with Max. I have
no intention of ever seeing him again. It was just a fling."

"I'm not breaking up with you over this," Alan said. "I'll help you
get back on track. You were doing so well, so many months. You
mustn't let one slip-up ruin everything!"

"I wasn't doing well. I was having sex with other men almost
every day."

"No."

"Yes! You thought I was jealous about this weekend. Well, you
were wrong. I was upset with you going away, because I wouldn't
have the willpower to resist sleeping with a dozen men."

Alan thought he might collapse. He staggered to his borrowed car
and sped off.

Without so much as a word or a glance back at Max, Jessica
rushed to her rented car and followed Alan, not only because it was
in her nature to follow, but because she wanted to make sure he
wouldn't do anything self-destructive.

Alan cried as he drove. He could feel his stalking urges, but he
tried to fight them. He would not stalk Jessica. He did not want to
want her. Anyway, he knew that the urge to stalk her was an absurd
urge, since at the moment he could see in his rearview mirror that she
was stalking him, and on top of that, after learning of her ongoing

infidelity, he didn't really want her back at all. And not wanting her back was strangely more painful than wanting her.

His only comfort was that he had been sexually abused as a child. It was a relief to blame his problems on his abuser. Since he had an urge to fix something in his messed-up life, he suddenly made the decision—which lifted his spirits slightly—to go and confront his abuser, scream at her, show her how she had ruined his life. Things could only get better after one lashed out at one's abuser.

Alan drove straight to Cross, forty-five minutes away. He tried calling Roland to tell him he'd be at least an hour late for their meeting in the field of Lynn's love, but Roland didn't answer his phone, so Alan left a message.

He parked his car at his abuser's house. Jessica parked a ways away.

He rang Miss Tuttle's doorbell.

Miss Tuttle had aged a lot in thirty years. She stood in the doorway, tying her bathrobe.

"Am I disturbing you?" he asked, and before she could answer, he added, "Not that I care."

She looked him up and down in a snobby way, he thought, and said, "You caught me in the middle of taking monthly nude photos of myself to observe the aging process."

"You are a sick woman. I'm surprised you haven't committed suicide."

"Why say such a horrible thing to me?" Miss Tuttle asked.

"You made me touch a *mangofish*. Remember? I was only five years old, for God's sakes! At least Seymour never made the little girl touch the bananafish."

"That's because there is no such thing as a bananafish," Miss Tuttle said. "But I did have a mangofish. I still do. It's in my bedroom. Go in and see, if you want."

He went into the bedroom, expecting her to either strip for him or attempt to murder him.

But in the bedroom was a fifty-gallon fish tank that shone in the darkness like a gigantic jewel. Inside was a fish that was about six inches long, and had whiskers and wrinkled skin, like a basset hound.

"But how did you have the fish in the water with you? You can't hold a fish on a leash."

"I had it in a plastic bag, and I opened the bag a little under the water to let you pet it."

Alan apologized to Miss Tuttle for having accused her of such a heinous crime. He had an irrational urge to apologize to the fish as well but knew it wasn't the exact fish, because fish didn't live that long.

They went back into the living room. Alan seemed deflated. In an attempt to make him feel better, she brought in a muffin from the kitchen, and asked, "Do you want to taste my pussy? It's nice and warm."

He blanched. She burst out laughing. "I'm teasing! You are too funny. You must come and visit me again. People around here are so jaded, let me tell you. But you!" She left it at that.

He confessed to her that he would have liked her to have been his abuser and that now he couldn't help resenting her a little because she wasn't. He explained how bad his life had been, and how it had gotten better, and now bad again, and how blaming it all on her had eased his suffering.

And he rushed out, disgusted with himself.

. . .

Ten minutes later, Alan had to pull over on the side of the road to cry some more. Jessica pulled over behind him. She looked at him through her binoculars. She felt sorry to see him cry but knew this was how things had to be.

As he cried, Alan felt like Cinderella at the stroke of midnight. All the wonderful things in his life had turned back to crap. He had lost his girlfriend and his abuser. And to top it all off, he hadn't even registered for the fall semester. If only he had classes to fall back on, perhaps things wouldn't seem so dire.

He thought of calling Lynn and using her for sex, but first he would check his messages to see if any suicidal friends called who might cheer him up. There were nine new obsessive messages from Lynn, which made her unappealing, and therefore useless, even for a rebound.

He would meet with Roland, and they would commiserate: two dumped men.

Alan started up the car and headed to the field of Lynn's love.

As he drove, Jessica looked at him through her binoculars. Even though she could only see the back of his head, he seemed calmer now. So she turned her car toward Manhattan to start an ordinary day of private investigating and a new life as a single sex addict.

While Alan had been confronting his abuser, Roland had his meeting with Max.

Max was surprised to see Roland at his door. They sat in the living room, to chat. Roland was visiting him under the guise of wanting to hear how the weekend went.

"Have all your guests left?"

"Yes," Max said.

"This house is very quiet when it's totally empty."

As Roland had hoped, Max did not contradict the part about the house being totally empty.

"Don't you have cleaning people who work for you or any sort of help? It must be so much work to do everything yourself."

"A cleaning person will come this afternoon," Max said.

"So, do you think you were able to shine a bad light on Alan?"

"Yes."

"You know one thing that really annoys me about him?"

Max shook his head.

"It's that he drinks water so slowly," Roland said.

"What do you mean?"

"I mean exactly that. And if he tries to drink it more quickly, he chokes. Maybe because I drink water very quickly I expect it of others," Roland said. "I never knew I drank it quickly until I noticed that certain people could not drink it as quickly without coughing. You'll see, I'll show you." He got up.

"Are you serious?" Max said.

"Yes! Do you mind if I go in the kitchen and get some glasses?"

Max chuckled. "Be my guest."

Roland came back two minutes later with two tall glasses of water. In front of Max, he placed the glass in which he had mixed the contents of his locket.

"What? I'm supposed to do this, too?" Max asked.

"Yeah, but hang on. Look at this, okay?"

Max nodded.

Roland drank the water very quickly—not extraordinarily

quickly, but like a normal human drinking a glass of water quickly.

Max nodded again, slightly, to acknowledge being mildly impressed.

"Oh, come on," Roland said. "You have to admit that was pretty damn quick."

Max snorted, said, "You're nuts."

"There's no way you could drink water even half as quickly as I just drank it. Anyway, I think French people have a natural advantage over Americans. I think we're able to drink water much more rapidly, on average." Roland plopped down in a chair, as if ready to leave it at that and move on to another topic.

Max languorously heaved himself into an upright sitting position and picked up the glass of water.

Roland's heart raced. He couldn't believe it was as easy as that. Now that Max was about to drink the cyanide, Roland's mind was free to worry further about his risks of getting caught and charged with murder. He blurted, "Where's your assistant?"

"What assistant?"

"The guy who, on the first day, told Lynn and me that you arranged for us to walk in on you having sex because you love feeling embarrassed."

"Oh, he was just a friend of mine who does that favor for me sometimes."

"Because you love feeling embarrassed."

"Yes. And blushing, especially."

"That's crazy, you know. But also stupidly endearing," Roland said, annoyed.

"I'm glad you think so. And let me be even more endearing by showing you how quickly I can drink this glass of water. Ready?"

Roland scowled, but didn't move. He didn't stop him, though it would have been easy. He could have taken the glass from him, said he had peed in it, or something harmless of the sort.

Max drank the glass of water very quickly. A few drops ran down his chin. He slapped the empty glass on the table.

"That water sucks," he said. "You got it from the tap?"

"Why did you betray me?" Roland asked. "When I phoned, not only did you tell Alan and Lynn it was me calling, but you lied and said I was asking if they had had sex! I heard it all."

Max only had a few seconds to live, and Roland wanted to satisfy his curiosity. "Why did you betray me?"

"Because you're a prick. Today, however, I find you more charming, with your special water criterion for evaluating people. Ow," he said, clutching his stomach.

"Why am I a prick? Because I asked for your help? Because I revealed that Lynn thought you were my sublime enhancer? Is that it? Your feelings were hurt? And you think that's enough reason to ruin my life?"

"Ow!" Max buckled over. And then he shouted, "You gave me something bad to drink!"

"Yes! Cyanide. In seconds you'll be dead."

"No!"

Max convulsed and slumped on his side. Roland knew it was the one-minute coma that preceded death.

As soon as Max was dead, Roland wiped his fingerprints off everything. He used all his willpower to restrain himself from dropping a paper clip—he didn't want to leave any evidence.

Roland returned his car to the rental place and took a cab to the field of Lynn's love to meet Alan. He got there before Alan, who had been delayed not only by the visit to his abuser, but by his poor sense of direction, which had been just moderately improved by the map-reading class.

When Alan arrived, he saw Roland sitting cross-legged, in the middle of the deserted field. As Alan got out of the car, Roland called out to him, "Is Lynn still interested in you?"

"Yes. She won't leave me alone. She left nine messages on my voice mail."

"You just couldn't get yourself to be more unattractive, could you?"

Alan didn't need to be criticized at the moment. He decided to get a quick ego boost. "I tried. But, you know, it's hard."

Roland approached Alan and screamed, "You are an asshole!"

"Really. Did you try to make Lynn dislike you when I wanted her?"

"Blah, blah, blah!" Roland screamed, and surprised Alan by punching him in the face. "Did you really think I came to this field to be in the place of Lynn's love?" Roland said. "You are so gullible. And dumb."

"I don't need this," Alan said, straightening himself, finger to bloody lip. "My girlfriend just broke up with me, I'm not registered in any classes, I've caused Lynn to be on the verge of self-destruction. And most troubling of all, my childhood sexual abuser never abused me, which means there is no explanation for any of this, other than that I am a born loser."

Roland again punched Alan, who fell to the ground. He kicked Alan once, twice, but forced himself to stop. He had already killed one person that morning. He dropped a paper clip, hopped in his car, and sped off.

Alan dragged himself to the train station and took the train home, repeating affirmations that he was great, he was pure, he would remain well-adjusted, would not let himself slide back, would not stalk his girlfriend, would never again chase after someone who didn't want him.

He was repeating these mantras as he stepped out of his elevator and was jumped on from behind. Lynn had sneaked past the doorman and been hiding in the stairwell, waiting for Alan to come home. This was too much. He felt beaten down. He flung her into his apartment. She stumbled but was not deterred. She came back at him like a magnet, arms outstretched, to hug him. And she did. She tried to kiss him. She put her hand on his crotch.

Alan could feel his erection. He knew he didn't have to take it anymore, and he knew how he could fight back. He would rape her.

It would be difficult, but he would try. It's hard to rape someone who wants you desperately.

As he ripped off her clothes, she clearly misinterpreted his actions. She thought he was being passionate. He'd show her it was not passion. It was violence, it was rape.

Of course, that she opened her legs so willingly and widely didn't appear much like rape, but he'd fix that by thrusting hard.

"Yes!" she moaned.

Was she actually attempting to enjoy this? How dare she! She was hugging him, which spoiled the rape effect, got him dangerously close to coming, and also hurt him where Roland had kicked his ribs, so he took her wrists and held them down on either side of her head. He came anyway.

She moaned slightly. With pain. Or at least he tried to believe it was with pain.

That hadn't done the trick. She still wanted him. He got off the bed, feeling emasculated. He dared not inform her that he had raped her, for fear she'd laugh in his face. He didn't know what to do. He took his rat from the cage and stared into its beady eyes, and thought to it, *Did you see Jessica cheating on me, again and again?* He couldn't tell what response the rat was giving him, but he was sure the answer was yes.

The phone startled them both. It was a wrong number. Alan turned off the ringer and sat on his armless white easy chair in front of the window, staring out. He said to Lynn, "Leave me alone for a bit, will you?"

She sat on the couch and read a magazine, glancing at him regularly.

"What happened to your face?" she finally asked.

He didn't want to tell her Roland had beaten him up. "I fell."

After a while he went and took a shower. At noon he said he was going out for a walk.

Perhaps if he allowed her to stay in his apartment, she wouldn't follow him down the street. It would be a welcome respite.

An hour later, when he opened the door to his apartment, he was assaulted by a delicious smell of cooking.

He felt oppressed and comforted at the same time. He happened to be hungry. *Dammit,* he thought. And when he finally got a glance at her, she was wearing nothing but boxers and an undershirt, and she looked damn sexy.

She came out of the kitchen with a saucepan and presented him with the wooden spoon, asking him to taste her sauce. She pushed it against his mouth more gently than he had pushed himself into her. He parted his lips reluctantly and tasted. Mmm. His stomach growled. He hoped she hadn't heard it, but her smile seemed to indicate she had.

"Sit down. It'll be ready very soon," she said, and sauntered back into the kitchen, her firm butt jiggling in that special way only firm butts can.

Five minutes later, she placed a meal on the dining table.

He dug into the pasta. It was good. He felt embarrassed by the pleasure it brought him. He ate, his eyes focused on the plate. He looked up at her only once, just out of curiosity, and she was looking at him, smiling. He looked back down, irked. He ate a few more mouthfuls, pushed his plate away, and was about to get up when she said, "There's more." She got up and came back from the kitchen carrying a warm crème brulée. *Damn,* he thought. He didn't know she cooked. He pressed his palms over his face. What was he going to do? She giggled. She must have guessed his thoughts. Yes, he would eat some crème brulée. But that didn't mean she had won. The grilled caramel on top looked crispy. And the smell. The smell was perfect, too.

He just stared at it.

"Eat it," she said.

He picked up the spoon and tasted the crème brulée. He frowned. How had she become such a good cook? Had she taken secret classes? He ate all of it.

"Please make love to me again," she said.

'Make love to me again'? That's what she thought he had done before? *I fucking raped you.* What was the point of even trying? He looked at her coldly.

"Please make love to me again," she repeated.

"I never made love to you," he said, getting up from the table.

"Ouch."

Ah, now, finally, she said ouch. It was about time.

"Please take me again," she said, stepping in front of him. She held his face in her hands and kissed him gently on the lips. He didn't move. His arms hung limply at his sides. She raised them and attempted to wrap them around herself, but when she let go of them, they fell.

"I don't want to," he said. "I didn't want to before, and I don't want to now."

"You didn't want to before? You could have fooled me," she said.

"That was an act of violence, not of sex," he informed her, hoping she knew he had just uttered the definition of rape.

But she didn't pick up on it.

"I wish you would go home and leave me alone," he said.

She kissed his ear, licked his earlobe. He hoped she couldn't feel him getting hard. She stuck her tongue in his ear.

He wished she knew the art of seduction. How to play hard to get, blow hot and cold. At least then he'd get momentary respites from her stalking while she blew cold. It would be so refreshing. He would search his course catalogs for a class for her. It might even teach her how to give up.

Alan pushed Lynn away. She stroked his jawline, caressed his left buttock. He pulled his hips back slightly, so she wouldn't feel his erection.

"God, I love you," she murmured.

He had backed up against the bookcase, and he couldn't back up any farther. The shelves dug into his back.

"You're hard!" she said.

She rapidly unbuckled his belt, unbuttoned and unzipped his pants, lowered them and his underwear.

"God, you turn me on," she said.

He pressed his lips shut, his arms spread at his sides, hands resting on shelves. He was looking away from his penis, the way he would look away when blood was being drawn at the doctor's office.

She was rubbing her thumb around the tip of his penis. He held his breath. He would not move an inch.

She pulled him to the bedroom and to the bed, laid him on his back, and straddled him. He stared fixedly at the ceiling.

She slid her tongue between his lips, licked his teeth. Nothing worked. She gave up trying to kiss him, and just rode him, her cheek against the side of his head. He could hear her panting in his ear. Her breath was warm. And then she sounded different. The panting turned to sobbing, and she rolled off him and curled up on her side, her back to him.

"What's wrong?" he asked.

"You're not responding," she said.

He sighed, got dressed, and moved to the living room. She followed him.

Alan was starting to think about Jessica again, and it made him sad. He suddenly remembered that Lynn didn't know he and Jessica were broken up.

"You've made yourself quite at home, cooking a meal, and everything," he said. "What if Jessica walked in?"

"This is the first time you brought her up. You haven't used her as an excuse for why we shouldn't do what we were doing. That's a good sign."

"A sign of what?"

"That she doesn't have such a strong grip over your affections. Or maybe a sign that she doesn't satisfy you completely. I mean, you know, you're cheating on her."

"No, I'm not. I would never cheat on her."

Lynn frowned, then her features softened into a smile. "You're not?"

He shook his head.

"That's great news!" she said. "When did it happen and over what?"

"It's not great news. I'm very upset." He sat on the couch.

"Oh, don't be!" she said, hugging him from behind. "I'll make you better. You're my honey."

"No, I'm not."

"Yes, you are. Everyone can decide who her honey is. The honey can't object. The honey has no say. The honey can only decide who *his* honey is, not whose honey he is."

Lynn took off Alan's shirt. *Not this again.* He tried to resist, but with so much lassitude that she succeeded in undressing him completely within three minutes. She spread plastic from the dry cleaners under his butt and over the couch.

She had just put on a CD—Bach's Toccata and Fugue in D Minor.

She stood behind him. Using a dinner knife, she was spreading something on his arm. In her other hand, she was holding a jar of honey. Harmless enough. She covered his entire body with honey. His penis became erect, but he ignored it.

He picked up the newspaper and began reading an article on lawns.

"See, now you are literally my honey. You can't object to that," she said, continuing to futz about him, touching him, and when he looked down at himself again, he saw that she'd covered his body with fresh mint leaves.

"I really should be going to work," he said.

She next put Rice Krispies all over the honey, which made his body bumpy, as if he had a horrible skin condition. He suddenly wondered if she was going to eat him.

She then sprinkled cocoa powder over his entire body, turning him dark brown in addition to bumpy. He looked monstrous, she noticed with satisfaction. She'd always had a fantasy of having sex with a monster. She thought that this act of covering him with food might win him over: it was whimsical, spontaneous, playful, artistic, charmingly childlike, and sensual.

She used Nesquik on some parts of his body and Ovaltine on some others. She asked him to close his eyes. As she was sprinkling Nesquik on his face, he said, "I really should be going to work. What about my job? I can't go to work looking like this."

"It's already two-thirty in the afternoon. Don't you think it's a little late to get to work?"

"Better late than never."

She then brought out a can of whipped cream. The organ music was passionate as she sprayed whipped cream on his nipples and over his pubic hair and balls and all over his penis.

"If I don't go to work, I'll become homeless. I'm already a beggar. A beggar for mercy. For solitude."

Since there were no cherries in the kitchen, Lynn came back with a blueberry, which she placed on the tip of his vertical penis.

She had left his feet and the top of his mostly bald head clean. She knelt at his feet, covered them in olive oil, and started giving him a foot massage. He jerked his foot a few times because it tickled. She slid her fingers between his toes. The pleasure, which he was trying to ignore, kept infiltrating itself into his article about lawns.

The doorman buzzed. Alan and Lynn looked at each other.

"Can you get that?" Alan said.

Lynn put down his foot and went to answer the in-house phone. "Yes?" She listened. She looked at Alan. "The doorman says that Roland wants to come up."

Alan didn't respond.

"I'll tell him not to let him up," Lynn said.

"No! Don't."

"Don't what? Don't let him up?"

"No, don't tell him not to come up."

"You want him to come up?"

"Yes." Alan paused. "Yeah, tell him to come up."

"Why? Are you insane? And look at the state you're in. He'll be upset to see me here. He might lose it."

"Good, let him kill us. What else have I got to live for, anyway? Let him up!"

Lynn told the doorman to let Roland come up. She opened the front door. She perched herself up on the back of the couch, behind and above Alan, her legs on either side of him, the back of his head in her crotch. She began giving him a head massage.

Roland walked in, stared at the spectacle.

Alan was glad to be covered in food, because he realized it was a testament to Lynn's obsession, to the power he had over her. That was one way of looking at it, and he wanted that to be the way Roland looked at it.

And Roland certainly was looking. The way Lynn and Alan were sitting, she looked like his throne. Her fingers on his head were his crown. As she massaged his scalp, the skin on his face was being stretched, his eyes were pulled back into slits. Alan tried to shoo her away. But she stayed attached to him, the tips of her fingers clasped to his mostly bald head like tentacles, like a crown of clinginess.

Alan had clearly won. Nothing could have made Roland feel more defeated than this display. It went far beyond a scene of domestic bliss, which certainly would have been discouraging. Alan had become a powerful, grotesque beast, majestic. Roland blinked a few times. He had an urge to bow and leave but forced himself to stay.

"What do you want, exactly?" Alan asked.

Roland didn't answer at first. Eventually he said, "Can I take Lynn?"

Deliver me from her, deliver me from her, Alan thought. What he said was, "I'd rather you not take anyone by force, but in principle, yes, you can take her, if she'll go with you."

"You're so weak and spineless, no wonder your girlfriend dumped you," Roland said. "It's amazing she was with you to begin with."

"Lynn, please go into my bedroom and bring back what is at the bottom of the third drawer from the top."

Lynn obeyed. She came back holding Jessica's gun.

"Kill him," Alan said.

Roland stared at the gun in Lynn's hand, pointed at him.

Lynn didn't shoot.

"If you don't shoot him, I want you to leave and never return," Alan said.

Lynn still didn't shoot. Finally, she said to Alan, "If I kill him, I'll go to prison and never see you again." She placed the gun next to Alan on the couch.

Roland rushed toward it. Alan didn't move. He allowed Roland to grab the gun. Roland shot at Alan. No bullets. Roland tossed the gun back on the couch. "You wimp. You weren't going to kill me."

"That's right, I wasn't," Alan said, haughtily. "Now, please, the both of you, get out." He sounded tired.

Lynn sat next to Alan on the couch and begged him not to make her go.

"Could you please take her with you?" Alan said to Roland. "My feet are oily, and I'm afraid I'll slip. And I'm exhausted."

Roland dropped a paper clip, picked up Lynn, and carried her to the door, screaming.

"One moment," Alan said, and Roland stopped. Alan got up, the sheet of plastic clinging to his butt. He approached, careful so as not to slip. He stroked Lynn's hair, and said, "I was mildly excited by the idea that you would do anything for me. So I tolerated your presence. But you didn't pull the trigger. I'm not the least excited any longer." What he said was true, but one did not always utter something just because it was true. He uttered it in yet another attempt at being unappealing.

They left.

Alan fetched the bullets from his bedroom closet. He loaded the gun.

He took out a piece of paper and on it wrote Jessica's mother's phone number followed by the request that Pancake should be taken care of by Jessica. He added a few words: "No one is to blame for my decision to end my life. I'm just not a happy man. Mom, I love you very much. You were and are the best mother imaginable. Please, don't be too sad. I'm okay now. Love, Alan."

He left the note near the rat cage.

He said good-bye to Pancake. He knew Jessica would take good care of him. She was a rats-and-guns type of woman.

Alan pressed the barrel of the gun against his temple. He slid it down his cheek. He placed it in his mouth. He tasted the honey and

Nesquik that had gathered on its tip. He licked it clean, then stuck the barrel farther into his mouth.

The fire alarm went off. He dropped the gun, grabbed Pancake from his cage, and ran out of the apartment. He could smell smoke. He started racing down the stairwell, cocoa powder flying off him as he ran. He hadn't bothered closing all the stairwell doors in the building recently, and now there was a fire! He wondered who had started the fire, whether it could have been Roland. A few mint leaves flew off him like loose feathers off a bird. The Rice Krispies slowly rolled down his surface. They were still held on by the honey, but no longer crispy, and the whipped cream dribbled down his nipples and thighs. He slipped and fell a couple of times because of the olive oil on his feet. He was carrying Pancake in one hand and raised that hand high in the air every time he fell, to protect the rat.

He was surprised that nobody was in the stairwell, but since he lived on the top floor, he had always known he'd be last in line, with no one rushing past him in the event of a fire. Anyway, they were probably all taking the elevators down, the fools. They knew nothing about fire safety; they didn't even keep the stairwell doors on their own floors closed.

When he reached the sidewalk, panting and shaking, most of the tenants were already gathered there. They were horrified at the sight of this chocolate-covered naked man holding a rat. They assumed his skin looked the way it did because he had been scorched by the fire, that his skin was burnt to a crisp and already bubbling up, blistering and doing gross stuff. The whipped cream was some weird fluid the body produced when it got burned: The groin and nipples started foaming. The mint leaves were confusing. The blueberry was long gone. Had it still been there, the tenants might have understood.

Alan reassured them that he was just covered in food. He walked through the crowd, petting Pancake to calm him, and asking the tenants where the fire was, how it had started. They didn't know for sure. Some said it was on the fourteenth floor, but they kept changing the subject back to the chocolate covering his body. They seemed to be trying tactfully to remind him that he was naked. They asked him whether he might not like to cover himself up, but no one offered any clothing. Alan didn't understand why his neighbors concerned themselves with such a trivial matter as his nudity. Wasn't it clear he had been engaged in some kinky sexual game? Was it really the time to giggle about chocolate-covered nudity when there was a fire in the building? What about perspective?

It was a chilly afternoon.

A cop came by and told him to cover up or he would arrest him for indecent exposure.

"But there's a fire in my building!" Alan said.

"Exhibitionists always have excuses," the cop replied.

A rumor began spreading that the fire was started by a young woman from the fourteenth floor, technically the thirteenth floor, the bad-luck floor, who was burning a contract her boyfriend wrote and signed in his blood that he'd never lie to her again. And then he did. So she burned the paper and left the fire unattended to cry on her bed.

Alan approached the woman from the fourteenth floor—the fire starter. The crowd of tenants parted to let him through.

He stood in front of her and said, "How could you leave burning paper unattended? Are you insane?"

"I'm sorry it caught you at that bad moment, when you were doing whatever you were doing," she said, pointing to his chocolate-covered nudity.

"There is no good moment to cause a fire," Alan replied.

"I'm sorry. I was disillusioned."

"Why?"

"It's personal."

"Everyone already knows about it. You burned a contract in which your boyfriend swore he'd never lie to you again, but he did. Tough. So what?"

"Get away from me. You're naked and disgusting and infringing on my privacy."

"And you started a fire. I'm one of your victims."

She rolled her eyes.

"On candles it says, 'Never leave burning candles unattended.' Haven't you ever had a candle?"

"Get him away from me," she said, cringing. "You're naked and disgusting and holding a rat."

Alan puffed out his chest and loomed over her. He then hopped up on a little wall and spun around, facing the tenants, his rat in one hand. With his other hand he pointed to the disillusioned fire starter. "And whose fault is that? Am I the one who chose to leave burning paper unattended just when I happened to be naked and covered in food? What did you expect me to do? Stay in my apartment and burn to death with my pet?"

"Listen, I can understand why you're upset," the woman said. "You're feeling humiliated and frustrated because I obviously inter-rupted you in the middle of some perverted sex game, but you're not improving your lot by screaming."

A businessman from 3A said, "It does look like the fire alarm caught you in the middle of a titillating situation. It must have been a drag to be interrupted."

"No! I was in the middle of trying to kill myself, okay?"

A few tenants laughed, assuming it was a joke.

The businessman smiled. "What suicide method involves being covered in chocolate?"

"None. But being covered in chocolate does not stand in the way of suicide," Alan said.

"No? I think it should," the man said. "Finding oneself covered in chocolate periodically and for any reason is a sign that one's life is rather exciting and not worth ending, in my opinion."

"Well, you're wrong."

"If I'm wrong, why did you run out of the building to save your life, just when you were about to end it?"

"I was saving my rat, not my life."

People were silent.

Alan added, "Every day of my life I go up and down the stairwell, closing every door on every floor to protect myself and others from maniacs like her who leave burning, broken, bloody contracts unattended!"

After a moment, the businessman said, "And now, do you still think you'll kill yourself?"

"Possibly not. The moment passed."

"So the rest of your life will be thanks to her."

"Yes. And if my life is bad, which it probably will be, as it has mostly been, it'll be thanks to her, too."

"You can't blame things on others."

"Just watch me. I'm sure you're all very familiar with how comforting it is, how mentally helpful it is to blame things on others. You all have your childhood molesters, your bad parents, your abusive teachers, people to blame everything on. I never had one. I thought I did, recently, but I was misled. Now I finally have mine." He pointed his finger at the woman from 14C and proclaimed, "The rest of my life will be her fault!"

The ex-psychologist homeless man, Ray, looked on, askance, wearily transfixed. He felt beaten down, worn down by the flurry of questions coursing through his mind like a drug whose effect he was trying to resist. It looked to him as though Alan were auditioning to be his patient, and Ray had to admit it was a convincing display of insanity.

Alan suddenly heard a loud voice from the crowd shout, "Drop your weapon!" He looked in the direction of the voice and saw two policemen pointing their guns at him and asking him again to drop his weapon.

"No, it's not a weapon, it's my pet rat!" Alan shouted.

"Drop what you're holding!" they said.

"No! Look, it's not a gun, it's just my pet rat, Pancake. He's not like a dog. He'll run away if I let him go." Alan raised Pancake by his tail, letting him dangle. He held the tail between his thumb and index fingers, the rest of his fingers lifted high and spread out, to show that he wasn't hiding anything else. Pancake struggled at the end of his tail, and abruptly swung up and bit Alan's hand.

"Ow!" Alan screamed, dropping the rat, who scurried away. Alan leapt off the wall and chased his rat, shouting to people, "Catch him! Catch him! He's my pet!"

The policemen ran after Alan, who finally caught up with his rat and managed to grab him. Furious, Alan turned to the cops. "How dare you make me almost lose my fucking pet! What do you want?

I'm naked because there's a fire in my building, and I didn't have time to put on clothes, is that a crime?"

"We need to take you in for questioning."

"Because I'm naked?"

"No, it's about another matter."

"I'm not the one who started the fire. Everyone already knows it's the woman from 14C. She confessed."

"It's about another matter."

"What other matter?"

"Get in the car."

"But I'm naked and covered in chocolate and honey. I'll dirty your car."

"It doesn't matter. We've seen worse."

The police questioned Alan about Max, eventually revealing to him that Max had been found dead. Alan told them about his last exchange with Max and about catching Max having sex with Jessica. They questioned Jessica, who answered all their questions truthfully, and immediately fell into a deep depression, believing she had been the cause of Max's suicide when she had told Alan, in front of Max, that she had no intention of seeing Max again. They questioned Lynn. They also questioned Roland, even though as far as anyone knew, he hadn't been at the inn in over a week.

After their brief investigation of Max's death, the authorities chalked it up to suicide.

Jessica left New York and decided to stay with her parents in the Midwest for a few months to think about her life and the people she had hurt.

Twelve

Four months passed, the dead of winter came, and, remarkably, nothing changed, the stalking chain remained intact.

Alan's building hadn't been seriously damaged by the fire. All the residents were able to continue living there, except for the fire starter, whose apartment had been destroyed. Alan still checked the stairwell doors every day.

After the fire and the news of Max's suicide, it had no longer seemed so important to Alan that Roland had beaten him up in a field, had come to his apartment and shot at him with a gun that easily could have been loaded, and had then carried Lynn off over his shoulder.

Alan did mention those offenses to the police when they questioned him, which was what led them to question Roland, but Alan didn't bother pressing charges against Roland or putting a restraining order on him. His magnanimity was not brought on by a feeling of strength, but quite the opposite, by feeling overwhelmed and numb.

Misfortune eats at one's self-confidence. Alan's strong new self had gotten weaker. He had learned the falseness of the saying "What doesn't kill you makes you stronger." He now knew that what didn't kill you made you weaker and weaker. He was no longer in touch with the friends he had made during his new life, which was now old and gone. His recovering stalker friends had stopped calling him, because he lacked the energy to give them pep talks and help them resist the temptation to stalk. He himself had not been gripped by an urge to resume stalking, but so what? He wasn't happier now than when he was a stalker. He was depressed and lonely and he shamefully admitted to himself that being followed was somewhat comforting. So dim did his life seem to him that his stalkers had become sparks of light. Even though he rarely spoke to them, he thought of them as his support group.

It had taken Roland a couple of weeks to adjust to living without the cyanide, without the reassurance that he could end things at a moment's notice if he wanted to. He felt vulnerable. But he also felt closer to his fellow beings, as though they were all in the same boat. He and they now had something important in common: They weren't carrying cyanide on their persons. He still wore the locket so that he wouldn't be reminded, as often, of the cyanide's absence.

As for being a murderer, it wasn't much on his mind. He found the topic uninteresting; it wasn't suicide, after all.

He hadn't committed any grave offenses since then. Granted he had tried to shoot Alan with a gun that might have been loaded, but it hadn't been—thank God, because he couldn't have passed that off as suicide. He had carried Lynn out of Alan's apartment against her will, but he'd let her go as soon as they hit the sidewalk—it's not easy for a man to carry a screaming woman down the street. She had then taken a cab home. He'd been glad he'd at least gotten her out of Alan's building.

The next day the stalking chain had resumed as if nothing had happened.

Patricia was surprised that Lynn, despite stalking Alan every day and being in a perpetual state of rejection by him, was still applying to clubs that wouldn't want her as a member, just to play it safe.

Alan, Lynn, and Roland continued to give money to Ray the homeless ex-psychologist who still held his breath and closed his eyes when the stalking chain passed him, particularly now that he had seen one of its links act so strangely, perform chocolate-covered naked ranting on a wall with a rat, before being whisked away by cops.

One snowy winter day, Alan stopped in front of the homeless man longer than usual, wondering why his eyes were so often closed and his breath so often held. Alan took off his coat and placed it in the arms of the homeless man. It was a beige shearling coat that Alan had worn for three years and didn't want anymore. Ray held the coat, stunned. He didn't usually accept presents, since his homelessness was relatively intentional, but a present from a link in the stalking chain was hard to resist.

Ray cleared his throat. "What is this?"

"A gift. Put it on, won't you?" Alan said.

Ray didn't move. He had to admit he was somewhat curious, somewhat seduced, despite his better judgment, despite knowing full well that deep inside, this nut was probably terribly banal.

Alan took back the coat, walked behind Ray, and held it up for him to slide his arms into. After a moment's hesitation, Ray placed his hand in the armhole. He could not help relishing every second as the enticing crazy person slid the sleeve up his arm. And then the other.

"There, that looks good, it fits you well," Alan said. What he meant, of course, was, "It fits you well for a coat that's two sizes too small for you."

"Thank you," Ray said. It was the perfect opportunity for Ray to ask Alan why the stalking order had changed, but he did not permit himself to ask any questions. He would not pander to his curiosity disorder.

Alan smiled and walked away.

Lynn witnessed the gesture and ruminated. She came up with an idea that excited her. In order to impress Alan, she paid a gourmet store on the corner to give the homeless man two meals a day, in a paper bag, for a month. It was not an inexpensive gesture, but if it had any chance of impressing Alan, it was worth it.

After handing Ray his first lunch and informing him of the ones to come, Lynn said to him, "The only thing I ask in return is that you mention this to Alan. Alan is the man who gave you your coat. *Bon appétit.*" She smiled and walked away.

As soon as Lynn was far enough away, Roland stopped in front of the homeless man. "What did that woman say to you?"

"She said she paid that store to give me two meals every day for a month."

Roland walked away, dropping a button and ruminating. He came up with an idea that made him smile hesitantly and invisibly.

Roland rented an apartment for Ray. He broke the news to him on the street the next day.

"Listen, I don't know how you feel about sleeping on the street," Roland said, "and I don't want to seem presumptuous, but I got you a small studio for the winter if you want it. You'll owe me nothing except to speak well of me to Lynn, and to tell her about this little favor I've done for you."

Ray didn't respond at first. Finally, he said, "Sure, why not."

He had had the willpower not to ask questions, and still did, but he did not have the willpower to refuse these advances. He knew he should turn down the presents, he knew it was fate, taunting him, but he couldn't.

He went to the apartment wearily.

Despite his coat, meals, and studio, Ray still stood at the corner to beg. The next time he saw Alan, he felt somewhat obligated to tell him of Lynn's gift of the meals. And while he was at it, he also mentioned Roland's gift of the winter studio. Alan stood, dumbstruck, in the snow. Ray found it irresistible to add, "Feel free to visit me sometime."

Alan was upset by Lynn's and Roland's gestures, because he knew that this beggar would eventually feel let down when the two stalkers stopped supporting him. He felt responsible for having unwittingly started this chain reaction. To assuage his guilt, Alan bought Ray some clothes. And when he visited Ray's new place and saw the squalor he lived in, meaning no TV and not much furniture, he went shopping for a sofa, a table, and chairs, and had them delivered to Ray's.

When Lynn saw how much the other two had done for the homeless man, she wanted to surpass their gestures, in order to impress Alan, but she didn't know how to. Then she figured he needed a social circle, so she gave him one by throwing a party at Ray's place.

Roland was in a corner, at the party, talking to a man he didn't know. "We've created this creature by the force of our group energy. It's as if we've given birth to a being. It is our child," he said, referring to Ray.

"Isn't that a little presumptuous?" replied the man, popping a peanut into his mouth. "I mean, giving food and shelter to a homeless person suddenly makes you a creator of life?"

Ray talked to the guests politely, but they didn't interest him; they were just ordinary people—not like his nuts. His eyes couldn't help seeking out the nuts and observing them. He was falling for them, he realized. If he were to discover now that their core was banal (and he still thought it probably was), he would be frustrated. Therefore, he continued not asking them questions. People's business was their business. Knowing was disappointing.

Curiously, what was almost as extreme as Ray's curiosity about the nuts, was the nuts' lack of curiosity about him. They felt guilty about their complete disinterest in him. They knew they really should ask him one or two questions about his life, his past, whatever, just to seem polite, but they kept procrastinating, afraid of a long answer, a boring answer, afraid of getting to know him. During the party, decency didn't allow them to postpone asking him a question any longer. They formed a semicircle around Ray. Roland held his hand behind his back and dropped a paper clip.

"So, what did you used to do before you became homeless?" Alan asked. The others nodded.

Ray didn't want to tell them the truth, that he used to be a psychologist and could analyze them if he wanted to, and could even, perhaps, help them. So he told them he used to be a locksmith.

"Ah, a locksmith!" they said, with civil enthusiasm. "And what happened? How did you become homeless?"

"I became disillusioned."

"About life?" Lynn asked.

"No. About locks."

"Really? How so?"

"I used to think locks were complex and exciting, but the complexity hides dullness. I was hoping for a lock that was somewhat difficult to unlock, to understand, relatively unpredictable, and therefore interesting, but no such lock."

"What made you become a locksmith in the first place?" Roland asked.

"I like having the key to things. And unlocking things. If I had been Bluebeard's wife, I'd be dead, too. I would have done what she did. I would have used the little key to open the forbidden room and see what was inside."

"You're a very curious person?" Lynn asked.

Ray lowered his eyes and softly confessed, "Yes." He added, "But unfortunately, what's inside is almost always disappointing."

"You do sound like a disillusioned locksmith," Roland said.

Weeks passed. Ray gradually got to know a fair amount about the nuts' situation, because even though he never inquired, bits and pieces were inevitably revealed along the way. On top of it, the nuts were not particularly secretive about their feelings.

Ray still hadn't been disappointed in them, but he remained skeptical. Every time a new layer fell off, he was surprised that it hadn't hit dullsville yet. Anytime one of them said to him, "Let me tell you about myself," or the equivalent, Ray replied, "Ugh, please don't."

Eventually, Ray began having the urge to exercise his influence on them. He saw how deeply unhappy and dysfunctional they were, and he was curious to see if he could improve their lives. He reasoned with himself that this was not as dangerous as asking them lots of questions. Asking questions had landed him in jail, but he had never really tried actively to improve someone's life, unless one counted the therapeutic comments he had whispered to them in the street. The most obvious way he could think of to improve their lives was to find them mates.

For a month, he searched. He met singles on buses, gathered e-mail addresses and phone numbers, he recontacted old friends who used to be single back in the days when he was a psychologist, to see if they still were. He asked around.

Finally, he threw a matchmaking party at his winter studio.

The nuts did not find mates, but others did. He was encouraged to throw another matchmaking party. He did. More people found mates. Not the nuts. Ray got sucked into the matchmaking business.

The nuts started to find Ray more interesting. They were impressed when people clamored for another matchmaking party. The nuts became curious about him. It didn't hurt that they overheard an old friend of Ray's at one of his parties say to someone, "Ray used to be a psychologist." Stunned, they went up to the man who'd just spoken those words, and asked him if this was true. The man, realizing he had made a blunder (for Ray had instructed all his old friends not to reveal his true ex-profession and to stick to the story that he was a locksmith), fixed his blunder by saying, "No, you misheard, I didn't say psychologist, I said psycho locksmith."

"Ahhh, okay, that makes more sense," the nuts said. "But in what way psycho?"

"Compulsive need to open things. Picking at locks until they give."

Ray threw more matchmaking parties. Word spread. He began charging a fee. People sought out his matchmaking services. Someone helped him build an Internet matchmaking site called Chock-FullONuts.com, which took off beautifully even though people had advised him against that name, saying it would scare off potential clients, especially women. He was glad he had finally found a profession he was good at.

No matter how many times he repeated to himself that the nuts weren't that interesting, they were always on his mind. And to make matters worse, they'd been hanging around a lot since he'd become successful with his matchmaking business. They were growing to admire him.

They came up with excuses to visit him—not that they needed excuses, since the studio belonged to Roland, the furniture to Alan, and the food to Lynn. Sometimes they were all three hanging out at Ray's place at the same time. Their obsession with each other had been slightly diminished because a portion of it had been transferred to Ray.

Ray looked at them, seated side by side on his couch. He asked them nothing, listened to them, and answered their questions.

Eventually, Ray felt things couldn't go on this way anymore. No one should have to live in such skins. He could see they were still not happy, and neither was he, really. He spent many hours trying to come up with a solution to help his friends. He took long walks around blocks, staring at the pavement, thinking.

He came up with the solution—a cure of sorts. He hadn't worked out the details of his idea yet, but he had the general concept. It was an unusual one. It would make them happier and make them realize there was more to life than each other, while preserving their unique nutty flavor.

· · ·

At the attorney general's office, Roland was called into his boss's office, the solicitor general, Mary Smith.

She said, "I recommended you for the committee for policy on Section 71 cases, and now Suzan Kahn told me you haven't shown up for a single meeting."

"They don't need me on that committee."

"That's not an excuse." She stared at him in silence before going on. "And that's not all. It appears that you lie. You said you had an oral argument in Seligman against the Department of Health, but Jerry Corman was at court for an argument and told me that the Seligman case was submitted without argument."

Roland kept his eyes downcast.

"You say nothing. That's fine, I don't especially want to hear your excuses." She sighed. "Look, this is happening too much. You're sacrificing the interests of the client, you're missing court dates, and your mind is obviously somewhere else when you're editing briefs. I just don't have any other choice but to let you go."

Thirteen

Ray invited the nuts to dinner at a restaurant. They were delighted.

After ordering their food and engaging in some small talk, Ray got to the point. "I don't think we live wisely. We are bored. You may not think you're bored, but I believe you are, we all are. Our lives are the equivalent of a sensory-deprivation tank, and that's not healthy. It makes many of us go nuts." He gave them a significant look. They were not aware that he thought of them as nuts, but that look was meant to be a hint. He continued. "Human beings evolved in a manner that makes them well suited to a certain kind of lifestyle, which involves danger in daily life. Through the ages, human beings managed to significantly decrease the frequency of dangerous occurrences. Do you follow me?"

They nodded. They thought he spoke well for a locksmith.

He went on. "This decrease in dangerous occurrences may have seemed like a good idea. It made our lives happier and more pleasant on a certain, immediate level. But the lifestyle that originally made us into what we are was not a safe lifestyle. Therefore, by inflicting upon ourselves a safe lifestyle, we experience certain unfortunate side effects," he said, pulling a small chalkboard out of a bag. "These side effects are, I believe, the following." He wrote on the chalkboard:

1. Loss of vitality.
2. Loss of perspective.
3. Loss of sanity.
4. Loss of the full and rich spectrum of happiness that human beings have the potential to experience if only they were to be subjected to the lifestyle they were made for.

He propped the chalkboard up on the table next to his plate for them to see and said, "Have you noticed how even just reading a book about miserable physical conditions is enough to increase your appreciation of small ordinary comforts? Well," he snorted, "just imagine how much more potent the effect would be if we actually lived those miserable conditions. I think it's pretty clear where I'm headed, right?"

The nuts stared at him without responding. Alan was sitting on his hands.

"In a nutshell," Ray said, "once a year we should try to endure something extreme in order to come to our senses. It's psychologically hygienic. Just like getting your teeth cleaned, or taking a shower. To maintain optimum mental health, we've got to have strong stimulation occasionally. And since our modern life doesn't provide that, we must manufacture it. What do you think?"

"Well, it's an interesting idea," Lynn said, thinking of Judy. "It reminds me of a friend who got hit by a truck and said it was revitalizing. So eventually, she did it again, and died."

"That may well be, but can you imagine how much better off she would have been had she lived?" Ray said.

"Better off than dead?"

"No. I meant, if she had survived without being seriously hurt, she would have been better off than if she hadn't been hit by the truck."

"I disagree," Alan said. "I don't believe in that dumb quote 'What doesn't kill you makes you stronger.' I think the truth is the opposite."

"To a certain extent, you're right," Ray said. "What doesn't kill you usually makes you weaker. But some things that don't kill you do make you stronger. And happier."

"Like what?"

"Like certain types of dangerous situations."

"But like what?"

"I think we should pick one all together," Ray said.

"I think it's an excellent idea," Roland said, fingering his empty locket.

The food arrived.

"We could drink sour milk," Alan said.

Roland dropped his head in his hands.

"I'm not sure I understand," Ray said to Alan.

"Well, aren't we supposed to subject ourselves to more danger and unpleasant things?" Alan said.

"Yes, but I think we should pick something a little more dangerous than expired milk," Ray said.

"We could chain ourselves inside a burning house," Roland said.

There was silence.

"That's a bit extreme," Ray said. "Ideally, I think there should be a 25 percent chance of a negative outcome. Not much more and not much less."

"What do you mean by 'negative outcome'?" Alan asked.

"I'm not sure we should be speaking so explicitly," Ray answered, "but by negative outcome I mean death."

"I'm not wild about this idea, Ray," Lynn said.

Ray stroked the stem of his glass pensively and said, "Let me ask you an awkward question. Are you happy?"

"I've been worse," Lynn replied.

"That's great. I'm really happy for you," Ray said.

Of course he had a point with his sarcasm, Lynn thought.

"Listen, I don't think any of you are as happy as you should be," Ray said.

They could not argue with that.

He continued. "We want to put our lives at risk, not squash them. Do you have any ideas, Lynn?" Since she didn't answer, he added, "Hypothetically?"

Finally, she said, "I didn't mind Alan's idea so much, of eating something bad. Something we might pick out of the woods."

"Like what?" Ray asked.

"Poisonous mushrooms, of course!" Roland said. "That's a cool idea, Lynn. I think we should do it."

"Is that what you meant, Lynn, poisonous mushrooms?" Ray asked.

"It crossed my mind, but I think the risk is too high," Lynn said. "I'm sure it's higher than 25 percent."

"I'd say so," Alan said. "Count me out." He ordered a glass of wine in the hope of getting carded, but he wasn't.

Ray put his chalk away. "I think we should give it some thought until we come up with an idea we can all live with."

"Or die with," Roland said.

"Yes, or die with," Ray said.

The next evening, they were all in Ray's winter studio, coming up with more ideas that none of them could agree on. Even though the season was no longer winter and Ray was subletting the studio from Roland for a modest sum, they continued calling it "the winter studio."

"How about if we played Russian roulette with Alan's gun?" Roland said.

"It was Jessica's gun, and she took it after we broke up," Alan said.

"Anyway, Russian roulette would do no good," Ray said. "Our lives need to be placed at risk for more than a second. We need to remain in the dangerous situation for a while. That's when the mental good happens."

Alan and Roland were sitting on the sofa, and Lynn had gotten up from between them and was sitting on a chair, next to Ray. "Why do you want to do this with us, Ray?" she asked. "You're not in the same boat as us. You're not unhappy."

"I am in the same boat. We're all in the same boat, even though it may not seem so sometimes."

"Yeah, and I am, too, even though I know it may not look like it," said Roland.

They laughed. On occasion, Roland could be amusing.

Lynn said, "We could all go out in the same boat and jump overboard. And then the disagreement would be settled. We would no longer be in the same boat." She chuckled.

"We would have to let the boat go," Ray said. "We'd have to jump out while it's speeding."

"Why?" Lynn asked.

"So that we couldn't get back in the boat."

She nodded.

Ray went on. "So that we would float. And wait. And witness our life regain its perspective, its value. And witness ourselves regain our sanity. There's a very good chance we'd get rescued and reap the benefits of the risk we took. And I'd say there's approximately a 25 percent chance that . . . we would not." Ray's eyes were opened wide like vast oceans where floating people always got rescued.

It took a week for Lynn and Alan to decide if they wanted to go ahead with Ray's idea of risking their lives to improve their lives.

After spending some time on his armless white easy chair with his rat, thinking it over, Alan agreed to the idea of jumping off a boat with the others. He had learned to swim and was proud of it, was no longer afraid of water, and anyway, they'd be wearing life vests. Besides, he'd wanted to kill himself. Just because fate had beaten down on him recently and weakened him didn't mean he couldn't fight fate a bit. Once again, he'd take a few days off from work—or forever, depending on the outcome.

Lynn agreed to the idea, because Alan agreed to it. When she looked at her calendar, she objected to the date they had chosen. She was booked for a dinner she had been dreading for weeks but was obligated to go to. It was being hosted by an obsequious collector who had bought work from her many times. She had already tried to get out of the dinner by saying she had another engagement that night, but the collector had changed the date just so she could attend. Lynn told the others about the conflict and asked whether they couldn't all jump off the boat a few days later.

"Why not a few days earlier?" Ray said. "This way, if you die in the ocean, it'll be a perfect excuse not to attend the dinner, and if you survive, then the danger you will have experienced will make the dinner more tolerable."

Lynn considered this for a moment and agreed to move up the date of their semisuicide.

"Does the date suit everyone's schedule now?" Ray asked.

Alan nodded, and Roland said, "I have no schedule."

"What do you mean?" Ray asked.

"I'm free all the time."

"Within reason, no?"

"No, all the time. I got fired."

The days passed, and the four nuts quietly went about their lives with the calm awareness of a day that was approaching, and of the act that would take place on that day. They did not even think of it as an act so much as a sort of gesture. They rarely spoke of it to each other anymore, and when they did, it was always obliquely.

Before taking the plane, Alan left the same suicide note in his apartment that he had written before. He told his doorman he was going away for a couple of days and asked him to go into his apartment if he hadn't returned in a week, to give his "gerbil" more food. The suicide note would be next to the cage, so the doorman would understand what had happened.

Alan kissed Pancake, held him against his heart, and said good-bye.

Lynn told Patricia she was going on vacation for a few days. Patricia said, "The Harlem Globetrotters just rejected your application for a tryout. That should sustain you and keep you sane while you're gone."

The three nuts and the bum packed their bags and boarded a plane for the Bahamas at 8:00 A.M. They checked into Hotel Atlantis on Paradise Island. They sat on lounge chairs by one of the pools, staring tensely at the fake waterfalls and at all those people who were not going to jump off a boat the next day to make their lives happier, fuller, and more valuable.

They went to dinner at one of the restaurants in the hotel. They ordered a bottle of wine. The waitress asked Alan for some ID.

"I lost my driver's license a long time ago, and I left my passport in my room. I'll have a Coke," Alan said.

"He's thirty-five, you know," Roland said to the waitress. "And looks older, in my opinion."

As Alan sipped his Coke, he said to the others, "We are quite young, you know."

"Yeah? So?" Roland said.

"So nothing," Alan said.

During the meal, the four friends passed the salt and pepper while Ray made a few attempts at a conversation, but his heart wasn't in it, and he soon gave up. He couldn't get himself to ask them if they were still okay with the plan, since he himself did not feel completely at ease with it.

After dinner, they went back to the pool and sat on the same lounge chairs, side by side, in the dark, alone. It took a long time for one of them finally to speak.

It was Ray. "I thought eleven o'clock might be a good time. That leaves us with many hours of daylight during which we might be more likely to get rescued."

Alan said, "It's strange. It's kind of like committing suicide in reverse, or something."

"It's true," Roland said. "It's almost like suicide, but instead of being performed out of hatred of life, it's out of love of life, out of wanting to recapture it. It's a sacrifice for life."

The next day, out at sea, all in the same boat, wearing bulky red life vests and little white hats, they stared at the land that was now only slightly visible, extremely far away. They had no excuses. And it wasn't as if they hadn't been—and weren't still—searching for excuses. But there were none: The ocean was not rough; the air was not cold, nor the water; there were no jellyfish in sight; there were a few pleasant clouds to protect them from sunstroke.

Roland dropped a penny in the boat.

When the time came, Ray slightly increased the speed of the small motorboat they had rented for the day. The four of them climbed on the side of it, held hands, and jumped off.

Fourteen

They watched their empty boat speeding away, wondering if it would keep going, hoping it would not, but it did—there was no reason it wouldn't. And then they glanced around to see if they could see any rescue boats, but they couldn't.

"Well, here we are," Alan said, once they had settled into the water and found comfortable positions amongst each other.

"This was a mistake," Lynn said, after five minutes. "If we live through this, you really think we'll appreciate life more?"

"It's too late to ask that question," Ray said.

"I think it would be tragic to die in these beautiful, sunny surroundings," Lynn said. "Death, if you're going to die, deserves to have a certain amount of drama and importance, but this death would not be dramatic."

"It was your idea to do it this way," Roland said. "If we die, it'll be a beautiful death, and if we live, it'll be a beautiful life."

Alan started laughing. Then he realized he was also crying. The others waited, alarmed, to see how it would develop.

"Are you okay?" Ray asked.

"You know what's ironic?" Alan slapped the water a little.

"What?" Lynn asked.

"We're all, still, in the same boat."

Roland sighed, but the others smiled, to be nice, and said, "That's funny, Alan."

Lynn added, "The point was not really to be in different boats, but to be . . . in a better boat. Right?"

Alan calmed down.

In order not to get accidentally separated from each other, they had devised a system. They had brought the belts of their hotel bathrobes, tied end to end, forming a complete circle. They had each worn a regular leather belt and each brought a rock climbing clip, so that they could attach themselves, by the waist, to the circle.

After two hours in the ocean, Lynn, Alan, and Roland realized how nuts they were. They congratulated Ray on his helpful idea. They couldn't believe they had put their lives at risk, that they were bobbing around like corks, when life was so full of exciting and pleasurable things they could be doing.

After two and a half hours, insults started flying and accusations that Ray was a "fucking cult leader." He said he accepted their anger and that he had made this sacrifice for them.

At one point, he said, "If we don't get rescued, it's a terrible death. But even if that happens, we'll get the pleasure of knowing how great life could have been. We'll die with that knowledge, which is a very pleasurable thing in itself. It's a gift."

Lynn threw water in his face. Alan kicked him under the water.

. . .

After six hours, they panicked when they saw a shark swimming around them. Alan, Lynn, and Roland were flapping their limbs, screaming, and Ray was hysterically trying to quiet them down, warning them that their behavior was the most effective way to get the shark to attack. They froze, which, according to Ray, was not much better in avoiding an attack. He told them they had to move in a calm, confident, healthy way.

"Move in a healthy way? What the hell does that mean?" Alan hissed.

"Now is not the time to analyze," Roland hissed back. "Just move in a healthy way."

"Stop bickering," Ray said. "Bickering will also make the shark want to eat you."

"Is anyone bleeding?" Roland asked. "Sharks can smell blood from miles away."

"No, why would anyone be bleeding?" Alan said.

"That thing, there, is a woman," Roland said, pointing to Lynn. "Those things bleed from time to time. Are you bleeding?"

"I think I am," said Lynn, who knew she was not. "Why else would the shark have come? Others will probably come, too."

The shark seemed to go away. It was hard to be sure about things of that sort.

They were thirsty. Alan wanted to drink the seawater. Ray told him not to, that he'd be the first to die if he drank the seawater.

"How can we be in water and not drink it?" Alan asked. "Why

didn't you warn us we'd be faced with that kind of tempta-tion?"

"Don't do it, Alan. Exercise some willpower," said Lynn.

Two hours later, as the sun was setting, they saw what they thought was another shark, and Alan immediately resumed moving in a healthy-looking fashion.

"Sharks come out at night even more," said Ray. "To feed."

But it was only a dolphin.

Lynn couldn't believe she was bobbing around in the middle of nowhere. She was a supersuccessful gallery owner. She was mad at herself for having followed Alan into the ocean. A life with so much potential, wasted. Not to mention the huge amounts of time she'd wasted stalking. She thought she deserved to die.

Night came. They were tired, cold, still thirsty, and now weak from hunger.

"I'm cold," Alan said.

"Yes. Our bodies may be suffering, but our minds have never been healthier," Ray said, to everyone's exasperation. "Just think: The more we suffer now, the happier we'll be later."

"You're sick," Lynn said. "You need to see a therapist."

Roland took a penny out of his pocket and stared at it in the moonlight. He released it under the water, watching it flip, flip, and fade.

Then he began moving his limbs energetically in the water.

"What are you doing?" Alan asked.

"Trying to warm up."

"That's a good idea," Alan said, and began moving his body and limbs enthusiastically. Lynn and Ray did as well.

"But you have to make sure to move energetically and healthily," Alan instructed. "That's important. Lynn, your movements don't look healthy enough. They look weak and tired. Put more vigor into them, or stop moving."

"I'm tired," said Lynn.

"Well, please hide it," said Alan. "You might attract a shark who'll then eat any one of us, not just those of us moving unhealthily. It wouldn't be fair."

"The problem with moving energetically," said Ray, "is that it dehydrates you more quickly and burns a lot of calories, and those are not good things for us right now."

They all stopped moving.

"But I'm cold!" Alan said.

Ray shrugged. "Well, then, decide which discomfort you dislike most. If you hate being thirsty, tired, and hungry, then stop moving. If being cold is even worse for you, then move."

Lynn and Alan did not move. Roland moved. Ray was doing something in between.

Alan said, "Damn that girl who started the fire in my building, interrupting my suicide attempt. I could be happily dead right now, instead of dying."

Eventually, in an effort to warm up further, they each took turns being in the middle of their circle, while the other three huddled around him or her.

They slept a little during the night, despite their fear of sharks. When the sun rose, they noticed Lynn had lost her hat. The men thought they ought to be gentlemanly and take turns lending her their hats. Roland and Alan debated which of them should give her extra time with his hat. Alan said he should be allowed to lend her his hat less time because he was bald and because she was his stalker. He said Roland should lend her his hat more of the time, because he was her stalker and should want to please her.

Roland said, "But I have black hair. Black attracts the heat more than a bald white head."

"But my head will burn," Alan said. "I'll get a terrible sunburn as well as a sunstroke. Plus, you're her stalker. You should lend her your hat! Can't you do at least that for the person you're supposedly obsessed with? I mean, what kind of obsession is this, anyway?"

"It's true," said Lynn to Roland. "What kind of puny, wimpy, selfish obsession is this, anyway?"

Roland threw his hat in her face.

"Ah, that is so refreshing!" Lynn said. "Does this mean you'll stop stalking me?" She put the hat on her head.

"I'm getting tempted," Roland said.

"Bravo!" Alan said. "And what about you, Lynn, are you getting tempted to stop stalking me?"

"Yes, but for other reasons. I just can't believe I'm here. It's stalking that brought me here. I don't want to waste my life anymore."

"Why are we even speaking as if we assume we're going to live?"

"We have no choice," Ray said. "How could we go on otherwise?"

"How could we not?" Roland rested his head against the puffy red life vest and closed his eyes. "It's not as if we have a swift means of self-deliverance at our disposal."

. . .

The three nuts got pissed off that Ray had not secretly arranged for them to be rescued. It was hard for Ray to convince them that no, he had not. They found it difficult to believe that he would risk giving up his good new life with a home and a revenue-generating occupation. They felt he was much more insane than they were.

During the day they saw two boats, one in the morning, one in the afternoon, and both in the far, far distance. They waved both times. Neither boat saw them.

"Max was so smart, the way he killed himself quickly, with cyanide," Lynn said.

"Now that's going out in luxury," Alan agreed. "It's like taking the Concorde to death. Whereas we're getting there on the back of a tortoise."

"Speed can be one of the most luxurious things in the world," Lynn said.

Roland was not so interested in the topic, since he had murdered Max. "I know what our outcome will be," he said, to change the subject.

"How would you know?" Alan asked.

"I just know. I will die, and you will all live."

"Why do you think that?"

"Because I'm not a good person."

"So? We know you're not a good person. You're a complete jerk. But do you think life is fair?" Alan asked.

"No, but I'm even worse than you think."

"Oh yeah? How?"

Roland sighed. "I have a huge capacity to hate. And I act on it."

"It doesn't matter," said Alan. "You could be ten times more evil than you are, and that doesn't mean you're more likely to die than us, unfortunately. And it also doesn't mean you're less likely to have a happy life. That's how life is. It sucks. This isn't some Hollywood movie we're living in. This is life. Which means you'll probably live long and be happy, will never get punished for your assholiness, will never get what's coming to you, will not reap what you sow, and we the good people will probably be miserable or die young."

Lynn and Ray nodded in agreement.

"I appreciate your efforts at comforting me," Roland said.

"It's the grim truth," Alan said.

"Why don't they make more movies where the bad guys don't get punished? I mean, it's so much more realistic," Lynn said.

"Because it's depressing," Ray said.

"That's true," Roland said. "Why would people want to see anyone get away with murder?"

"Because it's real. How's that?" cried Alan. "Don't you think people could handle it? Don't you think it would in fact be beneficial to society to be aware that the world sucks?"

"They do know," answered Ray. "They just don't want to be reminded of it in their entertainment. It's not pleasant."

"Well, except for the Europeans," said Roland, treading the ocean with an air of superiority.

"What do you mean?" Ray asked.

"They frequently have two different endings for movies—the ending for the American market, and the ending for the rest of the world. In *The Big Blue,* the hero at the end drowns in the ocean, but for the American release, they made him swim off into the sunset with a dolphin."

"I don't believe you," Alan said.

"It's true! You can rent it, if you survive," said Roland.

Lynn said to Alan, "Don't you wish you were in a movie—an American one—so you wouldn't have to die in the ocean, and Roland would get punished for what a jerk he is?"

When Roland woke from his nap, they all began fantasizing about the things they'd do with their lives if they got rescued.

"I want to meet new people, eat succulent foods," said Lynn. "I want to indulge in all sorts of physical pleasures. Each second of every day is an opportunity to indulge in something incredible."

"Sounds like you're definitely over your desire problem," said Roland.

"Of course. I was over that ages ago."

"If I live through this, I'm getting more pets," said Alan.

"Pets? What kinds? More rats?" asked Ray.

"I don't know. But I wanna lotta pets."

"But why?"

"For the warmth and the love, I guess." After a moment, he said, "God, I need my hat back, my head is burning. It's someone else's turn."

Roland was looking away, as if lost in thought, even though he knew it was his turn to give Lynn his hat. When he heard no sound, he glanced at Ray, who was looking at him with an urging expression.

"I have black hair," said Roland.

Sneering slightly at Roland, Ray gave Lynn his hat.

Sneering slightly at Roland as well, she said, "Thanks, Ray."

Alan scooped water in his hat and put his hat on his head. "Ahhh," he said with pleasure, as the water cascaded down his face.

"If I pull through this," Ray said, "I want to see more movies, make more money, and be dry. Maybe take a vacation in a really, really dry place. Dry and shady. Maybe a desert, under a tent."

They waited for Roland to volunteer his desires. He didn't.

"What about you?" Ray asked him. "Is there anything you're dying to do if you survive this?"

"Interesting word choice," Roland said.

"Thank you."

"I'm dying to get a refill," Roland said.

"A refill?" said Ray. "Of what?"

"Something I used to have."

"Which was?" Alan asked.

"Oh, something that used to make me feel powerful, unique," Roland said.

"A drug?" Lynn asked.

"Sort of."

"Which one?"

"It's personal," Roland said.

"What effect did it have?" Lynn asked.

"It could create a state, the prospect of which was pleasant."

"The prospect of which? But not the actuality?" said Lynn.

"Well, who knows about the actuality," Roland said.

"What?" said Alan. "Then what are you talking about? I don't get it."

Roland shrugged, didn't answer.

"But you would take it now, if you had it with you?" asked Lynn.

"Maybe," Roland said. "Or I might wait till things got a little worse."

"How much worse do things have to get before you'd seek comfort?"

"Having the option to take it would be a huge comfort. But taking it introduces you to a new way of being that you can't really recover from."

"It damages you?" asked Lynn.

"I'm not interested in this line of questioning," Roland said. "All I know is that I was a fool not to get a refill. This whole ridiculous situation would be so much easier to bear if I had the refill with me right now."

"Thank God at least we have each other," said Alan. "Can you imagine how much worse things would be if we were each alone in this ocean? I mean, on top of not having the refill? We wouldn't have these amazing conversations to pass the time."

"Is that supposed to be a sarcastic, yet deep, thought, Alan?" asked Roland.

"Maybe."

To everyone's surprise, Roland took out of his shorts pocket a pack of tuna fish. As soon as they understood that he had no intention of sharing, they said his tuna would attract sharks, and they quickly unclipped themselves from the circle of terry-cloth belts and swam away from him in a healthy fashion. Roland gobbled down his tuna, and rejoined them, holding the limp circle out to them, urging them to clip themselves back to it. He preferred enduring their insults to being alone in the ocean.

. . .

Lynn lost consciousness first, or fell asleep, after they had been in the ocean a day and five hours. Roland suggested spitting in her mouth, to hydrate her. But they ended up not doing it, because they had never heard of such a thing.

She regained consciousness forty-five minutes later, just in time to hear Ray rant and rave about the stupidity of having jumped in the ocean. He was cursing himself for having thought of the idea and cursing them for having been persuaded.

"You guys are so malleable, I swear!" he said. "How could you have followed the advice of a homeless person? You guys are insane! Now we're all going to die because of it."

Lynn lost consciousness again two hours later. And when she regained it, she was the first to notice a boat the others hadn't yet seen.

They began waving wildly, but the boat had already spotted them and was coming for them. It stopped a short distance away. The motor was switched off. Six people were standing at the railing, staring down at them. They looked welcoming.

"Do you need help?" a distinguished-looking older man shouted at them.

"Yes, very much so," Ray shouted back hoarsely.

"Well, come on board," the man said, waving them to the back of the boat.

With eager exhaustion, the four survivors swam the length of the one-hundred-foot yacht, toward the back, where the distinguished man was lowering a ladder.

As they climbed, the name of the boat, written in giant letters, loomed before them: *Eyeball*.

The moment Ray's toe exited the water, his mood changed, his spirits soared. He and his nuts had done it! The experience had been invaluable! They would now reap the benefits.

"Sit back and enjoy," he told Lynn, Alan, and Roland as they climbed out after him. "Relish the magic. Few moments in your life will ever be as wonderful as this. Try to imprint it on your memory. Notice the ecstasy you're experiencing right now. Savor every nuance of it."

"You're not acting very dehydrated," remarked Lynn, who was barely able to stand.

They were given water and dropped off in Nassau. A cab took them over the bridge to their hotel on Paradise Island. They showered and put on dry clothes.

They each, in his or her own room, ordered room service. Lynn remembered a picture book, from her childhood, that said you weren't supposed to gorge yourself when you hadn't eaten in two days or you could get sick. Lynn ordered pasta and a shrimp-stuffed avocado. Alan ordered two cheeseburgers; Roland a steak, wine, cheese, and a chocolate mousse; and Ray ordered conch chowder, pasta, and a disgusting pineapple soufflé.

Lynn would have preferred not to be alone at that moment, but being alone was better than being with them. She'd have been happy with a good friend near her, like Patricia.

Alan was thinking about little other than his bodily needs. He wanted to eat and sleep as soon as possible.

Roland felt disgusted with himself for having gone along with these freaks. He felt embarrassed.

Lynn, Alan, and Roland all felt the same way about one thing. They were thinking, *Never toy with life. Never take life for granted and squander it.* As they heard the things they were telling themselves, they realized that it had worked. This new attitude was exactly the one they had been hoping to acquire.

After eating, they each put the DO NOT DISTURB sign on their doors and slept.

Fifteen

For a while their existence was diminished and enhanced at the same time. The smallest elements of everyday life seemed heavenly compared to floating in the ocean. They were so appreciative of the slightest things, that they settled for small things. At home they each sat in bed, and the mere feel of the sheets against their skin (in Alan's case, the rat's fur against his cheek) was bliss. They felt they could live like this for fifty years and be perfectly content, need nothing else out of life. They slept a lot. And they enjoyed walking. Walking on the hard ground was practically orgasmic.

The stalking chain had dissolved in the ocean. The nuts were too tired to care about stalking each other. And when the tiredness faded, the prospect of stalking still seemed tiresome, repetitive, monotonous, a waste of time—not entirely unlike bobbing in the ocean. Life was too short for stalking.

Lynn wanted to forget her ocean experience and resume normal life as quickly and thoroughly as possible. She wanted to drench herself in normalcy and routine. If routine were a liquid, she'd love to take a bath in it. No, scratch that—too close to their ordeal.

She went to the hateful dinner she had been hoping to avoid

through death, feeling self-conscious about her appearance. Her hair was dry and damaged from having soaked so long in the sea, and her skin didn't look its freshest. But Ray had been right: The dreaded dinner wasn't so bad compared to bobbing in the ocean for days. The host's obsequiousness struck her as charming.

As for Ray, he continued working on his matchmaking business Chock Full O'Nuts, which was as successful as ever. He loved how his ocean ordeal had sensitized him to the pleasures of life and desensitized him to its discomforts and pitfalls and bad days. He was so excited about it, he could hardly contain himself and was certain that in a year or so he'd want to do it again. Life was too short not to—even though doing it might shorten it more.

Ray was glad that the nuts didn't seem obsessed with each other anymore. His only disappointment was that because they no longer needed anything more than solid ground, they seemed a bit vacant, like shadows of their former selves. Maybe that was what sanity was—a less heightened self.

But that state didn't last long. The divine perspective they had acquired thanks to the grueling ocean experience wore off soon enough, as it tragically always does. As they lost the perspective, their appetite for more than solid ground was reawakened. They did some of the things they'd told each other they'd do if they survived.

Alan purchased more pets. In addition to his rat, he now had a rabbit, a dog, and a ferret.

Roland went to France to visit his dad and ask him for a refill of cyanide. When his dad asked him what happened to the cyanide in his locket, Roland said he'd emptied his locket one day when policemen were searching everyone in a park where a crime had just been committed. His father told Roland he'd made the right decision, that one could get into a lot of trouble for carrying cyanide around. He gave his son a refill. Roland's father had a small cyanide-filled chest that had been passed down for many generations, along with the lockets. It was useful when lockets were emptied for various reasons.

A month after her oceanic experience, Lynn was standing in line with Patricia at the local bakery when she heard, behind her, an attractive male voice uttering her secret, "real" name.

She could not get herself to turn around. She just grabbed Patricia's arm and squeezed hard.

"What?" Patricia said.

Lynn didn't answer, she let it pass and walked out of the bakery looking away from the voice. Lynn realized she would never know who it was. Perhaps that was better than being disappointed.

Later that afternoon, at the gallery, Patricia asked Lynn why she seemed so melancholy, and Lynn said it was because she had been within touching range of the man of her dreams, and not only had she not touched him, she hadn't even looked at him.

"When?"

"In the bakery, when I grabbed your arm."

"Which guy was it?"

"I don't know, but I heard him behind us say to someone, 'I love that scary elephant.'"

"*That* guy? I know who he is, Lynn. He's your neighbor. If he's the man of your dreams, you certainly haven't lost him. In fact, you've probably seen him around. I've often meant to ask you what you thought of him, because he seemed like your type."

"You know him?"

"Not really. But he's cute."

"Who is he?"

"He works at the flower shop, three doors down, but you never buy flowers, so maybe you've never seen him."

Lynn ran out the door.

Lynn entered the flower shop. There was a man in a far corner, sitting on a chair, working with string and flowers. He was an average-looking man with a gray mustache. She approached him, looking at him gently, her head tilted sideways, her expression generous. He looked up and smiled at her.

Perhaps there was another man who worked in the store. She had to make sure she found the right one, the one who had uttered her real name, and not jump to any conclusions. She turned around and found herself face-to-face with another man who was standing there, right behind her, wearing a dark blue apron and holding a vase. In one moment, she had absorbed his face, a feat that usually took her many hours.

In a voice she recognized as the one that had uttered her real name in the bakery, he said, "May I help you?"

The charm of his smile was almost painful.

"What flowers do you recommend?" she asked.

"For what occasion?" he asked.

"For this occasion."

"What is this occasion?" he asked, innocently, but his smile was more playful.

Since she could not possibly say, "The beginning of the rest of our lives," she said instead, "My entering this store for the first time even though I've been working three doors down for six years."

"Oh, really?" he said. "Well, then, for this wonderful occasion, I would recommend . . ." and he looked around, his hand on his chin. "I would recommend creamy roses. How do you feel about creamy roses?"

"Good."

He picked out the roses and wrapped them in silence, while she watched his every move. He handed them to her.

"How much are they?" she asked.

"It was nice to finally meet you," he answered.

"Yes, finally. How much?"

"Very much."

"No, I mean, how much do I owe you?"

"Nothing."

"Really?"

"How about a coffee?"

Before she could answer, the other man, who had been sitting in the corner, addressed the man of her life with, "Hey, what do you think of this?"

The man of her life glanced back at the bouquet the other man had just finished composing, and gave him a thumbs-up. "Very elegant," he said, before turning back to Lynn.

Lynn stared at him, baffled, and murmured, "You keep saying my name."

"I do?" he asked, fascinated.

"Yes, my real name."

He didn't ask her what it was. He thought perhaps she meant it metaphorically.

"I have to go," she said, rushing out.

"Shall we say six tomorrow?"

But she was gone.

. . .

That night, the nuts and the former bum had dinner. They still saw each other almost as frequently as ever. Now, instead of obsession, it was habit, grim mutual curiosity, and even a small degree of complicated friendship that drew them together.

Lynn brought Patricia. Midway through the dinner, the others noticed Lynn hadn't spoken much, so they asked her how she was doing.

"I met the man of my dreams," she replied.

"Really?" Ray said.

"Yes, he knows my name."

"So do we," said Roland.

"No you don't. I have a secret name, a more real name."

"Won't you tell us?"

"It's Airiella."

"And he uttered it?" gasped Alan.

"Yes."

"That's quite something," said Ray.

"What he uttered," Patricia interjected, "was 'scary elephant.' "

"Same thing," Lynn retorted.

"Is it?" Roland said.

"Yes," Lynn replied, and enunciated, "sc—airiella—phant."

"Ah. A bit of a stretch," said Roland.

"I don't think so."

"Clearly not," said Ray, annoyed that despite his expertise in matchmaking, he hadn't been able to provide Lynn with her ideal man. "What about hairy electrician?"

"What?"

"H—airiella—ctrician," Ray repeated.

"Leave me alone."

"We're just concerned," said Roland. "What about primary element? Oops," he added, clasping his hand over his mouth, "I just uttered your real name. Prime—airiella—ment. This must mean I, too, am the man of your dreams."

"Why are we trying to burst her bubble?" Alan said.

"It's not a bubble," Lynn corrected. "It's real. He also said, 'Very elegant.'"

"I hear it," Alan said. "V—airiella—gant."

"Lord," said Roland.

"What is this nonsense, Lynn?" Ray said, as if talking indulgently to an unreasonable child. "We've just demonstrated to you that your secret name can be uttered very easily and very frequently by anyone."

"Perhaps," Lynn said. "But I never heard it before. I only hear it when he utters it."

"And where did you get this secret name anyway?" Patricia asked Lynn.

"I was at a fancy birthday party when I was around six, and a fairy told me to think of a secret name for myself and that one day I would recognize the man of my dreams because I would hear him utter my secret name."

"A fairy?" Roland asked.

"Yeah, Miss Tuttle, the birthday party fairy."

"Miss Tuttle?" Alan asked, chills coursing through his body.

"Yeah," Lynn said.

"Was she also a hairdresser?"

"Yes. You knew her? She was from Cross, actually. Miss Ann Tuttle."

"You bet I knew her! Roland recently made me believe she was my childhood sexual abuser, but she was not," Alan said, looking sternly at Roland. "I went to see her, and she had a mangofish in a fish tank in her house."

In a blasé tone, Roland said, "That fish is probably a cover-up, a fish she bought to appease men who, over the years, have knocked on her door to confront her about having abused them as boys."

"I hadn't thought of that," Alan said. "I hope it's true. I kind of regretted finding out I hadn't been abused."

"You're a sick son of a bitch," Roland said.

"No. Abusers are like garbage cans. You can toss all your crap into them."

"If you would like us to, I'm sure we could find someone to abuse you," Roland said.

"It's too late. I'm not little anymore."

"You're still pretty little."

"Alan, I'm sure Miss Tuttle didn't abuse you," Lynn said. "I'm sure that mangofish in her house was not a cover-up. Miss Tuttle the fairy is responsible for my finding the man of my life. She's a wonderful person. I owe her, if not my life, then my happiness, and I am categorically certain that she would never harm a child. She is divine, and I mean that literally."

"Has anyone ever even heard of a mangofish?" Roland said. "I haven't. Rest easy, my boy, you've been abused." He patted Alan's hand, and under the table he dropped a paper clip.

. . .

The following day, at six, the man of Lynn's life was already there when she walked in the café. He had called her at the gallery and told her where to meet him.

He was sitting on a barstool at a high and little round table. He was not wearing an apron. She didn't understand how she could have managed never to see him in the neighborhood, never to run into him on the street. He had sandy stubble around lovely full lips in whose lines a wonderful personality seemed evident. And his gestures were the furthest thing from superficial.

She sat on a stool across from him, leaned over the table, and said, "I don't care about hairy electrician or primary element."

"Neither do I," he said.

They laughed.

Sixteen

Lynn was secretly envied by Alan and Roland, who were yearning to find the same magic she had found.

Roland, particularly, was on the lookout for an enchanting encounter. He kept waiting for it to happen, hoping it would, but nothing of the sort was happening to him. Until early one afternoon.

He had just walked out of his usual restaurant after dropping a paper clip near the door. Outside, the day was cold and sad.

He stood at the curb, wrapping his scarf around his neck, looking left and right, searching for a taxi.

He heard a female voice near him saying, "Usually there are more of them in the street at this time."

He looked at who had spoken. It was an attractive young woman standing next to him, alone. This was rather romantic, he thought. He told himself it was perhaps, even, as romantic as what had happened to Lynn. And it was happening to him, now, that mind-blowing romantic situation.

"Yes," he said. "Are you here every day?"

She looked at him and asked, "What?" in a manner that seemed almost annoyed. He then noticed she had a black cord coming out of one ear. "What?" she asked him again. "I'm talking on the phone!"

The traffic light changed, and she crossed the street with a youthful stride. He heard her fading voice say to her interlocutor, "Sorry, it was just another creep who thought I was talking to him or to myself like a madwoman." And she laughed.

Overcome with sadness, Roland could not move. He felt like a fool, and he felt old. Lynn's sappy, silly story had gotten to him. Disgusted with himself, he clenched his fists in his pockets and remained standing there a long time.

Just as he was finally about to cross the street, he heard a woman behind him say, "Excuse me?"

He turned. A magnificent woman with black hair topped by a lock of white hair, somewhat resembling a skunk or Susan Sontag, stood there.

"Yes?" he asked.

"You dropped something," she said.

"Yes?"

Her hand came out of her pocket, holding a paper clip. "I wasn't sure I should bother giving this back to you."

"Yes, you should." He took the clip.

"In that case," she said, "perhaps you'd like the rest of your things."

He frowned. "What things?"

"The things you've lost over time." She pulled out of her handbag a plastic baggie filled with more of his droppings.

"You must be mistaken," he said, suddenly horribly embarrassed.

"Yes, I probably am," she said, replacing his droppings in her bag.

He looked around, hoping to be comforted by the sight of something distracting during this awkward moment.

"Who are you?" he asked.

"I come to this restaurant every day to have lunch and work at my laptop. I've seen you here very often, losing things. You've lost so much over time."

He didn't know what to say.

She added, "I wonder why."

He thought about it, and for the first time the answer came to him. "To find something more precious."

Then, looking away, but holding his hand out to her, he said, "Can I have my things?"

She reached into her bag and gave him his lost things. The package was too big to fit in his pocket, so he held it discreetly at his side, in as small a ball as he could make it.

"I met my soulmate," Roland told the others at a dinner reunion he had insisted upon, two weeks after their last one.

"You did?" Ray asked.

Alan flagged down a waiter and ordered a cocktail to get either flatteringly carded or drunk.

"Do you have some identification?" the waiter asked.

"I lost my driver's license ages ago. Do you really think I could be twenty-one or younger?"

"It's possible," the waiter said.

"I'll have a Virgin Mary," Alan said, and turned to Roland. "You were telling us you met your soulmate."

"Yes. She had my things!" Roland said.

"What things?" Ray asked.

"The things I've been dropping for years."

"You've been dropping things?"

"Yes."

"What kinds of things?" Alan asked.

"Buttons, paper clips, pennies, movie stubs."

"How often?"

"Every day. Many times a day."

"Where?"

"Wherever I happen to be. Usually as I leave a place."

"On purpose?"

"Utterly."

"Littering?"

"No, losing."

"Why?" they all asked at the same time.

"In order to find something more precious."

"Like what, a woman who'll pick up after you?" Lynn said.

"No."

"Then what thing more precious?" Alan asked, holding his Virgin Mary. "What is this vague bullshit explanation?"

"I don't know," Roland replied, sipping his white wine. "All I know is that I always go around with something to lose. I can't stand having nothing to lose. I can never leave a place without leaving something behind, even if it's just lint from my pocket. Otherwise, I experience discomfort. If you've got a better explanation, then tell me."

"Yes, I've got one," Alan said. "You lose things. Hence, you're a loser."

"I lose things on purpose."

"Well, then, you're a double-duty loser."

"No," Ray said. "The subconscious reason you were dropping

things was to give anyone who wanted to meet you an excuse to. It was your way of reaching out to people. You wanted people to have access to you despite your cold facade."

"Maybe," Roland replied. "But then why did I sometimes drop things where no one could approach me, like in the middle of the ocean?"

"Dropping things had become a compulsive habit," Ray said. "Since you weren't exactly aware of why you were doing it, it's logical that you would sometimes do it when it didn't make sense. No?"

"God, you should have been a therapist," Lynn said, impressed.

"Yeah, I was."

"But you said you were a locksmith!"

"I lied. I was a psychologist."

"Why didn't you tell us?"

"Various reasons."

"How did you become homeless, if you were a psychologist?" Alan inquired.

"I was a bad psychologist."

"Bad how?" Roland asked.

"Oh . . ." Ray hesitated.

"Did you analyze people poorly?" asked Lynn.

"No . . ."

"You gave bad advice?" Roland guessed.

"No . . ."

"Did you betray confidences?" he guessed again.

"No . . ."

"Then what?" asked Alan.

"I asked too many questions."

They thought he was commenting on their interrogation of him. "Oh, come on, tell us!" said Lynn.

Ray was confused. "I just told you. I asked my patients too many questions."

"But a therapist is supposed to ask a lot of questions!" Alan said.

"Yes, a lot, but not too many. I asked too many. Too often."

"What do you mean, too often?"

"I'd call them up every hour at home and ask for updates."

"Oh."

"But I was pretty good at analyzing behavior and giving advice. Roland, if you had told me sooner of your compulsive habit of dropping things, I could have helped you understand it."

"That's easy for you to say," Roland replied. "If you had told us sooner that you were a therapist, I might have told you of my habit."

"It's a good thing neither of you did," Lynn said, "because if you had, Ray might have cured you of your compulsive habit, and prevented you from ever meeting your soulmate."

"Hey, Roland," Alan said. "See, didn't I tell you things would work out for you? I predicted you'd not only survive the ocean but probably also have a happy life. Just because you're an asshole doesn't mean you'll ever suffer for it or be punished. And what about me? I've made a real effort to turn my life around and be a good person, and what do I get? I'm all alone and unhappy, and I'll probably never meet anyone."

"Yeah, you might be right," Roland said. "You make a convincing argument."

"I comforted you in the water. Why do you have to be so negative?"

"I thought you were just being truthful back then. Now I'm just

being truthful back—realistic," Roland said. "It's true that life's unfair. I didn't deserve to meet this amazing woman. I don't really deserve to be happy. But she does. And I want to make her happy."

Alan was jealous of Lynn and Roland. He wanted to meet his soulmate, too. Now that Lynn and Roland had experienced the same
magic, they probably expected it of him. He felt the pressure. And it
was not agreeing with him.

He told them that he was worried because he didn't have a secret
"real" name or a secret wacko habit that only his soulmate could recognize. So what was he supposed to do?

Lynn replied, "You probably have one without realizing it. Everyone has secret quirks."

"Well I don't! All my quirks are visible."

"Don't worry, somehow it'll happen," she said. "And if it doesn't,
that's okay, too."

He was afraid it would not happen, afraid he would be discontent
forever. It wasn't fair. It drove him crazy, this trend, this craze of
soulmates popping up. He started acting erratically.

He went around doing all sorts of weird takeoffs on what the two
others had done. He invented various quirks for himself, and rituals,
to see if his soulmate would recognize him. For example, he threw
fistfuls of rose petals in the faces of women walking down the street,
then watched for their reactions. When that didn't work, he tried
throwing Godiva chocolates up in the air and behind him while
walking down crowded Fifth Avenue, and then he would turn
around to see if a woman had been hit, or perhaps had even caught
one, and seemed taken with him—his soulmate. But no. People were

either brushing cocoa powder off themselves and looking annoyed, or looking at the ground in surprise where a chocolate truffle had landed. Since nothing good came of that plan, he engaged in his next one. He bought small diamonds, rubies, sapphires, emeralds, and opals, and threw them lightly in women's faces.

He also considered walking around with his rat, holding it out to women like a soulmate detector, to see if any of them were charmed. But what was the point—if petals, chocolates, and precious stones hadn't worked, why would a rat? So he persevered with the pelting.

When Lynn, Roland, and Ray heard about what he was doing, they tried to explain to Alan that their own quirks were not manufactured.

And he said, "Well, I do have a natural quirk. I lightly stone women with beautiful little rocks. Why can't you accept that's my natural quirk?"

"You are crazed," Ray said to him with concern.

"So I'm romantically doomed because I don't have any hidden quirks, is that it?" He was having this conversation with them from jail, where he was being kept overnight after having finally been arrested for throwing stones.

Lynn brought her soulmate, Jim, to art openings and dinners and parties. When people asked him what he did, Lynn didn't mind that he was a florist and that he said so. She was proud, in fact. He was so obviously charming and intelligent that being a florist only added appeal in her judgment. And her judgment was excellent.

Ray, Lynn, and Alan found a couple of nicknames for Roland's girlfriend, Victoria. One of them was "the Translator," because, as Lynn put it, "She translates this French asshole into a nice person." They also nicknamed her "the Picker-Upper."

The Translator saw what was great about Roland and enabled other people to see it, too. If Roland did or said something that seemed unappealing, she'd be able to explain why it was actually appealing, or she'd simply rephrase his obnoxious statement in a manner that made it convincingly pleasant. She never opposed. She skewed.

Roland often said about her, "She gets me." He loved himself for loving her. A guy like him should normally never be evolved enough to be attracted to her, nor be attractive to her. She was smart. She was strong. She did not wear makeup. And she even had a touch of masculinity about her. She was a banker. He was intoxicated.

Alan gave up acquiring fake quirks. He tried to forget about romance and decided to redirect his attention toward small domestic matters, like cleaning his apartment and finally getting rid of his white easy chair. He put it out on the sidewalk for the garbage people to take during their next round. It was not an easy thing to do, emotionally. Since he had always identified with his chair, he almost felt as if he were putting himself out with the trash, throwing himself away. Sometimes a small sadness can distract us from a large sadness more effectively than a small joy can.

Hoping to distract himself from the small sadness, he went grocery shopping. On his way back, he saw a taxi parked near his white easy chair, and its driver was hauling his chair into the trunk with the help of a pretty girl. The girl was taking his chair. She found it desirable. Alan stood there with his plastic bags full of toilet paper and frozen dinners, looking at the spectacle. The girl was slapping dust off her hands. She turned and saw him. She held his gaze. She did not exactly smile, but had a pleasant expression nevertheless. And then she ducked into the cab, which drove off.

Alan wasn't sure what hit him. Or rather, he felt as if something had almost hit him but had missed. He had just been handed, by fate, an opportunity to experience one of those magical romantic moments, and he had let it slip by. He could have approached the girl and told her she was holding his chair. Even if it hadn't been his chair, it would have been a good line. But since it was his chair, it was an excellent line. That's my chair. You like my chair. You are taking my chair. No one else wants or likes my chair. But you do. We have the same taste in chairs.

He went up to his apartment. He slammed the front door, went straight to his couch, and sat there, with his plastic bags, staring at the empty space that used to contain his white easy chair. He buried his face in his hands.

He should have told her that was his chair. Maybe she would have admired his taste.

A few days later, Roland and his soulmate the Translator, Victoria, were having dinner with Lynn, Alan, and Ray. Lynn's soulmate hadn't been free to join them, but was planning to meet up with them afterward.

Midway through the meal, Lynn was noticing how happy Roland seemed. A series of thought connections made her ask him if he'd ever gotten his refill. They'd all been meaning to ask him—especially Ray, with his curiosity disorder—but kept forgetting.

Roland was speechless, stunned that Lynn knew about his cyanide. Then he realized she didn't know. He recalled telling them in the ocean that he wished he'd gotten a refill, to ease his oceanic suffering. That's all he'd said—a refill—without specifying of what or in what, without mentioning cyanide or his locket.

He sighed with relief. "Yes, I did. But I've lost interest in that now." He paused, wanting to appear as though he were changing topics. "Oh, by the way, look!" He opened his locket. Inside was a picture of Victoria.

They murmured with appreciation.

"What was in there before? You never did show us," Alan said.

"None of your business." Roland snapped his locket shut.

"Yes, your interest is much appreciated," translated Victoria, "but men who treat love wonderfully seriously aren't always ready to reveal the inside of their locket."

Later in the meal, they touched lightly on their ocean experience. Victoria already knew the story from Roland.

Ray asked them if they all still regretted having committed their semisuicide.

They all nodded.

Ray said with frustration, "How can you guys continue to regret it, when in fact you have to admit it gave you one of your greatest pleasures in life?"

Roland scowled. "Which was what?"

"Coming out of the water," Ray said.

"What kind of freak would come up with such ideas?" Roland said.

"It's true, only mad geniuses come up with this sort of stuff," Victoria reworded.

"Thank you," said Ray, charmed.

"Victoria is incredible," Alan said to Roland. "She not only picks up your droppings but wipes up your messes. You definitely don't deserve her. I don't know how you got so lucky. I'll never be that lucky. I was almost lucky, the other day. For a second, I had a chance to meet this amazing girl in a very romantic way in the street, but I didn't grab the opportunity, and now it's lost."

"You'll get other chances," Lynn said.

"Not like this one. This felt . . . unique." Alan shook his head. "Things aren't going so well for me right now. And it doesn't help that I've spent all my money on precious and semiprecious stones."

Roland said, "No one understands better than I the urge to leave a little something behind. But Alan, I left paper clips, buttons, and pennies, not diamonds, sapphires, and opals!"

Alan shrugged. "I'm less cheap."

"Better cheap than whine about it afterward," Roland snapped.

"Yes," elucidated Victoria, "one of the disadvantages of being a supergenerous person like you, Alan, is that if your gifts happen not to be appreciated, your suffering and loss are greater."

"And plus, you didn't have to leave the precious stones behind!" Roland said to Alan.

"I didn't have someone to pick up after me like you do, Roland." No one spoke.

Alan finally added, "Oh, I don't even care about being broke. I don't know why I mentioned it. I'm just sorry I let that unique romantic opportunity slip through my fingers."

"I'm sure it was unique," Ray said. "But each one is unique."

"Perhaps," said Alan. "But this one felt more unique."

The days were passing monotonously for Alan. He was depressed and lonely. It didn't help that removing his chair had left a hole in his living room, a void which Pancake, Bugsy, Toto, and Fuzz-fuzz were only partly able to fill. Alan had trouble getting used to that hole. It kept reminding him of the special opportunity he had failed to grab. He decided he would buy a new chair, another white chair, to plug up the hole and help him stop thinking of the girl he could have met. But he wasn't sure the new chair would do much good, because in his heart, he'd know it was not the same chair.

He told himself he'd pull through this bad period. The pets were a help. And he was forcing himself to go out more, meet new people. He would turn his life around. He had done it before; he believed he could do it again. There was a new beading class he had his eye on and was keen on taking. If he never found an ideal mate, or even a vaguely adequate mate, he could still be happy. If he worked at building a rich and fulfilling life for himself, happiness would come eventually, even if a soulmate didn't.

One late afternoon, his doorman buzzed him. "There's a woman down here who wants to see you."

"Who is it?"

"She says you don't know her, but that she has something for you."

He took the elevator down, not wanting to let any strange woman into his apartment.

In the lobby stood the pretty girl who had taken his chair.

Approaching her, he said, softly, "You have my white elephant."

She smiled, looking puzzled. "No, your driver's license. It was in the cushions of your chair. I wasn't sure how long ago you lost it and if you had already gotten a new one. I didn't know if I should even bother giving it back to you."

"Yes, you should. They card me incessantly."

She laughed, handed him his license.

Looking down thoughtfully, he murmured, mostly to himself,

"Sometimes, when you lose something, you find something more precious." Suddenly worried he had sounded corny, he said, "I lost my chair, but I found my precious driver's license." He looked up at her. "Listen, I'd love to get occasional reports on my chair. Can I give you my number?"

She laughed. "Sure. I'll just give you my card." She took a business card out of her handbag. "I'll write my home number on it. I don't always do that, because I've had problems with stalkers."

Flustered and off-balance, Alan chuckled. While she wrote her number on her card, he tried to think of what a normal, healthy, average man would answer.

Finally, he said, "Don't worry, I gave up stalking long ago."

She looked at him with a startled air and laughed.

They had dinner and drinks twice that week. He was carded each time and showed his driver's license.

Soon, he got to see his chair again. He got to sit in it. And do other wonderful things in it. And see his soulmate sitting in it. And see her sitting on him sitting in it. And him on her, in it. And him in her. And them in it.

THE END
(for the faint of heart, do not read further)

Seventeen

"I met the girl of my dreams, my soulmate," Alan told Lynn, Roland, and Ray.

"Tell us," Ray said.

"I don't know how to put it, in order to do it justice."

"Just blurt it out any which way," Lynn said.

"Very well. I was lost. And she returned me to myself."

"Nice," said Roland. "Could you be a little more concrete? We were concrete."

"She found me in the folds of what I had discarded."

"A little less poetic, please. More specific?"

"Just like your soulmate, Roland, she returned to me what I had lost."

Ray, Roland, Lynn, and even Patricia were eager to meet Alan's new girlfriend, Ruth. So they decided to have another dinner. "For a change," Lynn insisted on arranging a catered dinner at her gallery.

When the others arrived, they noticed Lynn's walls were bare again. Tactfully, no one commented on it.

They sat at a round table that was bull's-eyed by a magnificent bouquet of creamy roses brought by Lynn's florist soulmate. He was seated next to her, and Roland's translator soulmate was seated next to him. While they waited for Alan's to arrive, they asked him various questions about her, including what she did for a living.

"I don't know," Alan said.

"Didn't you ask her?"

"Yes, I did, but she's being evasive. That's the one thing that bugs me about her. She's hiding her profession from me."

"Ah, yes, that must be bothersome," Ray said.

"Actually, I'd be grateful if one of you could get it out of her during this meal."

"Maybe she doesn't have a profession. Maybe she doesn't work," Ray said.

"Yes, she does," Alan said. "She's often mentioning having to go to work or being exhausted from work. But she seems to work at irregular times."

"Does she like your rat?" Roland asked.

"Yes."

"That could be a clue."

"To what?"

"Her profession. You once said that women who have guns are likely to like rats. So what other types of women are likely to like rats? Perhaps women in gutsy, gritty professions. Maybe she's a cop, like Lynn's mom. Or a garbage collector, like Lynn's dad."

The Translator turned to Lynn and said, "That's what your parents do? That's so cool."

At that moment, Alan's girlfriend Ruth arrived.

Everyone at the table, except Alan, was stunned.

Finally, Lynn said softly, "Alan, she's practically a supermodel."

"I know, she's very pretty." Alan smiled fondly, stroking Ruth's arm.

They all lowered their eyes, embarrassed.

Ruth kissed him on the lips and said, "Sorry I'm late."

"Alan, she's not hiding her profession from you," Roland said, through clenched teeth.

Alan looked at him indignantly. "First of all I told you about that in confidence, and second of all, what the hell are you talking about?"

"She's just not telling. She's not hiding it. She couldn't hide it if she wanted to," Ray said.

"Alan, literally, she's practically a supermodel. She's a very famous model, practically a supermodel," Lynn said.

Alan still seemed to take this as some sort of compliment.

Lynn shook her head and vigorously started flipping through an *Elle* magazine she had in her bag.

"Her face is on billboards. I passed one on my way here," Roland said.

Patricia nodded and said to Ruth, "Sorry we're talking about you as if you're not here."

"It's okay. I understand," said Ruth, looking amused and sheepish.

"There!" Lynn exclaimed, and handed Alan the *Elle* magazine opened to a page with a photograph of Ruth modeling a brown pantsuit.

Patricia leaned toward Lynn and whispered to her, "That reminds me, this morning you got rejected by the Ford Modeling Agency."

"Oh," said Lynn. "That reminds me, I meant to tell you, I think I'm ready for us to stop sending applications to clubs who'd never have me as a member."

"Are you sure?" Patricia asked.

"Yes, I'd like to give normal life a try. I can always go back to madness later, if sanity doesn't keep me stable."

Alan scrutinized the photo a long time. He turned to his girl-friend and softly asked, "Why are you with me?"

"It's no big deal," she said, taking a seat. "Lots of great people are not observant."

"That's not what he meant," said Roland's Translator, who was also capable of translating other people. "What he meant was, since you're a model, why are you with him. You could have any man, et cetera. He doesn't find himself attractive, et cetera."

"Thanks," Alan muttered.

"What can I say? You do it for me," Ruth said. "You're to my taste. And to be honest, I have been drawn to your type in the past. My friends think I have perverse taste in men and furniture. Not that liking you or your chair are acts of perversion. Now I'm sound-ing insensitive."

"I think your friends are right," Alan said. "You are perverse. I'm lucky."

"And you, my friend, are shallow," Roland said to Alan. "I never realized you were so superficial, running after models."

"But I didn't know she was a near supermodel!" Alan exclaimed, indignantly.

"First of all, do I really believe that, and second of all, so what? It still shows that looks are the main thing you value in women."

Ruth looked a little grim.

Victoria said, "Oh, I completely agree, and that is so wise and good of you, Alan, because until you've been with someone a very long time and given that person a chance to reveal her innermost self, it would be premature and unfair to judge her on anything but her looks."

"Speaking of looks," said Jim, pointing to the gallery window, "who are those men giving us weird looks?"

They all turned and stared at the window. Three men were indeed standing outside Lynn's gallery, their foreheads pressed to the glass, looking in.

"Oh, they're just some stalkers I've got," said Ruth. "Alan, I hope you don't mind that I come with a little bit of baggage. They're creeps, but harmless."

"Lynn used to have a stalker, too," Patricia said.

Ruth nodded to Lynn sympathetically.

Roland said to Alan, "You should relish every minute of your relationship, buddy, because I'm sure you're aware that your days as the boyfriend of a near supermodel are numbered."

"What has gotten into you, Roland?" Lynn said. "Finding your soulmate has made you nastier than ever."

Ruth was pleasantly surprised that Alan and his friends were taking her stalkers so much in stride.

Victoria said, "You misunderstand him, Lynn. What Roland says is true. Having low expectations is always best. This way, when things turn out great, Alan will be pleasantly surprised."

"Speaking of low expectations," Roland said, turning to Lynn's soulmate. "Jim, haven't you ever had any higher ambitions than being a florist?"

"Because if you haven't," elaborated Victoria, "it's really impressive to be so unmaterialistic and genuine. That's a very rare quality nowadays."

"I'm afraid I can't claim to be completely unmaterialistic," Jim said. "I did get an MBA after college, and I did work in business for a couple of years, but I kept thinking I'd be happier living more simply. I love plants and nature, but I love people and the city too much to leave. I know it may not seem exciting to everyone, but I don't need a lot of money, and I'm very happy with the choice I've made. Particularly because it led me to Lynn." He squeezed her hand.

Roland lost interest and turned back to the easier target. "My poor Alan, I'm worried about you, about your expectations. Ask yourself, why would a near supermodel ever want to be with you, let alone stay with you?"

Alan looked pained. Everyone turned to Victoria, even though they didn't have much hope she'd be able to fix this vicious comment.

After a couple of thoughtful seconds, Victoria said, "Roland is right. Asking yourself why a supermodel would want to be with you is a very therapeutic exercise. You should make a list of all the reasons you come up with—and there will be many, no doubt—such as your kindness, sense of humor, charming innocence, piercing blue eyes, feathery blond hair, and you should study that list religiously. It'll keep your confidence up, your anxiety down, and enable you to enjoy your relationship more fully."

Ray placed his hand on her arm. "Victoria, I like you, and I don't want to see you get hurt. Every time you utter one of your lovely translations, I tremble for your safety. Roland has a temper. I warn you that one day he may turn around and slug you."

Roland's face turned red. "I don't like what you're insinuating!" he said, slapping the table and rising slightly out of his seat, threateningly. "Are you implying that her translations are annoying? That they'll get on my nerves? Well you're wrong! For the first time in my life I feel free! I don't have to watch what I say anymore. I don't have to walk on eggshells and be careful not to hurt people's feelings. As long as she's with me, I can just be myself, and she'll fix the damage before it even has time to register!"

"You were walking on eggshells?" Lynn said.

"Yes, for your information. Spare me your amazed air," Roland said.

Everyone was silent for a few long seconds, mulling over the concept that Roland had been walking on eggshells.

Later during that same meal, they talked of Max's suicide. Roland was not so interested in the topic, since he had murdered Max. Plus, the subject made him uncomfortable. Had it been a suicide, though, he would of course have been very interested, as was the case a moment later, when Alan's model girlfriend generously revealed that one of her old boyfriends who suffered from depression had committed suicide three years ago. Roland was dying to ask her how he had done it, but he restrained himself, fearing it was tactless. No one else asked either.

Alan was perturbed, because he had noticed that while they had been talking about Max's death, Ruth had begun staring at Roland rather insistently. Alan hoped it did not mean she was attracted to him. He told himself he was just being paranoid.

The days and weeks passed, and Alan worried about the looks his soulmate and Roland kept giving each other when they all got together.

Alan thought there was something terribly wrong in his relationship. That any human being could possess such a high degree of perversity as to be a near top model and be attracted to him seemed extraordinarily shady. Who knew what else she was capable of? Infidelity, perhaps. It was all too easy for him to imagine, after having lived it with Jessica.

Nevertheless, he chose to fight his fears. He believed that if he had strong enough faith, blind faith, his love would endure, and so would his soulmate. He wanted true love to be possible, and he wanted to be one of the lucky few who had it.

Alan had no way of knowing that the actual reason Roland was staring at Alan's girlfriend was not because of her pronounced beauty, nor because of her fame, nor because he was attracted to her (he was not especially), but because her ex-boyfriend had committed suicide and Roland wished he could think of a way to ask her how.

Alan had no way of knowing that the reason his soulmate stared at Roland so frequently and insistently was not that she found him handsome or charming or had any interest in dating him or even talking to him (she did not), but because of how obvious it was to her that he had killed Max. She was amazed that it wasn't obvious to the others, but then again, how could it be—they didn't know what it felt like to have murdered someone.

Her ex-boyfriend "committed suicide," but Roland hadn't picked up on the quotation marks when she'd mentioned it that night she first met Alan's friends at the restaurant.

But when they'd mentioned *Max's* "suicide," she'd noticed something about the way Roland moved, or blinked, or breathed, or perhaps it was a downward glance. She didn't know what it was, but whatever it was, she understood it, felt it viscerally. And she knew, at that moment, that Roland had killed Max. She hadn't said anything, because she didn't feel she was in a position to judge, having herself murdered her old boyfriend and passed it off as suicide when his lack of logic and tendency to contradict himself had become too annoying to her.

Alan was convinced his soulmate would dump him, leaving him to live the rest of his days alone, while Roland and Lynn would live happily ever after with their soulmates. Alan was dead wrong.

Roland soon discovered that his soulmate, his Translator, his Picker-Upper, was HIV positive. He had been looking for aspirin in her medicine cabinet and had found some Combivir, AZT, and other pills, which he knew were used by such patients. He double-checked on the Internet and confirmed it.

Furious at his Translator for not having told him, for not having cared about his safety, he said to her, "In case you weren't aware of it, AIDS is a fatal disease that is sexually transmittable."

"So are lots of things," she said. "*Life* is a fatal disease that is sexually transmittable."

After a long silence, Roland said, "I'm waiting."

"For what?" she said.

"For you to mention that you just quoted Jacques Dutronc. Or were you going to pass that off as your own?"

"Chill out," she said.

"You didn't *care* that I might catch AIDS!"

"I always insisted we use condoms. And plus, my viral loads are low."

"It's still risky!"

"Barely. And what were you doing snooping in my medicine cabinet? And what are you doing now, acting mad! You're supposed to be all sad that your soulmate might die!"

"My soulmate is supposed to be truthful and not hide that she has a contagious disease! Why didn't you tell me?"

"I wanted you to get hooked on me before I told you. So that you wouldn't leave me."

Roland walked out on his soulmate.

As for Lynn, an unfortunate day arrived for her and Jim.

"I can't see you tomorrow. I'm meeting Trista," he told Lynn.

"Who's Trista?" Lynn asked, thinking it might be a sister he hadn't mentioned or his accountant.

"She's a girl I see sometimes."

"A girl?"

"Well, a woman, whatever."

"You see her alone?"

Jim looked amused. "Yes."

"How do you know her?"

"I was actually set up with her on a blind date by a friend, three years ago."

"Oh? Did you guys ever date?"

"Yeah, I just told you I'm seeing her tomorrow night."

"That's a date?"

"Some people would call it that. I'm not sure I would. I mean, it's not as though we go through the whole official dinner slash conversation thing. That stage is long gone."

Lynn's body was suddenly freezing cold. "What do you mean? You're teasing me, right?"

"I don't think so. I'm not sure what you mean by 'teasing.'"

"Are you sleeping with this woman?"

"That's a vague question. It's hard to answer. I mean, the present tense you're using is confusing. I'm not sleeping with her right this second, as you can see."

Lynn's freezing body was suddenly becoming very hot. "Tomorrow. Will you be having sex with her?"

"I can't predict the future. I'm not a psychic."

"Have you had sex with her since I've known you?" Lynn asked.

"Yes."

Lynn was silent for many long seconds. "You've been cheating on me?"

"Cheating? Have we been taking a test? I don't understand how the word 'cheating' could even apply to the situation?"

"You weren't faithful to me?"

"You mean sexually exclusive? No. We never spoke of such a thing."

Lynn knew then that she couldn't be with this person. It broke her heart. What made it easier was the fact that it got worse.

"You mean we had to talk about it before you'd feel the desire to be faithful to me?" she said.

"No."

Fleetingly, Lynn felt a tiny bit better. Until he elaborated.

"Talking about it wouldn't make any difference," he said. "I'd never feel the desire to be faithful to you. Or to anyone. I'm not interested in monogamy. It's not for me."

"You misled me."

"How so? It's not my job to assume that you are presumptuous, nor to protect you from your own presumptuousness. I choose to think the best of people. Anyone who egotistically imagines that her preference for monogamy is everyone's preference and who gets hurt as a result has only herself to blame. Protecting those people will only slow down the progress our society is making, the process of becoming more evolved and accepting other belief systems. That progress has been made with holiday cards, which now rarely say Merry Christmas. They say Season's Greetings. That's the way it's gotta be with love, too."

Lynn told her friends what happened.

"What do you expect when you fall for a faggy florist," Roland said, untranslated and unsoftened.

Since Alan was the only one left with a soulmate, Ray, Lynn, and Roland waited to see what would happen. The question was, would she stay good or not?

A couple of weeks passed. Alan was starting to act victorious. Therefore, Ray, Lynn, and Roland decided to look into Ruth's background to see if she had a dark secret. They called up Jessica in the Midwest and hired her to do the digging. They said they were concerned about Alan and wanted to find out a bit more about his new girlfriend to make sure she was trustworthy and decent. Jessica, who couldn't resist the opportunity to do something for Alan, agreed to dig for free.

Jessica did discover a secret in Ruth's past, but it was a secret that made the model, if anything, more impressive.

They had suspected drugs or alcohol, maybe some extreme sexual kinkiness, which would explain her liking Alan. But instead, she had a doctorate in economics that she had gotten secretly in her spare time and which was all the more impressive considering that her life had been full of such traumatic events as the suicide of her boyfriend three years ago and the death of her sister in a fire the year before that.

When they informed Alan that they had dug into his girlfriend's past, he was angry.

They defended themselves. "We wanted to make sure she was as good as she seemed. We were looking out for you."

"How dare you!" he said.

"Our soulmates turned out to suck. We thought yours might, too. We care about you."

"You are such assholes."

"Well, she did turn out to be hiding something significant."

Alan stared at them with sheer hatred.

"Yes, there's something she never told you," they said, dragging it out.

Alan waited, lips clenched.

"She has a doctorate in economics."

"Assholes."

"What. Aren't you happy? She turned out to be even better than we thought."

"If it ain't broke, don't fix it!"

Feeling guilty and wanting to make up for having snooped, they told him they'd throw him and Ruth a party to celebrate the fact that their snooping hadn't turned up anything negative and that Ruth was not a bad soulmate so far.

The party took place at the home of one of Ray's clients, who was glad to lend his ground-floor duplex to the founder of Chock Full O'Nuts, for a celebration at which he was hoping to meet some good romantic matches.

Alan searched for his model soulmate at the party. She'd left his side soon after they'd arrived together. He found her on the second-floor balcony, sitting on the balustrade, looking down at the garden. When Alan approached her, he saw that she was gazing down, specifically, at Roland, who was standing alone with a glass of white wine, facing the potted trees. Every time Alan saw his soulmate staring at Roland, his gut hurt. He could already see it coming: roaming interest, flirtation, infidelity. He didn't want to go through that again.

In fact, Ruth did not have those specific impure thoughts or disloyal intentions. She was only marveling at that thing she and Roland had in common, which was visible only to her. Having things in common naturally increases people's interest in one another. That interest is not necessarily, or even usually, romantic. Just basic human interest. The more significant that thing which people have in common is, the more intense the interest is likely to be. Therefore, Ruth's degree of interest in Roland was perfectly continent and respectable considering that what they had in common was murder.

Ruth sensed that Alan was feeling jealous. She wished she could reassure him. With time, he'd understand she was a faithful person. If he knew she'd killed her ex and her sister, he'd probably be even more worried, but there was no need for him to be concerned about that either. His life would not be in danger as long as he didn't annoy her with (a) self-contradictions, (b) lack of logic, (c) an inability to hold his side of an argument, or (d) other irritants.

She told Alan she was going to get another drink and left his side.

In another corner of the party, Roland approached Lynn. "Have you noticed how Alan's girlfriend doesn't stop staring at me?"

"No," Lynn said, even though she had.

"She wants me," he said, looking at Ruth, who was now staring at him while standing near the drinks table, chatting with Ray.

"Well, you shouldn't stare back," Lynn said.

"Why not? She's hot for me. I may do a lot more than stare back."

Lynn looked at him sternly. "Just because things didn't work out for you and Victoria doesn't mean you should spoil things for Alan. You should wish him well."

"I do wish him well. That is why I want to test Ruth's fidelity. To make sure she won't cheat on him."

"I don't want to hear about this," Lynn said, and went to talk to Alan, who was near the staircase, alone, stirring his drink morosely.

"Congratulations on your relationship. I'm really happy for you," Lynn said to Alan.

He smiled faintly.

"Are you okay?" she asked.

After a moment, Alan said, "Have you noticed how much she looks at Roland?"

"Maybe a little bit."

"Maybe she doesn't believe in monogamy. She may be just like your ex, only less honest about it."

Lynn took Alan's arm and said to him sincerely, "I wish you the best, but if the best doesn't happen, the good still can. With someone else or just with friends. And the good isn't so bad."

Alan looked unconvinced, so Lynn went on. "I don't believe that finding a great love is guaranteed for everyone. I hope I'll find one, but I may not. And who knows, you may not either. But there are other things that are good. Friendships, relationships that are supportive and comforting and fun, even if they're not romantic or passionate. And you can find passion in other areas. No matter what happens between you and Ruth, you can count on me, on Ray, on your other friends to support you if you need us."

Alan nodded, too moved to answer.

Roland joined them. "Hey, your girlfriend keeps staring at me. Have you noticed?"

Alan turned red. "No, I haven't noticed."

"Yeah, right. Aren't you afraid she'll cheat on you? Kind of like Jessica did?"

Alan gazed at the triumphant banner strung across the ceiling, on which Ray had written "Not-A-Bad-Soulmate Party." Alan tried not to feel mocked by it. At that moment, he realized he had two choices.

He could expect the best and be rewarded by a long and happy life with his soulmate, who would love him with all his faults, forever, no matter what.

Or he could give in to his jealousy and negative thoughts, lose his girlfriend—the best thing that had ever happened to him—fall into a downward spiral, and perhaps even become suicidal again.

No.

He would not be defeated. He was victorious. He had everything he wanted and was determined to enjoy a long life of happiness with Ruth. Roland, Lynn, and Ray had tried to find something bad about her, but it seemed there was nothing bad to be found. She was a good soulmate, his soulmate. He would not let his paranoia ruin everything. Ruth was faithful. She loved him. She was not yearning for Roland.

Alan finally answered, "No. I love Ruth, and I trust her. I think only good things of her."

"That's great!" Roland said. "People say that attitude can really make a difference in how things turn out. You're harnessing the great American power of positive thinking!"

"Yes. I'll give it a shot. What have I got to lose? It can't hurt."

They gazed at him.

He added, "I know I'll be extremely happy with Ruth. I'm really looking forward to growing old with her."

His positive outlook seemed to suffuse the room with a rose tint. Lynn and Roland were feeling more optimistic about their own lives. They left Alan's side and mingled with the party.

Alan felt better, too.

Ruth brought him a refill of his Bloody Mary. They chatted intimately, commented playfully on the other guests. They were having a good time. Things were already lighter between them, less strained than at the start of the evening. His positive attitude really was working! If he stuck to it, Ruth would be more likely to stick to him. He wouldn't have to be single, ever again, looking for a new love, as Lynn and Roland were doing. He would try his best to stay on the positive path and wouldn't let small things, like Ruth's glances at Roland, bother him. She was so wonderful in so many ways.

Alan was right. His girlfriend had many wonderful qualities. She was intelligent, beautiful, faithful, supportive, protective, fun, funny, warm, athletic, artistic, cultivated, generous, logical, consistent, and nature-loving. Being evil was her only fault.

LA FIN

About the Author

Born in Paris, Amanda Filipacchi was educated in both France and the United States and has lived in New York since the age of seventeen. She earned an MFA from Columbia University and is the author of two previous novels, *Nude Men* and *Vapor,* both of which received widespread U.S. and international acclaim. Her work has been published in France, the Netherlands, Italy, England, Germany, Russia, Israel, Poland, Turkey, Slovakia, Sweden, Denmark, and Hungary. Film rights for *Love Creeps* have been purchased by United Artists for Single Cell Pictures. For more information, visit her Web site at www.amandafilipacchi.com.